Felicity's Eloquent Earl

Seven Unsuitable Sisters
Book 5

BY MAEVE GREYSON

ARE YOU SIGNED UP FOR DRAGONBLADE'S BLOG?

You'll get the latest news and information on exclusive giveaways, exclusive excerpts, coming releases, sales, free books, cover reveals and more.

Check out our complete list of authors, too!

No spam, no junk. That's a promise!

Sign Up Here

www.dragonbladepublishing.com

Dearest Reader;

Thank you for your support of a small press. At Dragonblade Publishing, we strive to bring you the highest quality Historical Romance from some of the best authors in the business. Without your support, there is no 'us', so we sincerely hope you adore these stories and find some new favorite authors along the way.

Happy Reading!

CEO, Dragonblade Publishing

Additional Dragonblade books by Author Maeve Greyson

Seven Unsuitable Sisters Series
Blessing's Baron (Book 1)
Fortuity's Arrangement (Book 2)
Grace's Saving (Book 3)
Joy's Willful Wager (Book 4)
Felicity's Eloquent Earl (Book 5)

The Sisterhood of Independent Ladies Series
To Steal a Duke (Book 1)
To Steal a Marquess (Book 2)
To Steal an Earl (Book 3)

Once Upon a Scot Series
A Scot of Her Own (Book 1)
A Scot to Have and to Hold (Book 2)
A Scot To Love and Protect (Book 3)

Time to Love a Highlander Series
Loving Her Highland Thief (Book 1)
Taming Her Highland Legend (Book 2)
Winning Her Highland Warrior (Book 3)
Capturing Her Highland Keeper (Book 4)
Saving Her Highland Traitor (Book 5)
Loving Her Lonely Highlander (Book 6)
Delighting Her Highland Devil (Book 7)
When the Midnight Bell Tolls (Novella)

Highland Heroes Series
The Guardian (Book 1)
The Warrior (Book 2)
The Judge (Book 3)

The Dreamer (Book 4)
The Bard (Book 5)
The Ghost (Book 6)
A Yuletide Yearning (Novella)
Love's Charity (Novella)

Also from Maeve Greyson
Guardian of Midnight Manor (Novella)
Once Upon a Haunted Highland Mist (Novella)

Chapter One

Lady Atterley's Dinner Party
England's Lake District
Early July 1825

LADY FELICITY ABAROUGH, sixth sister to the most infuriating Duke of Broadmere, sidled along the outermost edge of the parlor, keeping to the shadows. Occasionally, she swept a glance across Lady Atterley's expertly planned festivities. Even more often than that, she noted where her sister Serendipity was and whether or not Seri was looking her way. Just a few more yards, and she would be able to dash into the kitchens and escape this unbearable torture of shedding her status of devout wallflower long enough to attract a suitable husband. Since four of her older sisters had married for love, she, Felicity, was next on the matrimonial chopping block that would supply her brother Chance with yet another percentage of the family's coffers he had yet to inherit.

Thank heavens, he only inherited that additional percentage if she married for love. That was the only saving grace to their parents' will that had set this fine mess into play and prevented Chance from receiving the entirety of the estate's vast fortune. Praise be for that little legality, since her only current love was food and concocting delicious new recipes. Eventually, she wished to marry. Truly, she did, but just not yet. And at two stone heavier than she should be, according to the modiste, and virtually invisible to most in the *ton*, she should be safe. *Should be.*

But that didn't mean that Chance and Serendipity, the eldest of the seven sisters and Chance's assistant in this Marriage Mart madness, had stopped doing their level best to throw her into the path of every eligible gentleman of Polite Society.

"Come along now, Seri," she muttered. "That is your second or third glass of lemonade since supper. Wouldn't a visit to the ladies' cloakroom be in order by now?" She craned her neck, willing her sister to retire for some relief. Then Felicity could escape to the kitchens before Lord Smellington…er…Lord Pellington cornered her with his malodorous presence. Currently, he was across the way, gagging a trio of young ladies with his unbearable odor.

As usual, their hostess had outdone herself. The dinner party had provided not only an exemplary meal, but some of the guests were presently amused by a rollicking game of charades. Those not interested in that diversion had the choice of several card games. Tables for whist, quadrille, and cribbage had even been provided. Music and dancing rounded out the evening's entertainment.

Felicity had sorely hoped to escape these gatherings, since the Season was now officially over, and they had retired to their summer leisure at Broadmere Hall in the Lake District. Alas, it was not to be. Heaven forbid that the matriarchs of the *ton* should become bored, no matter where they might find themselves.

"At last." She breathed a sigh of relief as her sister allowed a servant to take her empty glass, then turned and gracefully swept across the room toward the ladies' cloakroom. As quick as a flash, Felicity darted after the servant and followed him to the kitchens.

"Bless my soul, there she be! I had begun to wonder," said the grandmotherly woman at the head of the long worktable.

"She did just say that, Lady Felicity," said the kitchen maid, chopping dried fruits with a loud, banging fervor. The cheery girl paused in her labors and winked. "I was just telling her to give you time to escape your keepers."

"You are so right, Marcie," Felicity said to the maid before rushing to catch hold of the floury hands of Mrs. Amesbury, longtime cook for the Atterley household and also longtime friend. "It took me forever to slip past Seri." Felicity indulged in a wicked grin. "And thank you for having the footmen ply her with lemonade. You know it is her weakness."

"Well, now…we do what we can for our cherished friends." With a pleased-with-herself wiggle of her ample girth, the amiable cook quickly let go of Felicity's hands. "Now, now. Flour on your gloves. That will never do."

Felicity couldn't care less about a little flour, but she brushed her hands together and slipped off her gloves, stuffing them into her reticule after removing a tightly folded parcel she couldn't wait to show to her dear friends. For that was exactly who they were—her dear friends. After taking refuge in the kitchens of all the best households and helping the staff churn out their recipes, all the kitchen servants of the *ton* adored Lady Felicity as much as she adored them. "See here what I stitched together? My very own apron." With a flamboyant snap of the cloth, she held up the linen garment that would cover most of her gown and shield it from any errant splashes. "Now, what are we making? I know you need help. Between the vicar and Lady Urnstall, there is not a single rout cake, tart, or biscuit left on the refreshment table. How on earth could they possibly devour so much after that scrumptious banquet you prepared?"

"Ah, the vicar." Mrs. Amesbury nodded. "I wondered if he was here. Not a soul can eat like that man. I swear his legs must be hollow."

"We be glad for your help," Marcie said. "Them folks eat more than me brothers, and that be truly saying something."

The familiar aromas of herbs, spices, and the mouth-watering roasted meats that had been served for dinner buoyed Felicity's spirits as she donned her apron, hung her reticule on a peg by the door, and joined the women at the worktable. This was her element. The kitchen was her place.

"I could make some marchpane cakes," she said. "I worked

out a new recipe where they do not take nearly as long and are quite lovely when I form them into little shapes like fruits. Those would hold the guests until everything else gets out of the ovens. I know you must have rosewater, sugar, and flour. Have you enough almonds? I could start blanching them."

"We have almonds aplenty." Cook gave one of the scullery maids a nod. "Fetch our lady whatever she needs. Be quick about it now."

"Yes, Mrs. Amesbury." The girl scurried to the pantry. Harried thumps and bumps from the adjoining room attested to her diligence in doing as she was told.

"I do beg your pardon," said a rich, deep voice from the kitchen's doorway.

Felicity froze and stared down at her fisted hands, fearing that Serendipity had sent someone to fetch her.

Mrs. Amesbury and Marcie curtsied.

"Yes, my lord?" Mrs. Amesbury moved toward the door, wiping her hands on her apron.

Finding what little courage there was to be had, Felicity cautiously turned to see who this *my lord* was and what on earth he was doing in the kitchens.

Tall and so broad-shouldered that he filled the doorway, the dark-haired gentleman offered Mrs. Amesbury a polite bow. "Do forgive the intrusion, but I fear I missed what I am certain was a divine supper because my rascal of a horse slipped free of his stall. Dratted devil. Took me forever to catch him. But thankfully, I did and made haste to keep from missing this lovely party."

"And how can we be helping you, my lord?" Mrs. Amesbury said, apparently not quite certain how she might remedy his unfortunate situation.

Without thinking, Felicity stepped forward. "He is hungry, Mrs. Amesbury, and the refreshment table is quite empty." She ventured a soft curtsy toward the breathtaking man who possessed the kindest eyes she had ever seen. Or maybe it was his lopsided smile that perfectly set off the manly cleft in his chin. "Is that correct, my lord? You are in search of something to eat?"

The captivating sir beamed at her. "Yes, you understand me perfectly, Miss...?"

"Felicity." She purposely left the *lady* part off. After all, one must never overplay one's hand. Her sister Joy would be so proud of her. "I fear we are in the process of preparing more refreshments, but nothing is yet ready." Then an easy solution came to mind, as long as it was agreeable to him. "Might I tempt you with some coddled eggs and soldiers? I could prepare those for you in no time at all." Chance loved her coddled eggs and soldiers. Surely, this gentleman would too.

He glanced heavenward as if she had answered his prayers, then gave her a formal bow. "I would forever be indebted to you for your kindness."

Mrs. Amesbury cleared her throat and cast a pointed look at the maids. "Come along, girls. Back to your tasks. Marcie, gather what is needed for the gentleman's repast, then return to helping me. Our lady...our *Felicity* will see to Lord...?"

His lordship jumped as though shot. "Do forgive me. Where are my manners? I am Mr. Drake Pemberton...er...sorry. No, I am not. I am now the Earl of Wakefield." He rolled his shoulders and fidgeted in place like a child about to be scolded. "I fear I have yet to adapt to the title. Once a member of the gentry, always a member of the gentry and all that, you know? My uncle was the sixth Earl of Wakefield, and I was the only male heir to be found at the time of his passing."

Mrs. Amesbury slowly nodded at the man's babbling, then turned and ambled away with a clap of her hands. "Be about it, girls. We have guests to keep happy. Our Felicity has everything else well in hand."

"Do have a seat, my lord, and I shall get your eggs and soldiers underway." With her insides fluttering to the point of giddiness, Felicity pointed his lordship to the stool at the end of the worktable, then hurried to help Marcie gather the silver egg coddler, eggs, bread, butter, and seasonings. Surely a man of Lord

Wakefield's size would need at least two eggs, maybe more. "How many would you like, my lord?"

There was that lopsided smile of his again, and her insides stopped their giddy fluttering. They melted. "While I could eat a dozen, I shall not be greedy, Miss Felicity. Two will surely hold me until the refreshment table is replenished."

"Two it shall be, then." Felicity swallowed hard. *Mercy.* She needed to stop squeaking like a mouse every time she spoke. What would he surely think of her? Clearing her throat, she bent to set the flame beneath the coddler that Marcie had already filled with steaming water from the fire. "And you recovered your horse, you said? Try not to be too angry with the stable lads. Sometimes the gates do not latch properly."

"Oh, I cannot lay the blame at the stable lad's feet." Wakefield raked a hand through his gorgeously thick hair, settling it into a dashing arrangement of disarray. "I was the last at the stall. The fault is mine."

A man who admits his own mistakes? Impressive. After cracking the eggs into the porcelain cups that fit inside the egg coddler, she eased them down into their holders, then popped on the lid. "It takes a rare gentleman to admit his own mistakes," she said, then blushed and turned away. She should not have said that.

The dashing earl laughed. "I am not so rare." He rose and joined her, leaning so close that it stole her breath away. "So that is how you coddle eggs. I never knew."

She stood there, blinking like a hopelessly tongue-tied owl. He was actually talking *to her* and not *down to her.* "Uhm…yes. The water comes to a boil, heats the cups, and cooks the eggs to the perfect jamminess for nice, toasty soldiers to dip into." The soldiers. She needed to toast the bread. "Heavens! I must make haste, or the eggs will grow cold waiting for your toast."

"You are a wonder, Miss Felicity. My angel who has saved me from starvation."

His angel? Her cheeks burned as hot as if she had touched them to the silver coddler. "I am sure if I were not here, Mrs.

Amesbury or Marcie would have been more than happy to feed you." She concentrated on cutting the bread to avoid looking into those hazel eyes of his that seemed to be filled with so much sincerity; she wondered if she were dreaming. He was being *nice* to her. Her. Felicity. The least desirable and fattest of the litter, as she had overheard one cruel lordling say.

"Ahh...but would they have done it with such care?" He returned to his seat, seeming to sense that his nearness made her nervous. "I am quite the eloquent earl, you know."

She glanced up from the bread she was carefully toasting over the fire, certain he was making fun of her this time. But he wasn't. "Is that so?"

"Yes, and the tempting aroma of that buttery toast threatens to make me wax poetic."

"Indeed?" She had no idea how to respond to that as she transferred the slices to a plate, cut them into soldiers, and set the plate in front of him. When he reached for one, without thinking, she threatened to smack his hand away. "Not yet. Wait for the eggs so you may dip them."

He grinned and folded his hands in front of his plate. "Yes, ma'am."

"It will only be a moment." With the greatest of care, she lifted the porcelain cups out of the coddler and set them on a plate. After seasoning them to what she considered perfection, she placed them in front of him and nodded. "Now."

After the first bite, he closed his eyes and groaned so loudly that Mrs. Amesbury and the rest of the maids at the far end of the kitchen turned and stared.

"Bliss," he said. "Pure, unadulterated bliss." He proceeded to finish off the first egg with such alarming speed that Felicity wondered if she should've coddled four instead of two. When had the poor man last eaten?

"Shall I prepare more for you?" she asked. "The rout cakes have just now gone into the oven and will be some time."

"Nay, Miss Felicity." He pressed a hand to his heart. "The first egg took the edge off; the second is to savor. But first, I must recite the verse that sprang to mind while I was lost in the wondrous delirium of those exquisite bites. Would you be offended by an impromptu poem?"

She couldn't help but arch a brow as she wiped her hands on her apron. "It depends on the poem."

He grinned. "'Tis naught but an ode to the fair maiden's coddled eggs."

Felicity noticed that all the scullery maids had, surprisingly, disappeared into the pantry. Only Mrs. Amesbury remained *somewhat* in the large kitchen, and the dear old soul stood in the pantry's doorway with her back to Felicity and her guest. Rather obvious, if she did say so herself. She would be having a word with the matchmaking cook. Felicity accepted Lord Wakefield's offer with a gracious nod. "I would be honored to hear your poem."

He wiped the corners of his mouth and sat straighter with his hand pressed to his heart once more. "'Ode to the Fair Maiden's Coddled Eggs' by an importunate breakfast admirer—namely me:

> *Oh, gentlest lass of aproned grace,*
> *With blush upon thy lovely face,*
> *Thy dainty hand, so deft, so fleet,*
> *Prepares a most celestial treat.*

> *No feast of kings, nor banquet grand,*
> *Could tempt as doth thy silver hand—*
> *To crack the shell with tender care,*
> *And stir with spoon both light and fair.*

> *In porcelain cup of purest white,*
> *Thy eggs do bask in steamy light,*
> *Like clouds that dream in buttered skies,*
> *And melt beneath thy watchful eyes.*

> *Thy spices fall with noble air—*

A pinch of salt, a peppered prayer;
A whisper of the nutmeg's kiss,
A sigh of thyme, a swirl of bliss.

No evening chorus quite compares
To thee in thy domestic lairs,
As thou dost tend the simmering flame
And gently call each yolk by name.

For not alone thy eggs are warm—
Thy smile too holds a softened charm;
Thy kitchen is a hallowed space
Where hunger yields to art and grace.

So here I sit, with heart o'erthrown,
Beside thy dish, my love full-blown.
Not for the eggs—though rich, divine—
But for the hand that coddles mine."

He finished with a dramatic flourish of his hand. "And that, Miss Felicity, is what you inspired."

Eyes stinging with tears of delight, she was rendered speechless. "Oh...my." The last stanza played over and over in her mind. *So here I sit, with heart o'erthrown, beside thy dish, my love full blown. Not for the eggs—though rich, divine—but for the hand that coddles mine.*

She swallowed hard and shook some sense into herself. *Good heavens.* The man was jesting because she had cooked him some eggs to make up for his missing dinner. When one was fed, it automatically put one in a jolly mood. She was a ninny for taking it to heart. "You were quite right, Lord Wakefield. You are most certainly an eloquent earl." She heartily clapped as if at the theater. "Bravo! Bravo!"

"I meant every word," he said as he popped the last bit of toast into his mouth and chewed as if it were the most delicious morsel on earth. "I cannot thank you enough for this delightful repast that will certainly go far in holding me over until the rout cakes come out of the oven." As he rose from the stool, he wiped his mouth and hands with the kitchen rag Felicity provided, then gave her a heartfelt bow. "I suppose I should return to the other guests now, even though the company here in this room has been most enjoyable."

She bowed her head to hide another furious blush as she curtsied. "Thank you, my lord. I do hope you enjoy the remainder of your evening."

He nodded again, waved to Mrs. Amesbury, then dashed out of the kitchen.

"Go after him," the portly cook said while pointing at the door. "Never in all my life has anyone ever recited a poem to me for my coddled eggs."

"Yes, indeed," Marcie chimed in as she rushed to peek after him. "Such a handsome man! He had all the girls sighing. And him an earl too, my lady. You best go get him afore one of them other ladies snaps him up."

Felicity shooed them away, refusing to take their words to heart. "He was merely flirting because he thought me one of the servants. You know how some gentlemen can be. If I went out there and revealed my true identity, he would be beside himself trying to find a means of escape."

Mrs. Amesbury shook her head and clucked like a nesting hen. "You have the wrong of it, my lady. Surely you do. Have you no mirrors at Broadmere Hall?"

Felicity ignored her even though she wished upon all her being that what Mrs. Amesbury and Marcie hinted at were true. That Lord Wakefield *was* attracted to her, and if he knew who she really was, he would seek her out for her company and not merely her ample dowry. Past experience had taught her all about that awful tendency, too. The road to matrimony for love was treacherous and cruel.

She shook the unhappy thoughts away. Time to return to her

first love: cooking. "Marcie, are the almonds finished blanching? If so, I can start grinding them and get those treats out that door before Lady Atterley decides to make a personal visit to the kitchens."

"She will understand," Marcie said. "She knows well enough how the vicar and Lady Urnstall have never met a bit of food they would turn away."

"But Lady Felicity be right. If no food goes out that door soon, Lady Atterley will come in here and discover her, then Lady Serendipity and His Grace will soon follow, and they'll be giving her a harsh scolding." Mrs. Amesbury shooed the maids back to work. "We do not wish our visits with our Felicity stopped. Off with you now. Check those rout cakes, and surely those biscuits are done by now too."

"And I shall get to those almonds." Felicity busied herself with setting the egg coddler aside and clearing away Lord Wakefield's plates. She needed to be helpful. Just as she had promised. It didn't matter that she didn't possess the courage to run after the earl and tell him who she really was. No matter how badly she wanted to, she just couldn't bear to see the truth in his kind eyes when he discovered that the kitchen maid who had cooked his eggs was really a plump wallflower, sister of a duke, and worth a hefty dowry. His ode to the fair maiden who had coddled his eggs would change to a sonnet dedicated to gold. It would be crushing indeed to discover him to be a silver-tongued devil looking for coin rather than the pleasure of her company.

She crushed the blanched almonds in a stone mortar and added a little rosewater to keep their oils from separating. But try as she might, she couldn't keep her mind on her work. Lord Wakefield's kind eyes and that infernal poem filled her thoughts, making her wish…

She shook her head. "Silliness," she said under her breath as she added the sugar and ground the paste even more. "Do we want pretty little square cakes or shall I shape them into fruits?"

"Little square cakes be fine," Mrs. Amesbury said, then shook a finger at her. "And then you wash your hands and be getting yourself back out there and finding your earl. Please, my lady. Do it for us. It will give the footmen something exciting to share at the table tonight when we all sit down to our supper."

"He is not my earl."

"Seems to me the man would follow you to the ends of the earth for your coddled eggs," Marcie said as she filled another tray with raw rout cake dough.

"He was hungry. A famished man will follow anyone for food. They are much like dogs."

"Felicity Bethianna Jasmine Abarough!"

Felicity cringed. Serendipity had such a powerful way of saying her name. Just like Mama had the time Felicity caused quite a fire in the kitchen and nearly burned down the townhouse.

She turned and smiled at her sister standing in the doorway. "Yes?"

The high color to Serendipity's cheeks and her pinched expression spoke volumes. "We need to return to the festivities, sister." She spat the words like a hissing cat.

Felicity sighed. This battle was lost, and she didn't wish to get Mrs. Amesbury or Marcie into trouble with Lady Atterley. She wiped her hands clean, removed her apron, and carefully folded it back into the tidy little bundle that fit inside her reticule.

"Where are your gloves?" Serendipity reached for the apron, but Felicity refused to let her take it.

"They are in my reticule. Give me a moment, Seri. What is your hurry?"

"The party misses you, sister. Gentlemen are lining up to fill your dance card."

Felicity huffed as she pulled on her gloves, stuffed the apron back inside her bag, and cinched it shut. "Mama would not approve of your lying."

"Mama also would not approve of your hiding."

"It is not really hiding when you always know where I am,

now, is it?" Felicity refrained from smirking, knowing it would incense her sister even more. "I was out there for dinner and quite a while afterward, and not a single gentleman spoke to me other than Lord Smellington, the Marquess of Debt."

Marcie snorted, and Mrs. Amesbury shooed her into the pantry. "Beg pardon," the cook said before following the maid and closing the door behind them.

"The new Earl of Wakefield finally arrived," Serendipity said. "You have yet to meet him, and dare I say, he is quite the handsome fellow. His uncle, the sixth earl, was an enormous cod's head when it came to understanding the dangers of gambling, but I have yet to discover anything ill about the seventh. He is reported to have come from landed gentry and was quite successful in his own right."

Felicity nearly choked on the butterflies that immediately left her stomach and flew up into her throat. She could not enlighten Lord Wakefield about her true identity tonight. While she understood it was inevitable, she simply wasn't ready at this moment. But how on earth could she escape it? Serendipity seemed overly determined to oust her from her hiding place. So much so that Felicity doubted that an excuse of feeling unwell would be accepted.

Then it came to mind: a wardrobe mishap. An impossible-to-deny excuse. After all, it wasn't as though she hadn't strained a few seams in the past. Madame Couire, their modiste for many years, would attest to that. She took as deep a breath as her corset allowed, doing her best to expand her ribcage to epic proportions. The bodice of her pale-pink gown was already snugger than she liked. With just enough twisting as she bent to retrieve her *accidentally* dropped reticule, the softest ripping sound was music to her ears.

She caught her side and straightened. "Oh dear."

"Oh, Felli." Serendipity groaned. "Not again?"

Keeping the split seam modestly covered with one hand, Felicity shrugged. "I am afraid so. Might I trouble you to fetch my shawl? Then I shall wait in the carriage while you gather everyone else."

"You did that on purpose," Serendipity accused.

"I would never," Felicity lied, assuming a most convincing innocence.

Her sister blew out a heavy sigh. "Wait here. I shall return momentarily with your shawl."

As Serendipity left the kitchen, Felicity didn't dare look toward the pantry in case Mrs. Amesbury or Marcie were peeping out the door. Their disapproving glares had already burned like fire. It couldn't be helped. She would officially meet the eloquent earl at another time, just not today.

Chapter Two

S AFELY ENSCONCED IN the family carriage, Felicity watched for the others through its window. All in all, the evening had not gone as poorly as she had feared it would. After all, her cooking had drawn the sweetest poem from a handsome, eloquent earl. She couldn't help but smile at the memory but still wondered how he would behave when he discovered her true identity, for the discovery was inevitable. If not here in Binnocksbourne, then back in Town when they crossed paths at some festivity that Serendipity and Chance insisted she attend. Perhaps by the time they met again, and she introduced herself properly, he would already be well on his way to becoming an *ineligible* gentleman with a future wife on his arm. That thought made her sad and wonder if she should have listened to Marcie and Mrs. Amesbury about rejoining the party and chasing him down—not exactly chasing him down, but at least making herself known to him.

"Well, there is naught to be done about it now." She propped her chin in her hand and continued staring out the window. Apparently, Merry had found somewhere other than the nursery to hide. Chance and Serendipity must be having difficulty finding her. She smiled again. "Good on you, Merry."

As the two youngest of the seven sisters, she and Merry were closer to each other than the others. She didn't know what she would do without Merry's sparkling nature and spirited antics to make her laugh. Her sister made difficult days easier.

Felicity perked and sat straighter, stretching to see as far as she could up the curving driveway to the Atterleys' front veranda. That voice. She would know it anywhere. It was as rich and delicious as the perfect caramel licked from a spoon. The deep laugh that followed made her shiver. How could any man sound so...so...

She sighed. There were no words.

As he strolled into view, she leaned back, watching from the shadows as she always did. What a finely made man he was. Then a pair of last Season's flighty young things swirled around him like silky moths to a flame. Damn their eyes, fawning over him as if he were the last available man in all creation.

The surge of jealousy surprised her. She had no right. Well, yes, she did. Hadn't the man recited a poem just for her?

The ladies on either side of him tittered like a pair of nervous birds, laughing at every word that fell from his lips. The longer Felicity watched, the lower her heart sank. Oh, why hadn't she gone back out to the party as Mrs. Amesbury had suggested? And now here she sat. In the carriage. In a gown she had purposely torn.

"I am such a fool." She sagged back in the seat and closed her eyes, refusing to cry over an evening gone so terribly wrong, much to her own doing. She should have gone back to the party and properly introduced herself. Of course, she had no way of knowing if Lord Wakefield would treat her the same when he discovered she was a peer, but it *might* have gone well. He might have been pleased to discover who she really was.

Another sigh left her. Now, she would never know.

More laughter from the ladies walking alongside him had her wishing they would either choke on bugs or stumble on the path and land face first in the roses. Then she felt ashamed for harboring such horrid thoughts and truly hoped that Mama was so busy up in heaven that she hadn't heard them. Those girls were simply behaving as they had been trained by their marriage-minded mamas, while Felicity sat in the shadows of the carriage because she was a coward, the shy Broadmere mouse.

"Fool, fool, fool."

The carriage door opened, and a slightly out-of-breath Merry popped inside. "Who is a fool?"

"I am."

"Why?"

Felicity wasn't ready to share all the evening's details just yet. She turned and displayed her ruptured seam. "This."

Merry frowned. "How does tearing your dress make you a fool? It was the dress's fault. Not yours."

"I should have been more cautious. Madame Couire will not be pleased. She warned me about this silk."

"Madame Couire needs to learn some grace and curb her tongue. She also needs to remember that there are other modistes in Town, and also here. I do not like the way she scolds you when you need a dress repaired or seams adjusted. It is most rude, and I just might decide to speak with her about it at our next meeting."

"Leave it, Merry," Felicity said while risking another look out the window.

"Chance and Seri will be a moment longer. Lady Atterley didn't seem quite prepared to bid them adieu. You know how she can be sometimes now that her daughter has married and moved to the Continent."

"I hope Lady Frederica is very happy," Felicity said while leaning forward and stretching to see the earl and his pair of adoring hens.

"Who are you watching?"

Felicity snapped back and straightened in the seat. "No one. Why?"

Merry stretched and stuck her head all the way out the window for a long moment, then pulled back inside and settled in place. "Lady Carolee and Miss Maralee are making fools of themselves over that gentleman. Who is he? I have never seen him before. Did you happen to notice him before you escaped to the kitchen?"

"Mrs. Amesbury said his name was Lord Wakefield." Which wasn't exactly a lie, because Mrs. Amesbury had asked him his name.

"Lord Wakefield," Merry repeated, then wrinkled her nose. "Is he the one whose uncle died in the carriage accident and left him the title?"

"The very same, is my understanding." Felicity hated lying to Merry, but the evening was still too raw to spill all the details and all the mistakes made.

"Hmm…" Merry stretched back out the window for another look. "He appears to be leaving. On foot. Is that not rather odd?"

Felicity shrugged while fighting the urge to hang out the window and see for herself. "It is a rather nice evening."

"Yes, but to walk? Why did he not ride his horse? That would have been just as pleasing, and far less exertion in his best clothes and shoes."

"Perhaps he likes to walk?" Felicity wished Merry would be quiet, but a quiet moment with Merry was a rare occurrence. "Any sign of Chance and Seri? I do not look forward to the ride home."

Merry waved away her worries. "You know how it will be. Chance will sulk, and Seri will bathe us both in disagreeable looks and hissing sighs. Tomorrow will be worse. I am sure Chance will call one of his *meetings of the flock*."

"His flock is shrinking fast, and I am certain our dwindling numbers have him champing at the bit." Felicity pointed at her sister. "Best take care—since you have reached the ripe old age of one and twenty, he might not be satisfied with only one marriage this year."

Merry wrinkled her button nose again. "Chance needs to be thankful for that which he already has." She shook a finger. "And he also needs to remember that Seri must marry as well. When is he going to turn on her and hang her in the available-to-wed window along with the rest of us?"

"Seri knows how to handle Chance," Felicity said. "She discreetly steers him in whichever direction she wishes him to go. I very much doubt he will turn on her until you and I are gone."

"Well, I am not ready yet." Merry gave a curt nod, making her blonde curls bounce. "I wish I could get the babies without having to deal with finding the right sort of husband. They are all so…so…irritating and full of themselves, expecting us to fawn all over them and place them on a pedestal."

"Mama placed Papa on a pedestal," Felicity gently reminded her.

"That is because Mama adored Papa as much as he adored her." Merry's smile turned sad. "And Papa was never a pompous arse with her. He listened and took her thoughts to heart."

"Would it not be wonderful to find a man like that?" Felicity wondered if the earl might remotely satisfy that requirement.

"It would be heavenly," Merry said.

DRAKE PEMBERTON, THE secretly impoverished and fake seventh Earl of Wakefield, walked home from the Atterley dinner party, claiming the night much too glorious for riding in a carriage and his Thoroughbred much too spent after escaping the stall earlier in the day. In truth, his carriage was in dire need of repair, and his Thoroughbred was yet to be properly re-shod because he had barely scraped together enough blunt to pay the farrier, who had refused to grant the Wakefield estate any more credit.

Hands in his pockets, a heavy sigh escaped him as his footfalls thudded and crunched on the crushed stone of the roadway. The balmy evening did nothing to comfort or lift his spirits. Old Uncle George had surely drawn him into a fine kettle of fish, and he was about to drown in it.

Heaven help them both if anyone discovered that his uncle, the sixth Earl of Wakefield, was still alive and hopefully safely hidden away at Wakefield Manor, which was actually Drake's property that he had inherited from his father. Uncle George had gambled away the original Wakefield Manor, then coerced Drake into agreeing that it could be released from entailment to pay other household debts that had been ignored. Drake had no choice. It was either that or Uncle George would be dragged away to debtor's prison; therefore, the barring of entail had been done to satisfy at least a few of his uncle's creditors.

Unfortunately, the old man's gambling debts with the moneylenders, Rum and Catherty, were not so easily remedied, and the creditors took umbrage with Uncle George's unpaid notes. So much so that a carriage accident, which was no accident at all, stole away the use of Uncle George's legs. Afterward, forever bound to a bath chair and as conniving as the shrewdest cheat, he had convinced Drake to help him stage his own demise to save his life, even going so far as to erect a fine headstone on his empty grave in the kirkyard.

Upon settling the Wakefield estate, some but not all of Uncle George's legal debts were satisfied, but there was nothing left to pay off the gambling debts owed to Rum and Catherty. As the next earl, neither Drake nor the estate was legally bound to pay those, which left the moneylenders exceedingly disgruntled.

Drake sensed trouble brewing with that pair of usurers who had no compunction about taking their payments in blood. As yet, nothing had happened, but they still believed Uncle George had died of his injuries in the carriage accident they had *arranged*. They had no idea that Drake's uncle now posed as Mr. Charles Pembroke, a dear old friend of the previous earl that Drake had taken in, since the man was not only crippled, but poor as a church mouse.

"Damn and blast it all." Drake squinted up at the moon while sauntering along, thoroughly disappointed with his current lot in life. The evening had been a disaster as well. After much research, he had decided to win the heart and hand of one of the esteemed Broadmere sisters, not only because of their alleged loveliness but the plumpness of their dowries. Rumor had it, their dowries were among the most generous of the *ton*. By his count and according to everyone he had *carefully* spoken with, there were three sisters left on the Marriage Mart. Surely, he could convince one of them to marry him and be done with this damnable insolvency.

Alas, this evening had done nothing to forward those goals. The eldest Broadmere sister had regarded him with an almost hawkish coldness, and the other two were nowhere to be found. The only bright spot in the entire dinner party was the lovely blonde angel in the kitchen.

Another heavy sigh left him, but this one was a smidge happier. Such a sweet, gentle maiden she was, and her cooking? Exemplary. Perhaps once he married, he could hire her away from the Atterleys. Oh, to have a cook again would be the sheerest delight. Not that their housekeeper's boiling of the vegetables didn't fill one's belly, but Mrs. Pepperhill tended to cook the potatoes until they were more like gruel than a hardy, satisfying bite. Meat was an impossibility unless he had a successful hunt, which he had not had of late. Thankfully, the kitchen garden was flourishing and providing more choices for their pitifully sparse plates.

He had to win a Broadmere sister, marry her, and hire that kitchen angel away from Lady Atterley. More's the pity, the delightful girl had no worth other than her beauty and ability to coddle an egg. If only she had a dowry. Now, *there* was a woman he would happily pursue. Sadly, as a servant, the best he could do was appreciate her cooking, since he would never sully a maiden as sweet as her by making inappropriate advances or suggestions. He might be desperate and a bit of a cad because of his current situation, but at least he had kept a few scruples. Uncle George hadn't completely debauched him. He ground his teeth until his jaws ached. No, he was not debauched at all. He had simply done and was doing all that was necessary to keep his uncle alive. After all, the man had always doted on him and was his father's only brother, the eldest of the family. And, gads alive, Drake missed his father. He took care of Uncle George in honor of his father and the memory of how he had often bailed out the errant brother of the family.

As he rounded the bend, a single lit window at one end of the large manor house greeted him. Good. Mrs. Pepperhill and their butler, Yateston, had finally heeded his order to conserve the candles and lamp oil as much as possible. Such things might be necessities, but they were expensive and had to be handled judiciously.

"Evening, sir," Yateston said as he opened the door before Drake even reached it.

"Good evening, Yateston. Is the old man in his room or the kitchen?" The window with the candle was in the vicinity of the kitchen, and Uncle George had a tendency to go foraging this late at night. With his bedchamber on the main level, even though Yateston was available to push him through the home, Uncle had become quite adept at wheeling his bath chair to wherever he wished to go, even though it was rather awkward.

"In the kitchen, sir. Eating the last of the stale bread."

All the bread had gone stale, but they could hardly afford not to eat it. Mrs. Pepperhill only attempted baking every two weeks in order to make the flour go farther. Her loaves and buns were hard and heavy, more suitable for cannon fodder than human consumption. But, again, they could ill afford to let anything go to waste.

"Tomorrow is baking day," Drake said, after counting backward to make sure. Baking day was always a good day. It made the house smell as if they actually possessed something worth eating. He wondered how well Lady Atterley's lovely young kitchen maid baked. If her breads and other baked goods were as sweet as her nature, her foods would be beyond compare.

As he entered the kitchen, his uncle was brushing crumbs from his lap.

"Sorry, lad. I et the last of it." Uncle George belched as if he had just enjoyed a feast. "I believe she is getting better." He squinted one eye shut as he picked his teeth. "Last time I nigh on broke a tooth on that crust. This time it was not nearly so tough."

"Good to hear." Drake pulled out a chair from the worn table, sank into it, and stretched out his long legs, crossing them at the ankles. "I fear tonight was a complete loss. The only maiden I managed to charm was the one in the kitchen."

"What the devil were you doing in the kitchen? You should have been on the dance floor or playing one of those ridiculous games Lady Atterley contrives to torture gentlemen with each year." Uncle George tried to clean his glass of its coating of milk, but upon failing to claim the last of the creamy-white residue, he ran his finger around its insides and sopped up the rest. "Soured its way to buttermilk, but milk is milk." He slid the glass back onto the table and settled more comfortably back amongst his cushions. "Were the Broadmeres not in attendance? And again, I ask, why the blazes were you in the kitchen?"

"I was in the kitchen because I missed the meal and was famished, and yes, the Broadmeres were there. Or at least the eldest sister was, but the look she gave me left no doubt whatsoever that I would do well to keep walking and leave her alone."

"Perhaps she was being coy."

Drake slowly shook his head. "I think not."

"What about the other two? Or some of the other ladies. Their dowries might not be as ample as a Broadmere bird, but no amount of blunt would go amiss."

"I could not locate the other two Broadmere ladies, and do not call them birds. You understand they have to marry for love for their brother to allow it?" Drake scrubbed a hand across his eyes. The night had wearied him.

"They are all of age," Uncle George retorted with a gravelly laugh. "They can marry whomever they wish. The dowry would still be paid whether or not they received the duke's blessing."

"They would desire their brother's blessing." Sometimes, Uncle George's crassness was more than Drake could bear. "And I am certain the remaining sisters desire a love match. From what I am told, the first four achieved that rarest of states."

His uncle snorted a disgruntled huff and folded his spindly

arms across his chest. "You, dear boy, are a hopeless romantic. Just like your father."

"Thank you. I consider that the highest praise." Drake couldn't resist poking the old bear. "That hopeless romantic saved you many a time because he loved you."

Uncle George bowed his head while pulling in a deep breath and exhaling a heavy sigh. "God rest his soul."

"God rest his soul," Drake said, then pushed up from his chair and went to the window. With the moonlight shining in, he was tempted to pinch out the candle, but decided against it. Uncle George's arms were already battered and bruised from bumping into things in the dark. "It is late, old man. Time for rest."

"Yes. Time for rest," his uncle repeated softly. He stretched forward and took hold of the wheels, then dropped his hands away and fell back into his chair. "Push me, boy. This old man is weary."

"Glad to, Uncle. Glad to."

DRAKE ROSE EARLY and trudged out to the stables before he had even had his tea. The horses needed tending, and with only John choosing to stay on at Wakefield for nothing more than room and meager board, help was needed for mucking out the stalls and seeing that everyone was fed and brushed. Thoroughbreds were costly, and fine draft horses for carriages were not much cheaper. The animals would be seen to before Drake saw to himself.

"Morning to ye, m'lord," the aging Scot said as Drake grabbed a pitchfork. "How be ye this fine day? Any luck in yer hunt for a wife?"

"Not yet, John." Drake went to the first empty stall and started scooping up the soiled hay and dumping it into the wheelbarrow. "Dancer still limping? The farrier should be here today."

"Aye, the rascal is not having any weight on that foot, to be sure." With a curled hand gnarled by years of working in the stables, John gave the gleaming black stallion beside him an affectionate rub. "He be a good 'un, though, my lord. Glad I am that ye be getting him seen to."

Drake traded the pitchfork for a push broom and continued cleaning the stall. "I am doing my damnedest to take care of everyone, John. Truly I am." Could he possibly sound more pathetic? Time to find his backbone again and stop complaining. "I found us a fine cook to hire once I marry." His mouth started watering at the memory of the coddled eggs and soldiers. "And she is an absolute angel to look upon, too."

"Is she now?" John chuckled. "Not one of those skinny maids, is she? I dinna trust a cook what looks as if she never eats." He made the shape of a curvy woman in midair. "As me da always said, 'Gi' me a woman with enough soft plumpness about her to keep me warm on a cold winter's night.'"

Drake grinned, remembering the lovely young miss with the ample figure. "Curves aplenty, John. Golden hair. Eyes the sparkling blue of a fine sapphire, and a fetching smile that draws you in and threatens to make you forget your manners."

John shook his head as he led Dancer back into the freshly cleaned stall and gave him some feed. "Sounds to me as if ye got more in mind for her than the position of cook at Wakefield."

Drake leaned against the broom's handle and shook his head. "No. This angel is much too kind to sully in such a way. She deserves better."

"Ye remind me of yer father when ye talk like that." John shook a crooked finger. "Stay that way, aye? Dinna let that uncle of yers change ye." When John had stayed on at Wakefield, he had made it clear that he only did it because of Drake's father. The man made no bones about disliking the earl and not possessing an ounce of respect for him.

"Father's voice is always in my head, John. But I have to protect Uncle George. You know Father would have done the same."

"Aye. He would at that." John went to the next stall over and started cleaning it. "We'll be needing to let them out in the pasture more. Feed's getting low, and so is the hay. In the old days, we wouldha had the grass from the cuttin', but with no men in the fields, I reckon it'll have to be bought as soon as ye can."

Drake repressed a sigh. Yet another expense that had hit the wall on credit. "I am going into Binnocksbourne today. I shall see what I can accomplish."

"If I had any blunt to spare, ye know I would help," John said, his voice somber as he shoveled out the stall.

"I know, John, and I am grateful to you for staying on."

The older man nodded, then set to work in silence. It took the two of them more than an hour to get the horses properly cared for and set to grazing in the grassy pasture behind the stable.

Drake dusted off his hands. "After a good wash and some tea, I shall head into the village."

"Dancer canna be ridden just yet, ye ken? Could do permanent damage."

"I know." Drake kept his head held high. "It's just a good stretch of the legs. I shall walk." He turned to head back to the house.

"M'lord?"

Drake paused and looked back. "Yes?"

"God be with ye."

"Thank you, John." Drake knew the man meant so much more, and it made him even more determined to set things right for the Wakefield estate. Too many lives depended on his finding a wife with a fine, fat dowry for him to fail.

Chapter Three

FELICITY EYED LAST night's damaged gown draped over the chair. A vibrant shade of orchid, it had been one of her favorites until the bodice had become so snug. Daisy, her lady's maid, had apologized profusely, fearing she had drawn the dress's ribbons too tight or not pulled the laces tight enough on Felicity's stays. Felicity knew better. Once again, she had *outgrown* a Madame Couire creation.

She turned back to her glum expression in the dressing table mirror, wincing as Daisy twisted her hair into a fashionable braid that encircled her head.

"Forgive me, my lady," the maid said. "I didn't mean to pull."

"I know—I just need you to go slower. Getting dressed for the day is my only excuse for not already being down in the parlor as His Grace commanded." Chance had done his usual—summoned a meeting of his sisters, affectionately and sometimes not so affectionately known as *the flock*. And he had done so at an unholy hour of the morning. She hadn't even enjoyed her first cup of chocolate. "I am in no mood for my brother today. Does Cook have any fresh eels? His Grace needs a bucketful of them in his bed. If not, I shall need to visit the pond."

Daisy snorted, then hurried to cover her mouth. But nothing could hide the laughter in her eyes. She squared her shoulders and cleared her throat, struggling to assume a serious air. "Now, now, my lady. You know His Grace only has your best interests in mind."

"His Grace only has his monthly allowance in mind," Felicity grumbled. She glanced at the bedroom door. "Have you seen Lady Merry this morning? Do you know whether she has gone down yet?" With four sisters married, the remaining three no longer shared rooms, leaving Felicity feeling disconnected. "I most certainly do not want to be the first in the parlor to face the interrogation."

"I heard Jenny in the hallway. Surely, that must mean Lady Merry has already gone down before you."

"I hope so. Out of the two of us, she forces His Grace to behave with a little bit of compassion and respect." Felicity wiggled a brow. "I believe he is afraid of her."

"All the maids believe you have the right of it there, Lady Felicity. We think he fears her almost as much as he fears Lady Grace and Lady Blessing." Daisy stepped back and returned the brush and unused hairpins to the table. "I am afraid we are all finished here. I am sorry I completed it in such a timely manner."

"Well, you made it last as long as you could, and for that, I am grateful." Felicity rose from the cushioned stool and meandered over to the window before heading out the door. She was in no mood for Chance this morning. No mood at all.

A sharp rap on the door interrupted her musings. Merry stuck her head inside and glared at Felicity. "Come along. We might as well get this over with."

"I make no promises as to my behavior." A sudden surge of defiance filled Felicity.

"Good." Merry looped her arm through hers. "With the two of us against Seri and Chance, the odds are even, but I like to think we outnumber them. After all, Chance is not nearly as quick on his feet as we are."

"True." Merry's outlook brightened Felicity's mood considerably.

As they entered the parlor, they groaned in unison. Chance already stood in his usual place, in front of the hearth, with two chairs strategically placed in front of him. Serendipity stood off to the side, reminding Felicity of an avenging angel ready to cleave them in two if they didn't make haste and find husbands. Arms still linked, they went to the chairs and flounced down onto them.

"I am very disappointed in both of you," Chance said.

"Then we are even," Felicity retorted, "because I am very disappointed in you, too. You could have at least waited to hold your ridiculous meeting until after breakfast. I have yet to have even a single sip of chocolate or tea."

"Then I shall speak to Daisy," Chance said, "about not taking better care of her mistress. She should have arranged that while you were dressing." He clasped his hands to the small of his back and started pacing. "You *must* refrain from hiding in the kitchens, or you will never find a husband. Do you wish to remain a spinster and live under the same roof with me all the rest of your days?"

"Father provided an ample allowance for all of us," Merry said, coming to Felicity's rescue. "She would not have to share the same home as you."

"And you!" Chance pointed at his youngest sister. "Hiding not in the nursery, but in Lady Frederica's former suite? Are you mad?"

"Freddie told me if ever I should go to her former country home that she had some lovely books I would enjoy," Merry said with amazing innocence.

Felicity was impressed with her sister's ability to keep a straight face while telling such an obvious lie.

"And you ruined another gown," Serendipity said to Felicity as she took a step forward. "Really, Felli. You must at least attempt to show some restraint. Thank heavens a new modiste moved to the village, so we'll not have to wait until we return to Town to not only have last night's dress repaired but to have the seams let out in your other gowns too. I assume they have become uncomfortably tight as well?"

As a matter of fact, they hadn't, and Serendipity's insinuation stung. "They are fine," Felicity snapped. "And if our straits are so dire, I shall pay for my gown repairs out of my own pin money."

"You shall not!" Chance roared. He rolled his broad shoulders, making his large frame even more forbidding. He would be a harbinger of doom to someone else. Felicity knew him to be harmless. "Our straits are not dire," he said, "but the extent of my patience is." He snorted like an angry bull and paced some more, apparently attempting to calm himself. "Forgive me for raising my voice, but you know we are not in dire straits, and you should never say that. Not even in jest. Many are having issues due to poor investment schemes and failed crops. Thankfully, Mr. Sutherland, the elder, keeps all that well in hand and offers me excellent guidance."

"I believe that is the kindest thing I have ever heard you say about our solicitor." Felicity shifted in the chair, longing for a cup of chocolate *and* a cup of tea. "Is that all, brother? We know you do not appreciate it when we hide. That is part of the reason we do it."

Merry giggled. *"Touché*, Felli!"

"No, that is not all," Chance said through gritted teeth. "If you two had seen fit to take part in the festivities last evening, you would have met the new Earl of Wakefield. He inherited the title upon the recent death of his uncle. The man is young, from the gentry class, and handles himself quite well, if I do say so myself. He is also in search of a wife."

"And I have yet to discover any untoward rumors about this new lord," Serendipity said. "Unlike his uncle, he appears to be averse to gambling and determined to restore the Wakefield name."

"Averse to gambling and determined to restore the Wakefield name," Felicity repeated while trying not to groan at this revelation. "In other words, he is also in search of a *dowry*. A fine, fat one. Need I remind you we are to marry for *love*? Not someone's desire for our money?"

"You could at least meet him," Serendipity said, clipping her words so sharply that she reminded Felicity of an angry hen.

"Is that all?" Felicity asked again. She wasn't about to share that she had already met the eloquent earl and liked him a great deal. However, the news that he was more than likely a dowry hunter dampened her enthusiasm. She wanted a husband who liked her for *herself*, not for her money.

"Yes, our dear, unhappy keepers, is that all?" Merry asked. "Felli and I are going into the village after breakfast, and we would like to enjoy the walk rather than be roasted by the hot midday sun."

"Take your parasols and wear your gloves," Serendipity reminded her. "And yes, that is all. I honestly do not know why we bother. You two are worse than Blessing, Fortuity, Grace, and Joy ever were. But please, I beg you, and so does Chance, please stop hiding. So far, your antics have gone unnoticed by the gossips, but that will not last forever."

Their antics had gone unnoticed by the gossips because the servants of the *ton* were their loyal and trusted friends. Those who took care of the aristocratic households were the lines of communication that fed the rumor business.

Both Felicity and Merry curtsied, then scurried from the room before Chance or Serendipity remembered something else to harp on them about. Arms once more linked, they headed to the garden after asking Walter to serve them breakfast there.

Once they were seated in the shade beside the reflecting pool, they both exhaled in relief.

"I believe we have worn Chance down," Merry said.

"Do not underestimate him." Felicity lifted her face to the gentle breeze and breathed in the refreshing aroma of their mother's roses in full bloom. "When I smell the sweetness of these flowers, I always feel like Mama is back here with us. She always smelled of roses, didn't she?"

Merry smiled. "She did—and I feel her too. I think she and Papa are watching over us."

"I hope so."

A bee lazily buzzed from blossom to blossom. Birdsong filled the air, and the musical trickling of the fountain filled Felicity with a calmness she sorely needed. She resettled herself more comfortably on the cushioned wrought-iron chair. "Do you think poor Walters will remember we are out here? Fipps was not with him when we asked to have breakfast here in the garden."

Their dear, aging butler grew worse every day, but none of them had the heart to force him to leave his post. Instead, Chance had hired Mr. Fipps as a *junior* butler to help keep Walters focused. At first, the elder butler had sulked and fought the new young gentleman. But finally, he'd grudgingly accepted Fipps's guidance and help.

"Fipps is never far, and the man has the hearing of an owl," Merry said. "Or so says Mrs. Flackney."

The rattle of a tea cart on the flagstones attested to Merry's words. Fipps was pushing it with Walters ambling along behind it, following the junior butler like a devoted old hound.

"Tea and chocolate, Lady Felicity?" Fipps asked.

"Of course she wants tea and chocolate," Walters growled in his gravelly voice. "She always does. Lady Felicity loves her tea and chocolate first thing each morning. Just pour it, man, or get out of my way, and I shall do it."

"Forgive me, Mr. Walters," Fipps said. "You are quite right." He took a step back, his expression stoic, but kindness and compassion shone in his eyes.

For once, Felicity was proud of her brother for his caring nature regarding Walters, and for his determination in finding the perfect *helper* in Mr. Fipps. Walters might be slipping with age, but he had served them forever and deserved every bit of dignity that could be offered. He poured the tea and chocolate, spilling only a little because of the constant tremor in his arthritis-torn hands.

"Thank you, Walters. Thank you, Fipps. That will be all." Felicity smiled at them both and gave Fipps a nod of appreciation.

"Chance found the perfect helper in Fipps," Merry said as

soon as the men were well out of hearing distance. "Good on him."

"He did indeed, and I am not surprised." Felicity took a sip of the rich, decadent chocolate and almost purred. "For once, I am proud of our brother for his diligence and over-attention to detail. He interviewed quite a few before settling on Fipps."

"Well, he owes Walters his life. Remember the time Walters pulled him from the pond when Chance's legs cramped so badly he couldn't make it back to shallow water? Walters didn't hesitate to jump in and save him."

Felicity nodded and dipped a corner of her toast into her coddled egg, swirling it in the liquid gold of the yolk. "I remember we all were sent to the nursery without our supper because we threw Chance's favorite wooden sword in that pond, and that is what he was after."

"And we were advised never to try to kill our brother again because he was to be the next duke." Merry giggled as she cut into a kipper. "We weren't trying to kill him—merely disarm him."

Felicity laughed. "I think that is why Mama and Papa were so angry not only with us but also with Chance, because he had other swords he could have retrieved from the playroom."

Merry nodded. "Seems like I do remember Chance receiving hugs *and* lectures about finding a bit of good sense and using his head for something other than a hat rack."

"I miss those days."

"So do I." Merry sighed, finished her kipper, then dipped a strip of toast into her egg cup. "So, are you going to stay out of the kitchens long enough to meet this new Earl of Wakefield?"

"I already met him." Felicity pushed her plate away and poured herself another cup of chocolate. This conversation required it.

Merry stared at her for a long moment. "When?"

"Last night."

"Where?"

"In the kitchen."

"In the kitchen?"

"He arrived late to the party, thereby missing dinner, and the vicar and Lady Urnstall had already emptied the refreshment table." Felicity shrugged, but it was more of a shiver brought on by the memory of the handsome earl.

"You are blushing clear to your toes," Merry said. She refilled her tea, then leaned forward with the cup balanced between her hands. "Tell me every bit. Every word. Leave nothing out. What does he look like? How does he act? Did you like him, or is he a groveling fool?"

"He is very handsome."

"How handsome?"

"The broadest shoulders. My goodness, he filled the doorway when he entered the kitchen. Dark hair. The kindest eyes. And a crooked little smile that says he knows he is handsome, but he is not haughty at all."

"Did you speak to him?" Elbows on the table, Merry leaned even closer, her tea still held in midair.

"Of course I spoke to him. As a matter of fact, I fed him. Coddled eggs and soldiers. He thought them so divine that he recited a poem about them."

"A poem?" Merry arched a brow.

"'Ode to the Fair Maiden's Coddled Eggs,' by an Importunate Breakfast Admirer."

"You liked him." Merry grinned. "You liked him a great deal. Should we stay home today in case he comes calling?"

Felicity bit her lip and set her chocolate down. "He only knows me as Miss Felicity, the kitchen maid."

Merry stared at her again, sitting so still that she appeared frozen. "What?"

"He asked me my name, and I said, 'Felicity.'"

"Conveniently leaving off the *lady* part?" Merry surmised.

"Yes."

"And he did not think it unusual for a kitchen maid to be

wearing such a fine silk gown?"

"It was covered by the apron I made. Unless he had happened to look at my feet, he never would have seen any part of the gown. The apron goes down to my shins because Serendipity became so infuriated when I ruined a gown with a wine sauce the week before last."

Merry leaned back in her chair and thoughtfully sipped her tea, all the while eyeing Felicity with a plotting look. "So, he has no idea you are the sister of a duke with a fine, plump dowry. How did he treat you as a penniless maid?"

"He was very nice." Felicity couldn't help but sigh. Lord Wakefield had impressed her greatly. "You remember how the heroes in Fortuity's books are always written to have those rich, deep voices that *feel* like a gentle caress? And he was so easy to talk with. It was as though I had known him forever."

"Oh, my sister. I do believe you are smitten." Merry straightened and fluttered a hand over the contents of the breakfast table. "Finish your breakfast so we can get to the village. Perhaps we shall see him on the green. The village council did its best to mimic Hyde Park and Rotten Row. Perhaps he chose this lovely day to promenade. Instead of the shops, shall we promenade?"

"I prefer the shops to the promenade. We shall save that for another day." The discussion had awakened the herd of fluttering butterflies that had taken up residence in Felicity's middle ever since meeting the earl. The breakfast she had eaten did nothing to slow the furious beating of their wings. How would the earl act when he discovered her true identity? Would last night become a precious dream never to be repeated because he would seek out her dowry rather than her?

She placed her napkin on the table. "After this discussion, I am well and truly finished with breakfast. Knowing Seri, she probably already had one of the maids fetch our gloves, bonnets, and parasols so we would have no excuse to leave them behind."

"I am sure they are waiting on the table beside the door." Merry placed her napkin beside her plate and hopped up from her seat, waving for Felicity to follow. "Come along now. I am eager to meet your earl."

"He is not *my* earl, and we might not even see him." Felicity took a deep breath, attempting to calm herself. The earl was probably riding. Or hunting. Or whatever it was men did to amuse themselves when not attending parties. They probably wouldn't see him at all. Then her heart got into the inner dialogue, whispering oh so softly, *I hope we see him.*

She hurried along after her sister, both excited and filled with dread. Without the protection of her safe space, her kitchens, and the company of the cooks and the scullery maids, she struggled with making conversation with gentlemen. She tugged on her gloves, pulled on her bonnet that matched the delicate blue of her spencer and her muslin gown, looped the ribbons of her reticule over her wrist, and retrieved her parasol that the maid had propped against the entry hall table.

"I am ready," she said, not feeling ready at all.

With a bounce in her step, Merry led the way out the door and down the front steps. "Seri will be beside herself when she discovers you have already met the earl."

"You mustn't tell!" Felicity hurried to catch up with her sister. "And do slow yourself. This is not a race. Do you wish to arrive red-faced and glistening with sweat?"

After an apologetic nod, Merry slowed. "Do not be fractious. You know I would never tell Seri anything you did not wish told." She made a dramatic bow while walking and almost tripped over her hemline. Giggling at her own clumsiness, she added, "I am honored you chose to tell me."

"Parasols up," Felicity said. "There is Lady Urnstall, coming to visit Seri. She will surely tell her she saw us."

Merry hurried to open her parasol and prop it on her shoulder. "There. She should report us as bonnets on, gloves on, and parasols at the ready. I hope Cook has extra biscuits made, or there will be none left for us at tea."

"Lady Urnstall does enjoy eating, but she is rail thin. How

does she do it?"

"Perhaps she has a worm."

"Merry!"

She shrugged. "Well, either that or consumption. The woman is little more than an assemblage of walking bones. More folks than we have noticed her appetite and the direct contrast of the sharpness of her features."

"Let us change the subject." Felicity noticed she was clenching her jaws so hard that they ached. *I must relax and calm down. We probably won't even see him.* She eased in a deep, calming breath and allowed it to drift back out. "It is a lovely day."

"A perfect day for a promenade," Merry said with unmistakable slyness.

"Shops first."

"You are no fun."

"If we are not too weary after the shops, perhaps there will be time for an abbreviated promenade." Felicity couldn't help but relent. All the sisters did when it came to Merry. After all, she was the baby of the family.

"Agreed." Merry swung her reticule at her side. "Mettlestone's first, then Creary's Bookshop, then promenade."

"No treats from Caruthers?" Not that Felicity was hungry, but she adored chatting about recipes with Mrs. Caruthers.

"If we go in there, it will be well past teatime before we leave." Merry gave her a pointed glare. "You do not know when to stop when it comes to talking about recipes."

Felicity couldn't deny the truth in that. "Fine. Only Mettlestone's and Creary's, then."

"Tell me more about this ode to a fair maiden." Merry's craftiness knew no boundaries.

"'Ode to a Fair Maiden's Coddled Eggs,'" Felicity corrected her.

"Did he expound upon the fair maiden part?"

Felicity sighed, knowing Merry would not cease until she had pulled every shred of information about the poem. "A little. The last two stanzas were quite nice."

"Recite them."

"I cannot say that I remember them word for word," Felicity lied.

"Felicity."

"What?"

"Did you know that you wrinkle your nose whenever you tell an untruth?"

"I do not."

Merry bobbed her head. "Yes, you do, and all of us know it. How do you think Chance and Seri always ferret out the truth from you?"

"Well, blast," Felicity muttered. She must remember that and strive to undo that telltale habit. "If I repeat the stanzas, you mustn't read too much into them. Understood?"

"Understood."

After a deep breath and a hard swallow, Felicity recited,

> *"For not alone thy eggs are warm—*
> *Thy smile too holds a softened charm;*
> *Thy kitchen is a hallowed space*
> *Where hunger yields to art and grace.*
>
> *So here I sit, with heart o'erthrown,*
> *Beside thy dish, my love full-blown.*
> *Not for the eggs—though rich, divine—*
> *But for the hand that coddles mine."*

Merry squealed in a most unladylike manner. "He likes you!"

"Merry!" Felicity shushed her as they traipsed into the village. "Control your outbursts, or I shall not speak another word to you the rest of the day."

"Another lie," Merry said with a giggle. "You know you cannot help yourself, and are you not excited that he expressed such fondness for you? He even mentioned *love*."

"He expressed a fondness for the coddled eggs, not me." Felicity headed to Mettlestone's shop, which supplied the village with anything anyone desired. If they didn't keep it in stock, they ordered it. "And as far as he knew, he was flirting with the kitchen maid. You know how lordlings can be."

"Did he make any untoward advances or say anything he should not have?" Merry sounded uncharacteristically serious.

Felicity pulled open the door to the shop, causing the bell to jangle merrily. "He did not. That is one thing that truly impressed me about his character."

"Lady Merry! Lady Felicity!" Mr. Herbert Mettlestone came running out from behind the counter, trundling as fast as his portly self would allow. "I was just saying to Mrs. Beatrice that I hoped for a visit from the Broadmere family today." He turned and bellowed, "Mrs. Beatrice! Lady Merry and Lady Felicity are here! Mrs. Beatrice!"

Felicity almost covered her ears but refrained from doing so because poor Mrs. Beatrice suffered from hearing loss and so missed being an integral part of any conversation.

Mr. Herbert's wife came flying out of the backroom, her hands raised in delight. "Ladies! It is so good to see you. What might we tempt you with today?"

"Gossip about the new Earl of Wakefield," Merry said loud enough for half of England to hear. "What have you heard?" Felicity was ready to kick her.

Both Mr. Herbert and Mrs. Beatrice exchanged meaningful glances, then went strangely solemn. "The young lord is very personable," Mrs. Beatrice said with a tight smile. "I fear that is all we know of him as yet."

Felicity smelled a lie but didn't wish to make the older couple any more uncomfortable than they already seemed to be. "Then tell us about the new modiste. Is she talented?"

"Mrs. Kerr is also quite amiable," Mr. Herbert said. "Newly widowed, she moved here to Binnocksbourne for a fresh start. She and her daughter are purported to be very talented and up to date with the latest fashions."

The doorbell jangled again, making Felicity turn to see who had joined them. It was none other than the Earl of Wakefield. She clutched her hands in front of her middle and prayed for the shop's floorboards to open up and swallow her.

"Well, good day, Miss Felicity," he said. He removed his hat and offered a proper nod as if he already knew her to be a lady of the *ton*. His gaze shifted to Merry, and he nodded again.

"*Miss* Felicity," Mrs. Beatrice repeated, surprising them all that she had actually heard it. "Surely you mean *Lady* Felicity, my lord"—she motioned at Merry—"and Lady Merry, sisters to the Duke of Broadmere, one of the most esteemed families here in Binnocksbourne."

"*Lady* Felicity?" he repeated, the softest glint of accusation in his expression.

Felicity curtsied. "Yes, my lord. Forgive me for not being more forthcoming with my status. Surely, you understand why I chose such caution."

His smile broadened, and then he bowed. "No apology is necessary, my lady. None at all." His gaze lingered on her as he shifted his attention to Merry. "It is a pleasure to meet you, Lady Merry. I failed to meet you at the Atterleys' party last evening."

"Yes," Merry said with a wily grin. "You did." She didn't offer any explanation, just stood there looking as smug as the cat who had just eaten all the cream in the larder.

He tipped a subtle nod, taking her unspoken message to return his attention to Felicity. After a glance over at Mr. Herbert and Mrs. Beatrice, he cleared his throat and smiled. "Might I call upon you, Lady Felicity? Tomorrow, perhaps?"

Felicity tried to see through any subterfuge, knowing her heart and her hopes were blinding her. She curtsied again and turned slightly toward the door. "That would be lovely, my lord. Good day."

"Lady Felicity?" Disappointment dripped from Mrs. Beatrice's voice. "Leaving already? We have some lovely new ribbons with which to tempt you."

"I fear we must," Felicity said. "We are off to visit Mrs. Kerr after your glowing recommendation. We shall return another day for a longer visit. I fear we are short on time today." She offered the earl a smile, then forced herself to exit the shop at a graceful pace, rather than the breakneck run she wished for.

As soon as the door banged shut behind them, Merry caught hold of her arm. "Why are we leaving so soon?" she hissed. "You should stay and talk with him."

"I have said quite enough." The knot of emotions in Felicity's throat was about to strangle her. "Did you not see his eyes light up as soon as Mrs. Beatrice mentioned *Broadmere*?"

"His eyes lit up as soon as he saw you." Merry yanked on her arm. "Slow yourself. You are about to break into a run."

"He wants the dowry. Not me."

"Why could he not want both?"

"Because I am me. The fat, unattractive one of the litter, remember?" Felicity clenched her teeth and continued stomping along, hating herself even more for wallowing in self-pity.

Merry yanked her to a halt. "You are not! Just because you overheard that horse's arse say such cruel things that night does not make them true. You are beautiful, Felicity, just too blinded by what those idiotic lordlings said and Seri's constant nagging about what you put on your plate. And our modiste needs to learn to keep her opinions to herself as well. Now, stop it this instant, or you shall be the one with eels dumped into your bed."

"You are afraid of eels."

"For you, I will make an exception." Merry shook her by the shoulders. "You are beautiful. The earl thinks so too. I saw it in his eyes."

"You saw him gleeful that he had found the solution to his problems."

Merry released her. "Fine. Be pitiful." She whirled about and shook a finger not an inch from the end of Felicity's nose. "What would Mama say? And Papa?"

"They would tell me to spit in those gossiping lordlings' faces." Felicity huffed and blinked hard and fast against the stinging threat of tears.

"And what would they say about Lord Wakefield?"

"To give him a chance," Felicity muttered.

"What?" Merry cocked an ear as if she couldn't hear her.

"To give him a chance," Felicity repeated louder. "You are beginning to sound like Chance and Seri. Do you realize that?"

Merry grinned. "There is no need to be insulting." She shook her finger again. "Now, if I ever hear of you taking to heart what those insufferably cruel coves said, there shall be eels in your bed. Understood? And ignore Seri and the modiste. Do you understand?"

Felicity sighed. "I understand." Then she lengthened her stride. "But we are going home. No promenade today."

Merry snorted and looped her arm through hers. "Fine. No promenade. *Today.*"

— ❧ ❧ —

Chapter Four

"I AM AFRAID that is all I can pay you today, Mr. Herbert." Embarrassment and humiliation pounded through Drake like a terrible poison, making him ache to be done with it. He straightened his spine and carried on. "I do apologize and swear to continue with future installments, if you will but find it in your heart to allow it."

The shopkeeper's troubled expression deepened, and he shook his balding head. "I know these debts are not of your making, my lord, but we are businesspeople and must survive on our profits. The Wakefield estate owes us payment in full. We are talking quite an amount here."

"I understand that." What the shopkeeper didn't realize was that Drake had already sold everything he could part with other than the land his father had left him. As much as he hated to, he decided to offer one of the few precious items he had remaining from his parents. "We have a fine silver service at Wakefield Hall. If I were to bring it here for you to sell and keep the proceeds, would that settle the debt completely? It is very fine." He cleared his throat again. "It is from my mother's side of the family. A wedding present from when she married my father. It is not engraved with any initials and is quite elegant."

The compassion in the old man's eyes gave him hope. Finally, the shopkeeper nodded. "Bring it by for a look, Lord Wakefield. We will see what can be done."

Drake exhaled. "Thank you, Mr. Herbert. Again, I am very sorry."

"I am sorry you found yourself saddled with such debt, my lord." Mr. Herbert closed the account ledger and returned it to its shelf behind the counter.

"As do I, sir. As do I." Drake nodded again, then exited the shop as quickly as possible. The shame of the conversation tasted bitter, almost making him gag. Mettlestone's shop had been the final stop on his list of creditors that he was trying to pay just enough to silence them for a little longer. Or at least long enough so they might extend a bit more credit for absolute necessities. Drake hadn't asked Mr. Herbert about that. As far as he was concerned, they would do without and continue to try to survive on what hunting and the kitchen garden provided. Praise be that Mrs. Pepperhill's brother owned the village gristmill and gave his sister whatever short and coarse brans other customers refused to buy. While the middlings were not as refined as good flour and were normally used for animal feed, the housekeeper did the best she could to further grind the grains with a mortar and pestle and bake barely passable loaves of bread.

Thank heavens the shy Lady Felicity had chosen to leave the shop in haste and hadn't been privy to the unpleasantness of his begging Mr. Herbert for more time. "Damn you, Uncle George," he said under his breath as he strode out of the village. "Damn you straight to hell."

He didn't really mean that, but in a way, he did. Uncle George had paid the price for his poor choices. They had cost him his legs and his identity. Drake raked his hair back out of his eyes, making a note to ask Yateston, the butler, to do his best to trim it once again. He could make do without a valet when it came to most things, but he couldn't properly cut his own damn hair.

He tried to roll the tension from his shoulders and forced himself to think of more pleasant things. Lady Felicity was the first *pleasantness* to come to mind. He smiled. So, the shy, lovely kitchen maid was a Broadmere sister? How could he not have realized it? He thought back to last night and the modest apron she had worn. Then it hit him: the jewelry. How could he not have noticed her earrings and necklace? Amethysts, maybe? Whatever they had been, even though they were simple, he remembered them as being quite fine. What a fool he was. No, not a fool exactly. He hadn't noticed her jewelry because he had been too entranced by the sweetness of her smile.

"And I was starving," he said, remembering that the coddled eggs and soldiers had been the first meal he had eaten all day. He had been too busy for anything more than tea and a toss of brandy right before walking to the party.

So, his golden-haired angel with the luscious curves was a Broadmere sister? His heart lifted. Had he not wished several times that the delightful kitchen maid possessed a dowry? What providence was this? Not only was Lady Felicity witty and most pleasing to the eye, but her family was flush in the pockets. The Broadmere sisters possessed the best dowries of the *ton*—or so the rumormongers said.

He would call upon her tomorrow and every day thereafter until she agreed to marry him. Not only did he already possess a liking for her and an undeniable attraction, but something deep inside told him he might someday come to love her. He had never really thought about finding a wife to *love*, but what a boon that would be. To love the woman able to solve the lion's share of his problems and live a happy life, debt free?

Spirits well and truly lifted, he pushed through the Wakefield estate's back gate that led to the gardens. Merciless thuds and groans came to him, quickening his steps through the maze of overgrown shrubbery.

"Uncle!" Damn, he should not have shouted that. "Mr. Pembroke, take heart! Get off him, you bastards!"

A pair of ruffians broke away from the figure lying beside the overturned bath chair and escaped over the garden wall before Drake reached them. He went to his knees beside his uncle's battered body.

"Uncle?" he whispered, fearing the worst.

Eyes already swollen shut, nose, mouth, and ears streaming blood, Uncle George barely managed a feeble groan. Hugging himself, hands clutching at his ribs, he ducked his head and curled into a tighter ball, not even realizing the beating had stopped.

"Uncle, it is me. Drake." Drake gently lifted the old man and rushed inside with him, leaving the bath chair in the garden. He doubted very much if his uncle could sit upright. As he eased the softly moaning man down onto the bed, he prayed they could tend to the injuries without having to send for the surgeon. There was simply no money for a doctor. "Mrs. Pepperhill! Yateston!"

Mrs. Pepperhill skittered into the room first. "Oh, dear heavens, what happened?"

"I am guessing Rum and Catherty happened," Drake said. "I fear they somehow discovered our poorly played lie about Uncle's death." This time, from the looks of his uncle, the lie might become a reality, but he didn't say that aloud. Both Yateston and Mrs. Pepperhill were more like family than servants and had served the Wakefields for quite some time. "We need fresh water, bandages, and the last of the brandy to clean some of those scrapes and gashes properly." He removed his uncle's shoes and helped the old man straighten his useless legs, tucking them under the covers. "And any herbs you think might help," he called after her as she hurried from the room.

Uncle George moaned louder.

"I know, old man. You have taken a right sorry beating. Can you speak? Did those men say anything?" Drake wet a rag in the basin beside the bed. The water wasn't cool, but it was all he had until Mrs. Pepperhill returned. Ever so gently, he cleaned the blood off his uncle's face and out of his ears. "Uncle George. Can you hear me? Can you speak?"

"Barely," his uncle whispered.

"Did you know those men?"

"No."

"Did they say anything? Do you know why they attacked you?"

Uncle George flinched and bared his teeth, causing the split in his swollen lip to bleed even more. "Owe them money, I reckon."

"Did you try to tell them you were Mr. Charles Pembroke? That you were an old friend of the dead earl and not the earl himself?"

His uncle snorted, then groaned again and clutched his ribs. "They did not appear to be interested in introductions."

"If they have discovered our subterfuge, if Rum and Catherty sent them—" Drake shuddered and raked both hands through his unruly hair. Not only could his uncle be in grave danger once again, but Drake himself could be as well for posing as a peer. "Are you certain they said nothing? Did you at least attempt to tell them you were not the earl?"

"They were not very chatty, and neither was I."

Yateston burst into the room, wringing his hands. "I saw the overturned chair in the garden. Do forgive me, Lord Wakefield. I was in the stable helping John." He paled when he drew close enough to the bed to see Uncle George's state. "Good heavens," he whispered.

"When I arrived, ruffians were pummeling him," Drake said. "There is no money for a surgeon. Pray we can handle his injuries."

Yateston stepped forward, bowing as he tried to move Drake out of the way with a politeness born from years of service. "Allow me, my lord. I will do what I can."

Drake gladly stepped back and let the butler take over. He knew how to tend to animals' injuries from helping his father on the estate. But when it came to tending to people, he feared he was sorely lacking. "Thank you, Yateston."

Mrs. Pepperhill reappeared with a bucket of water, bandages, crocks, jars, and the last bottle of brandy in the house gripped under her chin. "I believe I have everything, my lord," she said, straining to speak without losing the bottle.

Drake helped her set it all down on the cabinet on the other side of the bed. Thinking it might help Uncle George to weather the treatments, he decided to share his best news of the day. "Uncle, do you remember my telling you about the kitchen angel who fed me last night?"

Hissing at the sting of the brandy against his cuts, Uncle George groaned. "What of her now? Has she promised to come cook for us for free?" He winced again. "No offense, Mrs. Pepperhill."

"None taken, my lord." The housekeeper added more brandy to the cloth and continued cleaning.

"As sweet as she is, she more than likely would, if I asked her." Drake flinched in sympathy for his uncle as the butler and housekeeper cleaned away additional blood and grime. "But I doubt Lady Felicity, sister to the Duke of Broadmere, would wish to fill the post permanently."

"Broadmere," his uncle repeated, arching his brows higher over his swollen eyes. "Truly?"

"Truly." Drake drew closer to the bed. "I saw her in Mettle-stone's today, and Mrs. Beatrice properly introduced me to Lady Felicity and her sister. I believe her sister's name is Lady Merry."

"Then why are you still here, standing in my bedchamber?" His uncle coughed and grabbed his ribs with a pained groan. "You should be calling on the lady, fool. Waste no time. By our reckoning, there is naught but three of them left, and you said the eldest one wished to have nothing to do with you." He cringed and bared his teeth as he slowly pressed on his ribs. "None broken, I think. Just badly bruised. Been down that road before. By the way, how do you know it was the eldest one who failed to succumb to your charms? Will she not be the first to need to marry?"

"Lady Atterley's dinner party was rife with gossip, and Lady Serendipity was pointed out as the eldest."

"If she is the eldest, the sisters who have already married must be younger. They do not appear to be pairing off in the usual order." His uncle had already returned to his sly, calculating self.

Drake was glad to hear the old codger's ribs weren't broken. It would take several weeks for Uncle to heal, but he would eventually be back in his bath chair, complaining about his lot in life.

"Full steam ahead, boy. Get thee to Broadmere House and call on Lady...Lady..." Uncle George frowned. "What did you say her name was again?"

"Lady Felicity."

He grunted. "Means *intense happiness* or *eloquence*. Did you know that?"

"I did not, but I find it quite fitting. The lady is most pleasing to chat with."

Uncle George waved him away. "Go see her today. Do not wait until tomorrow."

"I asked permission to call upon her tomorrow, and she granted it. It would be rude and presumptuous of me to show up on her doorstep today." Drake was as eager for his next meeting with Felicity as his uncle was, but he did not wish to overplay his hand.

"Well...I suppose you are right." Uncle George cleared his throat, then grimaced and caught his ribs. "Keep her away from here. She must not discover the state of things until you have properly snared her, and she cannot escape."

And that was where misgivings had started gnawing at Drake's gut. Felicity was so kind and considerate. Didn't the lady deserve to know the truth about his circumstances?

"I know that look," his uncle growled. "You are just like your father. Get it out of your head right this very moment. If you tell her the entirety of the truth, you will lose her."

"What look? Your eyes are swollen shut."

Uncle George snorted again. "You know very well what I mean. Your conscience is your downfall, boy. Once you receive her dowry and set things right, she will never know the difference." The old man managed a lopsided grin. "And if there is any to spare, perhaps we might go gaming and increase our investment."

"Never again, and you know it. I forbid you." Drake had taken everything remotely worth being gambled away and ensured it was out of his uncle's reach. In fact, most of it had been used to lessen the depth of their pit of debt.

His uncle gave an insulted huff and waved the words away. "Let an old man dream. What else is left to me in this life?"

Drake wanted to remind the man that his poor choices had led him to where he was today, and he had no one to blame but himself. But he didn't. It wouldn't do any good. How many times had his father begged his uncle to do better? "Try to get some sleep while I see about your bath chair. We can ill afford another."

"Stop talking to me about what we cannot do!" His uncle threw an arm over his battered face and turned away.

It would be time for the tantrums now because Drake had dared to remind his uncle that he had left them with nothing but a mess.

Drake left the room, unwilling to listen to the foolish prattling of an ill-tempered old bastard who thought of no one but himself. As he headed back to the garden, he pulled in a deep breath and let it back out with a groan. Heaven help him in this venture, and God forgive him for pulling dear Lady Felicity into it. But he had no choice, and he did like her very much and would never treat her poorly. Hopefully, in the young lady's eyes, that would be enough to at least start courting.

One of the bath chair's iron rods was slightly bent. Nothing John couldn't take to the forge and hammer back into place. Drake righted the thing and left it there, refusing to deal with it today. Besides, it wasn't as though his uncle would leave the sickbed for a day or two.

He foraged deeper into the overgrown garden, hoping some of the flowers, maybe even a few roses, had survived the onslaught of the weeds. He couldn't very well call on Lady Felicity with nothing to offer other than a smile and the sincerest hope that she would find him as pleasant as she had seemed to last night in the kitchen. The memory befuddled him. Why in heaven's name had she been in the kitchen instead of among the crowd enjoying the games or the dancing? A beautiful woman such as herself would be surrounded by likely suitors. Perhaps she was shy? Or worse. Perhaps she was hiding away because she was saving herself for someone else. He sincerely hoped not.

She is mine. A possessiveness for her came to him as naturally as breathing. The tense knot in his chest eased a bit and calmed for the first time in a long while, because of her. And not just because of her money. Yes. She was his—or soon would be.

"SINCE WE ARE not too far and spent hardly any time at all in the village, I say we walk by the Wakefield estate and have a peek," Merry said, sounding entirely too excited about her plan.

Felicity knew from her sister's tone that she would never be able to steer her toward another option. "Merry."

"Do not say my name like that. Since Lord Wakefield intends to come calling tomorrow, it is only prudent that we see what you might eventually be mistress over, if all goes as I think it will."

Felicity rolled her eyes and wished the day's timing had not crossed their paths with the Earl of Wakefield. Now that Merry had seen him, she was like a hunting dog tracking her prey. "We should be getting back. I promised to help Cook with tea."

"Cook can lay out a proper tea with her eyes closed," Merry said, "and that includes the baking of seven different kinds of biscuits. Under her command in the kitchen, the tea practically prepares itself." She tugged on Felicity's arm. "Come along now. You know you want to see it too."

"I do not."

"Liar. You just wrinkled your nose."

Dash it all. Felicity did her very best to keep her nose from twitching again. "I am not lying."

Merry snickered, covering her mouth and pointing as she danced down the roadway. "Now you look as though you are trying to dislodge something stuck up your nose!"

"Oh, stop, Merry. Do!" Felicity halted in the middle of the road. "I refuse to take another step until you promise to be nice."

Merry made her way back and assumed an almost convincing expression of contrition. "I am sorry." She held out her hand. "Come along now. I promise to be nice, if you promise to peep over the Wakefield garden wall with me."

"What if someone sees us?" Felicity couldn't believe her sister's brazenness. Here they were, two young ladies in their twenties, acting like—or at least threatening to act like—a pair of childish hoydens.

"We are out in the country and no one is around." Merry twirled in a slow circle with her arms extended. "I see no one for miles. The day is quiet as can be."

"A Wakefield servant might see us. Then what?"

Merry shrugged. "We run."

"Run? Are you serious?"

"Quite."

"What would Mama say?" Felicity asked in a last attempt at curbing her sister's enthusiasm that would surely be her undoing. She had to admit, maybe a little sneak peek over the garden wall wouldn't hurt. "And Papa?"

"They would say, 'Do not get caught.'" Merry gave her a wicked grin. "You know Mama and Papa always loved a good lark themselves."

Felicity closed her eyes and pinched the bridge of her nose, suddenly feeling quite sorry for Chance and Serendipity in their roles of trying to maintain order in the Broadmere household. With a resigned sigh, she dropped her hand away. "Fine. I give up."

Merry hopped in place, beaming with excitement. "Yes?"

"Yes."

Merry caught hold of her and tugged. "Come along, then. I believe it is just a little farther and down this lane to the right."

Caught up in Merry's sense of adventure, Felicity scurried alongside her, unable to keep from giggling. "If we get caught and word gets back to Seri…"

"We won't, and it won't," Merry said. "We are much too sly, you and I." She pointed at a modest stone manor house at the end of the lane. "There. I believe that is it."

"You believe? I thought you were certain." Felicity halted again, eyeing the home that seemed unusually quiet. It was much smaller than Broadmere Hall, and no gardeners or other servants could be seen moving around the grounds tending to their duties. For lack of a better word, the place looked deserted. "This cannot be it. There is no one about, and the shutters are still closed on some of the windows. I do not believe anyone is in residence."

Merry insisted on pulling her off to the side while pressing a finger to her lips. "Shh…look at the nameplate. *Wakefield.* See? And where else would he live? If he had a room at the inn, we would have heard about him long before Chance and Seri spoke up."

There was no denying the name on the gatepost. Felicity ducked lower as they moved along the solid stone wall, even though it was taller than both of them. "How are we to see over it when it is higher than we are tall?"

"We shall find a rock or something on which to stand." Merry stretched and hooked her fingers along the top stone block but couldn't pull herself any higher. "Drat. I have snagged my gloves. Promise not to tell."

"How in heaven's name could I tell when it would incriminate me along with you?"

Merry grinned as she scampered farther down the wall. "Here. A rock that should just do the trick." She climbed onto what amounted to a small boulder that should have been cleared away by the gardener or sentry long ago. A fit young thief would have no problem at all using it to vault over into the garden. That is, a fit young man not tangled in muslin and petticoat skirts.

"Well, what do you see?" Heart pounding in fear that they might get caught, Felicity pressed a hand to her chest. "Merry? What do you see?"

Frowning, Merry hopped down and reached for Felicity's reticule and parasol. "Have a look for yourself."

"You do not sound the least bit impressed."

Merry wrinkled her nose and tipped a nod at the wall. "Have a look."

Dreading what she was about to see, Felicity stepped up onto the rock and cautiously peeped over the wall. "Oh dear," she said under her breath. Choking in weeds and vines, the dilapidated garden had suffered badly from neglect. Weeks and weeks of neglect. The only part appearing to have been tended to in the least was a patch of ground closest to the back entrance of the home. Vegetables and herbs thrived in a sunny spot cleared of weeds and the unwanted encroachment of the ivy that had taken over the remainder of the garden. A table with its paint peeling and a bench that had seen better days sat nearby. One of the back windows with a broken pane had been repaired by boarding it up.

Felicity almost choked on the pity that made her heart swell. Poor Lord Wakefield. Such a kind man, and look what he had inherited. It would take months of work and a team of servants to return the Wakefield estate to its former glory—if it had ever possessed any. Hadn't Serendipity mentioned that the old earl had lost everything in the gaming hells and the new earl sought to restore honor to the Wakefield name? This was so sad. The place cried out for care and attention.

She slowly climbed down from her perch, took back her parasol and reticule, and nodded at the lane. "Come along, Merry. We should not have come."

"The place is so…" Merry's voice trailed off as she trudged along beside Felicity.

"So sad," Felicity finished for her. "What a terrible mess the earl must have inherited."

"The home is so small. How can this be the Wakefield country seat? Did Seri not say that the young earl came from landed gentry?"

"Chance said that," Felicity said, her heart heavy. "I would lay odds this was his land before he became the earl."

"But why has he not taken better care of it? And how could the old earl lose the family's country seat? Would it not be part of an entailment?"

"Entailments can be dissolved if all parties are willing." Felicity slowly shook her head. "Poor Lord Wakefield. It looks as though he had to let everyone go because of the debts he inherited. He must have used all that he possessed to pay off what the estate could not cover upon his uncle's death."

"How on earth do you know these things?" Merry asked.

Felicity gave her sister a frustrated glance. "Do you never listen to the conversations when Mr. Sutherland the elder and Mr. Sutherland the younger come to dinner? You could learn a thing or two from our solicitors. Things worth knowing."

"Do not be surly." They trudged along in silence for a while, then Merry asked, "What will you do when he calls upon you?"

A heavy sigh worked itself free, even though Felicity attempted to hold it back. "I don't know." He had been so nice to her when he thought her a penniless kitchen maid. Had he truly liked her, or was he simply a charming flirt who played up to the help to get what he wanted? The maids had spoken to her about those sort of lordlings. And if he behaved as if he liked her now, how could she know if it was because he *truly* liked her or her dowry? For heaven's sake, he certainly could use every penny that came with her. "I do not wish to be the solution to someone's dire straits. It makes me question the truth of their intentions."

Merry nodded. "You need to be the problem. The entire problem. Not the solution."

"And what is that supposed to mean?"

"It means he should want you so badly, he will do anything to win you because you are the air he needs to breathe."

"You have been reading too many of Fortuity's books again."

"Actually, that came from one of Serendipity's forbidden books that she thinks she keeps hidden." Merry winked and linked her arm through Felicity's. "Will you send him away tomorrow when he calls?"

"I told you I didn't know. What would you do?"

Merry's mouth drew into a thoughtful pucker as she stared off into the distance as if the answer lay somewhere among the wildflowers in the meadow. "I would see him and confront him."

"I cannot very well tell him I spied on his garden."

Merry snorted. "Well, of course not. You must be a bit more tactful…and sneaky about it. Simply tell him you heard *rumors*. That is believable enough. Even out here in the country, gossip is rife amongst the *ton*."

"Or I could tell him I am not receiving callers."

"You already told him you would."

"Yes, but one never knows when one's health might keep one to their bed."

"*One* is the poorest liar in creation. Do you really think Seri and Chance will believe you and allow you to hide in your bedchamber when you have a perfectly nice gentleman calling?"

"Some days I do not care for you at all, Merry."

Merry grinned. "Thank goodness you just wiggled your nose, or I just might have believed you!"

Chapter Five

"I NEED ENOUGH milk to make a stiff paste of the flour, butter, and sugar." Felicity studied the calculation she had scribbled onto a note, frowning at her measurements. "The last batch was so very dry and bitter. Do you think too little milk was the problem, or not enough sugar?"

"Too little butter, and I think old Scratch bumped your elbow when you was measuring out that vanilla of yours." Cook ambled over and peered over Felicity's shoulder at the paper. She tapped a calloused finger on the note. "Did you steep them vanilla beans longer this time to make the extract? Mayhap the brandy you used last time was not the quality you needed."

"Oh dear."

The plump matriarch of the kitchen arched her graying brows nearly to the ruffle of her white cap. "Oh dear?"

"I used whisky to steep the vanilla beans last time, and it did smell rather…uhm…strong."

Cook chuckled and shook her head. "When you use whisky for the vanilla beans, you have to take extra care to keep your oven from getting too hot and overcooking your biscuits on the bottom before the middle sets. That batch was a bit dark on the bottom."

"You mean burnt."

"They did take a bit of scraping." Cook tapped Felicity's recipe again. "Make a note about your temperature and try again. At least you learnt from it."

A clock chimed in the distance, making the maids scurry out of the room for a last check of the parlors. Cook took inventory of the biscuits and cress sandwiches already prepared and waiting on the trays. "You best brush off now, my lady. 'Tis calling hour."

Felicity's stomach churned at the thought of sitting in the parlor, waiting for Lord Wakefield to arrive. "I cannot stop midway. It would be too wasteful."

Cook trundled back to her side and eyed the bowl of partially mixed dough. She leaned over and sniffed. "No vanilla at all this time?"

Felicity shook her head. "Lemon in this batch. I used cocoa in the ones that are in the oven now."

Walters appeared in the doorway and cleared his throat. "You have a caller, Lady Felicity. A Lord Wakefield."

"Thank you, Walters," she said to humor the dear old man. Lord Wakefield surely hadn't arrived as soon as the calling hour struck. No man had ever been that eager to call on her. In fact, no gentleman had ever called on her at all. Poor, sweet Walters was probably confused because Merry had told him about their expected visitor. "I shall be there shortly. Which parlor?"

The aged butler blinked his bleary eyes as though he had just awakened from a nap. Without a word, he turned and shuffled out of the kitchen.

Cook shook her head. "God bless him."

"Yes," Felicity agreed, laying odds that Lord Wakefield had not arrived at all. "God bless him, indeed." She returned her attention to her bowl of dough. "Now, should I add more zest from the lemon or the juice, since it still has no scent?"

"More zest, but scrape it good and fine. No one wishes to bite into a chunk of lemon peel. That'll turn bitter right quick, it will."

Felicity set out to take Cook's advice and finish up, since calling hours had just started, and Lord Wakefield couldn't possibly be there. After refining her notes, perfecting the dough, and cutting it into dainty squares and baking it, she smiled as she pulled that particular batch of biscuits from the oven. "Oh, these look so much better and smell divine. I adore lemon."

Cook nodded in agreement. "Those biscuits look quite nice, my lady."

Fipps showed up in the kitchen doorway. "Lady Felicity— your caller is waiting." He had a pained look, as if he feared he had gravely erred. "Walters assured me he told you. In fact, I overheard him before His Grace summoned me to the library. Do you wish us to send Lord Wakefield away?"

Felicity pressed her hands to her rapidly heating cheeks. "He is really here?"

Fipps remained as staid as ever. "Yes, my lady. Lord Wakefield awaits you in the front parlor."

"Oh dear. I thought poor Walters was confused again." Felicity pulled off her apron and turned to Cook. "Am I all right?"

Cook caught hold of her hands and brushed the flour from them, then wiped flour from her face as well. She nodded. "You are quite right now, my lady. No flour to be seen. Shall we send in a few trays and some tea? Or do you prefer lemonade?"

"Tea, please. And this newest batch of biscuits, since they are warm from the oven."

"Right away, my lady."

Fipps calmly waited at the doorway as if nothing was amiss. "Lady Merry is there also, my lady. Shall I fetch Lady Serendipity as well?"

"No, let us leave my eldest out of this for now." Wishing she had donned her blue muslin with the delicate white lace rather than the much more relaxed, soft green creation she wore, Felicity shook the thought away. It was too late now, and she had already kept the poor lord waiting entirely too long. She hurried down the hallway.

"Lord Wakefield," she said as she breezed into the room. "Do forgive me for keeping you waiting."

The smiling gentleman, even more handsome than he had been in Lady Atterley's kitchen, jumped to his feet. "Think nothing of it, my lady. Your sisters kept me quite good company."

Sisters? Felicity bit the inside of her cheek as she forced a smile at Merry *and* Serendipity. She should have known Serendipity would never allow Merry to remain in the parlor unaccompanied with a gentleman for very long.

"I would be lost without my sisters," Felicity said, only partially meaning it. As one of seven, sisters could be such a chore at times. She seated herself, trying not to think about the state of the man's manor and garden. It wouldn't do to bring up the subject in front of Serendipity. "I fear when I work out new recipes with Cook that I lose track of time."

"If this recipe is as sublime as those coddled eggs and soldiers you prepared, you are most assuredly forgiven." He captivated her with another of his mesmerizing smiles. Dear heavens, the man was gorgeous, even more so because he didn't seem to realize it.

Serendipity cut a sharp look Felicity's way, narrowing her eyes as if homing in on a target.

"Lemon biscuits this time," Felicity hurried to say before Serendipity could add to the conversation. "Cook and I worked out the perfect amount of zest to flavor the sugar."

"Were those not lemon biscuits you prepared the day before last?" Merry asked with unmistakable leeriness.

"These are better," Felicity said, willing her sister to be quiet. "Cook and I refined the recipe." She turned back to the earl, attempting to turn her nervous smile into a self-confident one. "It is such a lovely day. Would you care to join us for tea in the garden? Cook is already gathering refreshments. Fipps could bring them right out."

"The garden?" Merry started coughing as though choking.

"Merry? Do you need to excuse yourself?" Serendipity asked.

Patting her chest, Merry shook her head while flaring her eyes open wider at Felicity. "Forgive me. I do not know what came over me."

Felicity knew exactly what came over her silly sister. Merry was afraid that if they were in their garden, the topic of the earl's sad state of affairs might come up and unleash a full-blown interrogation of the poor man from Serendipity. While Felicity wanted to speak with Lord Wakefield in earnest, she did not wish to make him feel uncomfortable. "I think the garden would be lovely," she said, "and I would happily give Lord Wakefield a tour of the roses while you two ensure our tea is properly laid. Shall we?"

The handsome earl's already pleasant demeanor turned into an even more stunning display of happiness. "I most certainly would enjoy a tour of the roses, Lady Felicity, although I doubt very much if they could ever compare to your loveliness."

Felicity didn't know whether to blush or groan. She wasn't accustomed to such overt compliments. Lord Wakefield was trying too hard. It hurt her heart and her feelings. The man was obviously desperate for her dowry. "Thank you, my lord. I believe you will find our mother's flowers quite lovely. She tended them as carefully as she tended us."

Serendipity rose. "I shall inform Fipps and Cook while Merry accompanies the two of you to the garden." She offered the earl a curtsy and hurried out of the parlor.

Now that they were all on their feet, Merry waved them forward. "Lead the way, Felli. I shall follow."

Lord Wakefield offered Felicity his arm. "Felli?"

"A childhood pet name, my lord." She tried not to tremble as she took his arm. *My goodness, how muscular.* This was no soft lordling who lifted nothing heavier than a glass. And the golden-brown hue of his skin made her wonder if he had taken up the chores that he could no longer afford to hire out to servants. She clenched her teeth and tried to hold her smile. "With eight of us so close in age, pet names were quick to spring up whenever we were at play."

"Some pet names were nicer than others," Merry said from behind them.

Lord Wakefield snorted a laugh but quickly recovered. "Ah...as an only child, I fear I have no experience with such things."

"No cousins, either?" If Felicity could gently lead him to the topic of his uncle, perhaps she could discover what she hoped was his true motive—and not just the obvious one. She so needed him to like her for more than her money.

The earl shook his head as he held the door to the garden. "Father once spoke of some distant relatives in Wales, but I have never met them."

"I shall wait here for Seri and the tea," Merry said, waving them onward. "As soon as they arrive, I will call out."

"Thank you, Merry." Nerves stirring her middle like one of Cook's spoons, Felicity led the way to the path winding through the abundance of roses dressed in their showiest colors. Explosions of red, pink, white, and yellow filled the air with their sweet scents. "My mother loved her roses. They were her children, too."

"The garden is exquisite." He tipped his head and treated her to one of those smiles that drew her in and made her feel as though he thought her the most important creature in his world. "Almost as exquisite as you."

"Merry and I saw your garden, my lord," she blurted out before she could stop the words from tumbling off her tongue.

A stoic seriousness fell across him like a dark curtain. He bowed his head as their stroll through the garden slowed. "I see."

"I am sorry. I should not have said that." She took her hand from his arm and hugged her middle, willing the churning to cease. "It is just that Merry and I were walking home yesterday, and we had never seen your estate, and there was a large rock to stand upon and look over into your garden, and..." Heaven help her, could she not shut her mouth and stop speaking? Could the earth not open up and swallow her? "I am sorry," she mumbled. "I fear we were quite rude in pushing our noses into your privacy."

His mouth flattened into a taut line, and he twitched a half-hearted shrug. "You have nothing to apologize for, my lady. You were curious about the man who had asked to call upon you." He offered her a bow. "I suppose I should take my leave now. Forgive me for wasting your time."

She caught hold of his arm as he started to leave. "Wait."

A bitterness flashed in his eyes as he paused and looked back at her. "What can I do for you, my lady? Although, as you already surmised from the state of my manor and gardens, I am sure you realize I cannot do much."

Now was her opportunity. While still holding his arm, she pulled in a deep breath and braced herself. "Would you still have called upon me if you had known I had no dowry? If you believed I was a penniless kitchen maid, would you have pursued me? Still rushed to my door as soon as today?"

His scowl hardened as he looked away, either unwilling or unable to meet her gaze. "I would like to say 'yes,' my lady, but that would be a lie. I need a wife of means to repair the damage done not only to the Wakefield name, but to the estate as well. I fear my uncle left both in tatters."

"I see." The need to cry hit her so hard, she had to hold her breath to control it. "Why me, my lord? Did you figure I would be so desperate for a match that I would jump at the chance?"

He finally faced her, his scowl shifting to befuddlement. "Why would you be desperate for a match?"

"Answer my question, my lord, if you please. Why me?"

With a slow shake of his head, he lifted both hands as if surrendering. "When I discovered that the lovely young woman who had taken it upon herself to feed me was not a kitchen maid, but a lady in her own right, I had to call upon you as soon as I could, before another gentleman stole you away. I was thrilled to learn your true identity."

It was her turn to stare at him with a long, hard look. Was he lying? She so wished she were as adept as her sisters at sniffing out falsehoods. "No gentleman is about to steal me away, my lord."

She huffed a sad laugh. "Why do you think I was in Lady Atterley's kitchen in the first place?"

Now, he looked even more confused. "I had wondered that, my lady, but thought it none of my affair, and therefore did not ask."

"It appears you are more mannerly than my sister and me." She watched him closely, trying to read the shadows in those hazel eyes of his. The way he quirked a single dark brow—did that mean he was lying? How could she know for certain? "I was in Lady Atterley's kitchen because I was hiding."

"Hiding?"

"Hiding."

"From what?"

"Everything and everyone." She proudly lifted her chin. "When a wallflower tires of being ignored yet cannot escape from being dragged to parties, she finds other means of disappearing." She shrugged. "Mine is hiding in the kitchens and helping the cooks and maids with their duties."

"Why in heaven's name would you ever be ignored?" he asked so softly that it hurt her heart.

"It would seem I am not the pick of the Broadmere litter."

His scowl hardened. "Who spoke ill of you? I would have their name at once."

She shook her head. "They spoke ill of me when they thought I was nowhere nearby. When I confronted them, rather than apologize, the drink they had consumed that evening turned them defiant and proud of everything they had said. My brother, Chance, pummeled them, as did my brother-in-law Thorne." She wet her lips, suddenly wishing she had waited to have this discussion over tea. "It matters little, though. One cannot exactly un-ring a bell. The words remain with me to this day."

Lord Wakefield started to speak, but she stopped him. "Do not pity me. I know one cannot help or control what another thinks. However, my brother worries about it a great deal. You see, unless I marry for love to satisfy that specific part of my parents' will, Chance will not receive the percentage of his inheritance that is attached to me." Stomach churning like a storm by now, she led the way back to the table. "Surely, Fipps has brought our tea. Shall we rejoin Merry and Serendipity?" This terrible moment needed to end. It had held such hope, but now she knew it for the truth it truly was.

"Lady Felicity." He caught her by the arm. "Wait."

"I will never marry for anything other than love," she said with a defiance that surprised even her.

"You deserve that and so much more," he said with surprising gentleness. He kept hold of her arm. "My only hesitation in coming here was knowing I had nothing but a title to offer you in return. As I said, when I learned my lovely kitchen angel was a lady of the *ton*, I considered myself the most fortunate man in the world."

The heat of him standing so close, his scent of sandalwood and spice, his rich, deep voice—they all spun their spells and made it so difficult not to believe him. She so wanted to believe him, wanted to take in the sincerity in his eyes and accept it for what it was: the truth. She tried in vain to harden her heart against him. "We have only just met. Surely, you cannot claim to love me."

He shook his head. "I make no claim of love, but there is *something* there. Something that, if it is nurtured, might just grow into what we both want and need." He eased toward her, closing the distance between them. "Can you not feel it? That *something*?"

"I so want to believe you," she said, then immediately wished she hadn't. Joy would scold her for showing her hand.

"I want you to believe me, too, because it is the truth."

If she just leaned in a little more and lifted her face, her mouth would be so very close to his. Heart pounding, she struggled to speak clearly. "Even a liar swears their words are true."

"The only lie I have ever told is the lie of omission, and you surmised that when you saw Wakefield Hall."

His warm breath tickled across her lips, making her part them.

"Felicity! Tea!" Merry's boisterous shout rang through the garden. "Come along now. We mustn't lose his lordship in the maze of Mama's roses."

With a resigned sigh, the earl took a step back and offered his arm once again. "We should return, my lady. After all, I would never wish to compromise you."

That alone made her wonder if he was telling the truth about that *something* between them. If he compromised her, the dowry would be his in a handy marriage of convenience. Felicity swallowed hard at her choking knot of emotions as she took his arm. "I would never wish you to compromise me either, my lord." Then she would never know why they had ended up as man and wife. "Come and enjoy my lemon biscuits."

"I look forward to them, my lady." His smile was more tender now, his eyes penitent, reflecting a contrition that reached out, took hold of her heart, and squeezed.

She released his arm as they emerged from the roses and seated herself at the table. Serendipity had already poured and looked ready to pounce.

Felicity barely shook her head and whispered, "All is well." She prayed that was the truth. She offered the salver of her prized biscuits to the earl. "My lord?"

"Absolutely." He helped himself to not one, but three, piling them onto the small plate beside his teacup. But when he sank his teeth into the first one, his eagerness disappeared. He pressed a fist to his mouth and gave a single, barking cough. His face turned bright red.

"My lord? Are you all right?" Felicity rose from her chair and struck him between his shoulder blades, uncertain what else to do.

Lord Wakefield turned aside and coughed again, all the while chewing hard with his fist clamped to his mouth.

"Water. He needs water. Fipps!" Felicity called out. "Hurry!

We need water."

Merry hopped up and ran to the door, nearly running head-on into Fipps as he rushed forward with a glass and pitcher of water.

Serendipity snatched it from him, filled the glass, and handed it to the earl.

Wakefield grabbed it with both hands, drained it, then held it out again. "More, please."

Serendipity filled it again, then set the pitcher in front of him.

"Good heavens, my lord." Without thinking, Felicity rubbed and patted his back. "Are you quite well now? Did you choke on some loose crumbs?"

"Yes, crumbs," he agreed in a strained voice, almost wheezing the words. "Forgive me, but I must take my leave now."

"Of course, my lord." Felicity awkwardly stopped rubbing his back, realizing it was most unseemly. She stepped away. "Fipps, do see Lord Wakefield out and ensure he is quite all right."

Fipps bowed. "Of course, my lady."

With the butler's help, the Earl of Wakefield hurried from the room.

"Thank heavens the man did not die on us," Serendipity said as she plopped back into her chair.

"That would have made for some interesting gossip," Merry commented.

"Merry!" Felicity sagged into her seat and propped her head in her hands. What an afternoon it had been—a disturbing one in so many ways. She picked up a biscuit and bit into it.

Immediately, a bitterness so sharp and choking that it made her jaws throb filled her mouth. She jumped up and spat the mouthful into the bushes. "Oh, good heavens, what on earth did I do to them?"

Merry hazarded a nibble, then did the same, spitting the bite into a planter of lilies. She coughed and wiped her mouth with the back of her hand. "The man is going to think you wished to poison him."

Horrified, Felicity stared down at the innocent biscuit that smelled so lemony and was a beautiful golden brown. What had gone wrong? What had she done? And, oh dear heavens, what would Lord Wakefield surely think? Then it came to her, making her gasp. "The sugar. Walters came in just as I was about to add the rest of the sugar." She groaned, closing her eyes and seeing her mistake as plain as day. "I failed to add the sugar and doubled—nay, not only doubled but *tripled* the zest from the lemon and added some lime as well." She held her head. "He will think I tried to poison him to scare him away, because I told him we saw his garden."

"You what?" Serendipity looked sharply at each of them in turn.

Merry assumed a nonchalant air and sipped her tea. "We merely passed by the Wakefield estate on our way home from the village."

"The Wakefield estate is not on the main thoroughfare." Serendipity sat taller, obviously winding up to take them to task.

"I knew Lord Wakefield was coming to call today. He asked permission when we met in Mettlestone's." Felicity shot Merry a silencing glare. They might as well confess. Serendipity would discover the truth of it anyway.

"He asked permission to come calling as soon as he was introduced to you in Mettlestone's? That was rather bold of him." Serendipity's eyes narrowed. "Tell me the rest. I see it brewing, and you are wrinkling your nose."

Drat her infernal telltale nose. Felicity pinched it as if that would calm the traitorous thing. "I met him in Lady Atterley's kitchen on the night of her dinner party. Except he thought me a kitchen maid rather than a daughter of Broadmere."

Serendipity slowly pulled in a deep breath and held it, a sure sign she was doing her level best to control her temper. "And how did he behave when he thought you were a servant?"

"He was kindness itself and spoke to me as respectfully as he spoke today."

Her sister gave her a long, slow look, then aimed her scowl at Merry. "Felicity would have never taken it upon herself to spy on the Wakefield estate if she had not been encouraged."

With a defiant tip to her chin, Merry folded her hands on the table. "I simply thought it wise of her to have a look around. A lady must take in as much information as possible when it comes to suitors. Is that not why you have so many *resources* who keep you apprised of the latest gossip?"

"Well, apparently they are slipping, since I was not informed of the drastic state of the earl's manor, which you two discovered—in quite an unseemly way, I might add. How bad was it?"

Before Merry could elaborate, Felicity spoke up. "It appears the earl inherited an estate riddled with disrepair and in dire need of proper tending by a bevy of servants, which he does not have." She slowly pushed away her tea, which had gone cold, much like her poor, aching heart. "He needs my dowry. Badly. Either that, or he must find an heiress to marry."

Serendipity stirred her tea, quietly clacking the silver spoon against the sides of the porcelain cup. "I was aware he was determined to restore the Wakefield name, but I had yet to discover that his country estate was in a shambles. It makes one wonder about his property in Town."

"I would not describe it as a *shambles*." Felicity felt so bad for the poor earl, and even worse for herself. Now, she would probably never know if he truly liked *her* as he had said. "It simply needs a great deal of work."

After a sip of her tea, Serendipity nodded. "Well, perhaps it was providence stepping in to help you be rid of him. Felli. Your next caller will be more prosperous."

"My next caller?" Incredulous, Felicity snorted. "I am two and twenty, and Lord Wakefield is the only caller I have ever received. What does that tell you, Seri?"

"It tells me you should stay out of the kitchens during festivities and see to the task of finding a gentleman worthy of you."

"Even though I am two stone heavier than I should be and

not nearly as lovely as the rest of my sisters."

"I have never said that," Serendipity claimed. "You are obviously overset by this afternoon's events. Perhaps you should go upstairs and lie down."

"You are not Mama. Stop trying to send me to my room." Felicity rose from the table, determined to salvage the day and take hold of what little hope she had left in her heart. She liked Lord Wakefield—even if it was against her better judgment. She had to make things right. "I am going to make a batch of my best chocolate teacakes and take them to him."

"You cannot call upon him," Serendipity sputtered. "It is not done."

Her course set, Felicity dismissed her sister with a flick of her hand. "It is done now, and Merry will come with me. Will you not, Merry?"

"Most definitely," Merry said. "I wouldn't miss it for the world."

Chapter Six

DRAKE HAD NEARLY reached home before his tongue stopped burning, and the ache in his jaws eased from that vile biscuit. What sort of poison had Lady Felicity used? Damn and blast it all, he had nearly choked to death right there in her garden. That would teach him for not being entirely open about his circumstances. He scrubbed his jaw and worked his mouth as if he had taken a hard punch.

What would she have done to him if she knew his uncle still lived and breathed? That thought stopped him in the middle of the lane. What would Lady Felicity do if he told her the truth, told her that Mr. Charles Pembroke was really Lord George Pemberton, the sixth Earl of Wakefield, and that he, Drake, was no more than a member of the gentry who had sold everything except for his father's land to try to drag the Wakefield name out of its mire of disgraceful debt?

Drake snorted. His father's land. An estate that had once provided quite an income, but also required servants and tenant farmers to work it. The tenant farmers had remained, but the rents they paid barely covered Wakefield Manor's needs, and he would be damned straight to hell before he raised their rents because of his bloody uncle's selfish ways.

He shook his head, amazed at how he had mismanaged everything while trying to clean up his uncle's mess. He had failed everyone. Worst of all, he had failed the memory of his father.

Damn, but he hated money. It truly was the root of all evil.

He raked a hand through his hair and spat in the dust of the road. Without Lady Felicity's dowry, what the devil was he to do now? Worse than that, what would he do without Lady Felicity? His precious kitchen angel lived in his thoughts and haunted his dreams. Not just because of her beauty, but for her kindness, her caring, and her soulful eyes that reflected the sweetness of her character. Now what would he do, since any hope of making her his was well and truly gone?

Her revelations about her mistreatment as a wallflower of the *ton* had shocked him, but also explained why he had discovered her in Lady Atterley's kitchen. What he wouldn't give for the name of the cur who had slandered her and put that pain in her lovely sapphire eyes. It didn't matter that her brother and brother-in-law had already pummeled the worthless cove. Drake wanted his own opportunity to teach the bastard how a genteel lady should be treated.

Hands shoved in his pockets, he shouldered his way through the front gate. The wrought-iron bars of the entrance were in dire need of painting, but it couldn't be helped—not until he paid down more of the debts against his credit. At least all the merchants had been kind and understanding, but the pity in their eyes stabbed him in the heart.

"Are you unwell, my lord?" Yateston asked as Drake dejectedly strode into the entry hall that was as stripped of every refinement and bauble as the rest of the manor.

"I am fine," he told the butler. "How is Uncle today? When I looked in on him earlier, he was sleeping."

Yateston brightened. "He insisted on rising from his bed, so I assisted him into his bath chair and placed him just outside beside the doorway next to the kitchen garden. He wished for a bit of fresh air."

"Well done. I shall join him out there." Drake handed over his hat and gloves, and then his coat. There was no reason for anything other than a waistcoat here, and one never knew when he might be called upon to help with a chore. As he passed through the kitchen, he noticed a bowl filled with shiny red apples in the center of the worktable. "Where did those come from?" he asked Mrs. Pepperhill. They couldn't have come from Wakefield land. Their trees had been stricken with a blight and died, much like the Wakefield coffers.

She curtsied and bobbed her kerchief-covered head. "My brother's missus sent them, my lord. Their trees are giving more than they can put up at a time, and they thought we might enjoy them."

"We will, indeed. Please extend my gratitude for your family's generosity. It is most appreciated."

The housekeeper dipped another nod, then returned to her task of chopping carrots and parsnips. "Got these from the garden today, and there be plenty more where they come from."

"More good news." But Drake didn't feel the sentiment. How was it he could coax the earth to grow things with abundance, but couldn't convince the ledger books to stop bleeding red ink? "I am out to the garden to visit with Uncle. Shall I take him some water?"

"Already seen to it, my lord." She scraped the chunks of root vegetables into a bowl and wiped her hands on her apron. "He seems in fine spirits, and glad I am to see it."

"Yes," Drake agreed, admiring his uncle's ability to survive any and everything with defiant jauntiness. He exited the kitchen and squinted as he stepped into the sunny garden. The day was bright. He just wished his spirits were as well. "Good afternoon, Uncle."

Uncle George looked up from his book. "Well? How did it go? Will the first of the banns be announced this Sunday?"

"She knows."

"She knows what?" Uncle George closed his book and set it on the table beside his chair.

"Lady Felicity and her sister peered into our garden yesterday. They saw its condition."

"Did you tell her we are simply caught midway in finding more servants to tend it?" Uncle George nervously patted his blanket-covered knees. "Good servants are often difficult to find. I feel sure she would find that an acceptable answer."

Drake snorted and flicked a hand at the weed-choked garden. "This mess cannot be explained away as a few weeks of inattention."

Uncle shook his head. "Nonsense. With the Wakefield charm, you can convince her of anything. Put some effort into it, boy."

"I do not like lying to her," Drake said through clenched teeth. "She deserves better."

His uncle's bushy gray brows knotted over his bruised and blackened eyes. He sadly shook his head. "You like her—a dangerous thing, boy."

Unable to sit, Drake paced up and down the path of cracked flagstones. "I do indeed *like her*, but it no longer matters. She made herself quite clear today. She wants nothing to do with me."

"She said that?"

"She did not have to." Drake scraped his tongue on his teeth, still tasting that deadly biscuit.

Uncle George shrugged and picked up his book. "Ah well, there are other dowries out there, and you do not necessarily need to *like* your wife, you know. That is what mistresses are for."

"That is disgusting."

"That is a fact of life, boy. Your father dying while pining away for your mother is a rarity."

"A rarity I would like to find for myself."

Drake's uncle blew out a huff that sounded like a hissing kettle. "Nonsense. Money first, boy. Everything else will fall in place as long as you have money."

Drake had never realized just how avaricious Uncle George truly was, and the longer he toiled to protect him and right his wrongs, the more he disliked him. This was not the man of his childhood, the man who had told such fantastical tales and always had time to sit with him and chat as if he were an adult. No, this Uncle George was a self-serving, money-grubbing scapegrace.

Yateston appeared in the doorway, tense with an uneasiness that shouted from him. "You have a caller, my lord," he announced, then cleared his throat. "Shall I return Mr. Pembroke to his room?"

Mr. Pembroke. Whoever had stirred the butler into such a state needed to be kept in the dark about Uncle's true identity. "Yes, Yateston. Show Mr. Pembroke to his room," he said, ignoring his uncle's growls. "By the by, who is it?" He had visited all their creditors. Or at least, he thought he had. Had he missed one? Was it another solicitor bearing news of more unknown debts? Drake braced himself for the worst. At this point, nothing would surprise him.

Yateston threw out his chest and stared straight ahead. "Lady Felicity of the Broadmeres and her sister Lady Merry." He held out his arm bearing Drake's neatly brushed jacket. "I thought you might want your coat, my lord."

Gads alive, had she come to finish him off with more poison? Drake grabbed the garment, yanked it on, and shrugged it into place. "Pray tell me you put them in the better parlor?" The other one had a broken window.

"Of course, my lord."

Drake pointed at his uncle. "Stay in your room and stay quiet. I do not wish to add to the lies of omission of which I have already been found quite guilty. Understood?"

With an unhappy smirk, his uncle huffed and rolled his eyes, shooing away Drake's request with a wave of his hand. "Go, boy. Charm the woman while you still have the chance."

Rushing inside, Drake paused in the kitchen. "Mrs. Pepperhill, we will need tea. I realize we cannot offer cakes or biscuits, but pray, do whatever you can."

Appearing as worried as he felt, the housekeeper bit her lip and nodded while glancing around the kitchen. "I shall find something, my lord. Never fear."

Not reassured in the least, Drake strode down the hallway, dreading what awaited him. Had she brought her brother and brothers-in-law to speak in her defense? Drake shook his head. *Do not be silly. Yateston would have said.*

As soon as he stepped through the archway, the lovely Lady Felicity hopped up from the settee and held out a basket covered with a checkered cloth that matched the soft green muslin of her gown. "Lord Wakefield, I am so glad to see you fully recovered. I most heartily apologize and swear on my own life that I had no idea those biscuits were so horrid. Please forgive me."

His heart rose the barest bit from the pit into which it had plummeted, lifting his spirits along with it. "Forgive you?"

"Yes—you see, when Walters told me you had come to call, I lost my place in the recipe and left out a great deal of the sugar that would have made those treats much tastier."

"That is debatable," her sister said, barely loud enough for him to hear. "Lemon biscuits appear to be the bane of her existence."

"Merry!" Felicity stamped her foot so hard that her golden curls bounced. She turned back to him, completely mesmerizing with her adorably humble sincerity. "Do ignore her, please." She lifted the cloth from the basket. "I brought you a basket of delicious chocolate cakes to atone for my mistake. I promise they are my very best. Everyone loves them." She cast a pointed look back at her sister. "Even Merry likes them."

"They are quite tasty," Merry said with an approving nod.

He eyed the basket, wanting to believe they were a peace offering after the earlier debacle. Not that he would blame her for trying to poison him. He deserved it. Accepting the gift, he offered her an apologetic smile. "You came here in haste," he said, then wondered if he shouldn't have said that.

"I had to." She gave the barest shrug. "I feared you would believe I had tried to poison you."

He forced a laugh that almost sounded authentic. "How silly, my lady. I would never have suspected you capable of such a thing." Well, he had—but since he deserved it, in his opinion, she was guilt-free. He offered her a contrite bow. "But if you had chosen to punish me, I would not have blamed you. After all, I had not expounded on my circumstances." He nodded for her to return to her seat. "Mrs. Pepperhill is bringing tea. We can enjoy these lovely cakes together. Would you and Lady Merry do me the honor? Have you got time?" While it was still well within calling hours, it was later in the afternoon.

Visibly relieved, Felicity rejoined her sister on the settee and nodded. "We would love to. Would we not, Merry?"

"Indeed." Merry grinned. "And we shall have Felicity eat the first cake, so we might gauge her reaction."

"Merry!"

Drake laughed, unable to keep from it. The sisters brought the brightness of hope into his day. "I am so thankful you called. The two of you bring laughter that has sorely been needed."

Yateston and Mrs. Pepperhill hurried into the room, each bearing trays. Drake noticed the housekeeper had removed her kitchen kerchief and patted her gray hair into a bun of somber submission that befitted her station.

"Your favorites, my lord," she said with a pointed look his way. "Cress-and-butter sandwiches."

"Thank you, Mrs. Pepperhill, and Lady Felicity brought us some of her delicious chocolate cakes to enjoy as well." He nodded at the basket on the large, round table that had once been used for extravagantly proper teas when they could afford them.

The housekeeper curtsied. "I shall fetch more plates and silver, my lord."

"Shall I pour, my lord?" Yateston asked.

"Yes, Yateston. Thank you."

"Cress-and-butter sandwiches are your favorites, my lord?" Felicity asked, her expression sweet and guileless, but he was still uneasy. Cress-and-butter sandwiches were known as poor man's fare.

"Indeed, they are." Or, at least, they had become his favorites because that was often all there was to eat with his tea.

"Mine too." Her smile grew, lighting up her face. "Sometimes, simple is best. Do you not agree?"

"Most definitely." He released the breath he had held as Yateston served the ladies, then handed him a cup of tea.

Mrs. Pepperhill hurried back in with a mismatched set of saucers and silverware. It couldn't be helped. It was all they had left. She deftly served the cakes and then hurried back out of the room, leaving Yateston behind to manage any further needs.

Just as Drake sank his fork into the rich, tender cake with its swirl of white icing, Merry cleared her throat. "Felicity first," she said with an evil grin.

"You are a troll," Felicity told her, then held her plate higher, cut herself a bite, and popped it into her mouth. "Mmm. Delicious, if I do say so myself."

Doing his best not to laugh, Drake took a taste, then groaned. "Oh, my dear Lady Felicity. This cake rivals the deliciousness of your coddled eggs and soldiers."

The way her eyes danced and the lovely blush across her cheeks made him wonder if compliments to her were rare. "I am so very glad you like them," she said. "I truly hated the biscuit debacle. Oh my goodness, those were awful. How humiliating."

"I spat mine into the lily pot," Merry said. "I fear it may kill them."

Felicity glared at her. "I am beginning to regret bringing you."

"Would you rather have Serendipity as a chaperone?" Merry wiggled her nose, then took a sip of her tea.

After a cutting look at her sister, Felicity turned back to Drake. "I hope you do not think it presumptuous of me, but I brought quite a few cakes. Serendipity mentioned that you are sheltering a disabled war veteran who served with your uncle. I thought the cakes might brighten his day as well."

Clenching his teeth at the mention of his self-serving uncle,

Drake forced a smile. "How kind of you, Lady Felicity. I am quite certain Mr. Pembroke will be most grateful."

"I am glad." Felicity took a bite of a cress sandwich, mesmerizing him with the way her lips embraced the bread. He nearly groaned aloud when she flicked her tongue out and licked a bit of butter off the corner of her mouth. She smiled and patted her napkin to her face. "I am sorry. Do I have more crumbs?"

"No, my lady. You have only beauty." He startled himself with such boldness. "Forgive my forwardness, but it had to be said."

Her cheeks took on an even rosier shade, and she wore the color well.

"Do you have a library, my lord?" Merry asked as she set her tea aside. "I adore books and would love to peruse your collection while you and Felli finish your tea."

Aghast at her sister's brazenness, Felicity turned to her. "Could you possibly be more obvious?"

"I am trying to be helpful." Merry rose and arched a brow at him. "Well, Lord Wakefield? Where might I wander for a bit? That is, as long as I have your word that nothing unseemly will take place in this parlor and that the doors shall remain wide open."

More than a little grateful for the opportunity, Drake rose from his seat and nodded at Yateston. "Show Lady Merry to the library, please."

"Yes, my lord."

Before the helpful young woman left them to themselves, Drake offered her a formal bow. "Thank you, Lady Merry, and let me assure you that I would never compromise your sister."

Merry attempted a sternness and failed when she grinned. "See that you do not." She flitted out of the room, chattering nonstop to Yateston.

Drake returned to the tea table. "More tea, Lady Felicity?"

She joined him. "There is no need to serve me, my lord. I should pour." As she leaned to fill their cups, one of her curls fell forward onto her cheek, and without thinking, he reached out and tucked it behind her ear.

She gasped and met his gaze, her sapphire eyes wide with wonder and her temptingly kissable lips parted.

He let his hand fall away. "Forgive me," he whispered. "I could not resist."

"No forgiveness necessary," she said just as softly, then seemed to shake herself. She held out his teacup, holding it between them. "Your tea, my lord."

"Thank you." There were so many things he wished to say to her, but the shadow of the greatest lie of all, the lie about his title, lay heavily on his heart. "I cannot tell you how much your visit means to me, my lady. I feared the bitter biscuits were your way of sending me away so that other suitors might take my place."

Her fair brows arched even higher. "Suitors?"

"Yes, I am sure you have many."

With a sad smile, she turned away, but rather than return to her seat, she took her tea to the window. "Wakefield Manor is quite lovely."

"There is no need to lie, my lady."

With a slow shake of her head, she kept her gaze locked on whatever was beyond the window's pane. "It is no lie, my lord. The estate but needs a bit of care. It has good bones, my papa would say. Good bones and a good foundation mean everything."

"Your papa sounds as though he was very wise." He joined her at the window that overlooked a luscious meadow of barley. The summer's breeze rippled across the sea of verdant green, making the grasses dance and sway.

"Papa always knew what to do. Very wise, indeed." A heavy sigh left her. "I miss him still."

"I understand, my lady. I too miss my father and his wisdom." Drake found himself staring at the way the light from the window played across her, setting her golden hair aglow as if she truly were an angel. "There was never a situation that stymied my father," he said, "and I could always go to him for advice." His father would not have approved of the dangerous lie Drake was living, even though it kept Uncle George alive. Unlike his brother, Father was an honorable man. But how could Drake tell Felicity the truth? To do so would surely dash any and all hopes of courting her.

"What would your father say about me?" she asked quietly, then huffed a soft laugh. "'Cast a blind eye to her many drawbacks, my son, and marry her quickly for her dowry'?"

He set his tea aside, then took hers from her and set it aside too. He gently took her hands and turned her toward him. "I see no drawbacks, my lady, and I wish I could tell you the dowry did not matter, but your own eyes can see that it does."

She stared up at him, looking into his very soul. "I will not marry for anything less than love, my lord. Love for me. Not love for my money."

"As I said before, you deserve nothing less." He ran his calloused thumbs across the softness of her fingers as he kept hold of her hands. "May I at least court you, my lady, so we might see if this *something* between us blossoms into love?"

"You may call me Felicity." Her shy smile grew a little bolder. "We shall start with that."

"Then I insist you call me Drake."

"Drake," she repeated. "A fine name."

"And may I call upon your brother for permission to court you?"

"You are very persistent."

"I am determined not to lose you," he said quietly, then grazed a tender kiss across her knuckles, making her gasp again. "You entrance me, Felicity. I cannot bear the thought of your going to another."

She eyed him with a disconcerting wariness. "I want to believe you," she finally said. "Truly, I do."

He realized it wasn't him or his circumstances that held her back, but the hurtfulness foisted upon her in the past. She was like a mistreated animal, afraid to trust, afraid to get hurt again. "I can only prove the truth of it to you if given time and the blessing of your company. Will you grant me that?"

From across the room came the distinct sound of someone clearing their throat.

Felicity snatched her hands out of his and turned back to the window. "Did you say that field was planted in wheat or barley, my lord?"

"Barley, my lady." Drake turned to see who dared interrupt them, relaxing as Merry crossed to the settee and had a seat.

She gave him an apologetic smile. "I thought it best to return. Mustn't shirk my duties as chaperone."

"Of course not." He offered his hand to escort Felicity back to the settee. "Is His Grace in this afternoon, or should I wait until tomorrow?"

"I am not certain," Felicity hedged, wiggling her nose as if it itched.

"Our brother is in," Merry offered. "Other than a meeting with our steward, his diary was quite open the rest of the day. I saw it when I returned a book to our library."

Felicity pinned her sister with a narrow-eyed glare. "Perhaps we should take our leave, Merry." She turned a kinder gaze on him. "And thank you ever so much for the lovely cress sandwiches, and also for the generosity of your forgiveness about the bitter biscuits."

He swept a bow. "Thank you for the generosity of your time, Lady Felicity. I cherish every moment you deign to give me." Before she could comment, he added, "As a matter of fact, I shall escort the two of you home, so I might meet with your brother today." He went to the doorway and called out, "Yateston, my hat and gloves, please."

"Today?" Felicity repeated with an endearing squeak. "Are you quite certain, my lord?"

"More certain than I have ever been about anything."

"YOU WISH TO court my sister." It was not a question, but a statement. The Duke of Broadmere paced back and forth behind his lavish desk, never taking his scowl off Drake. "I am aware of your circumstances, Lord Wakefield. Felicity deserves better. She deserves a man who can provide for her and her children, should her marriage be so blessed." His Grace's tone suggested he wasn't finished. "A woman's dowry should be set aside in case she becomes widowed. It should not be used by her husband to restore his family's coffers. Would you care to address that?"

Drake wouldn't lie to the man who reminded him of a mighty caged lion, wily and ready to kill. "I cannot deny that a portion of the dowry would be used to restore the Wakefield name, but I am better with finances than my uncle was. I hope to regain financial stability and would make as many provisions as possible for my wife and children."

"Better than your uncle was," the duke repeated. "Serendipity informed me you are averse to gambling. That is one thing in your favor." He studied Drake, his eyes a darker blue than Felicity's, a steelier blue that was far more cutting. "I am also aware that you treated my sister with respect when you thought her nothing more than a kitchen maid." He nodded. "Another boon for you." He scrubbed his jaw as though it helped him think. "Does my sister wish to court you?"

"Your sister has made it quite clear that she wishes to marry for love—love for her. Not for her dowry."

"And you love her?"

"There is *something* there, Your Grace. I honestly believe I could. Ever since meeting her in Lady Atterley's kitchen, she is always in my thoughts—even in my dreams."

The duke leaned across his desk, his scowl hardening. "I will not have my sister hurt. Of all seven of them, Felicity is the gentlest and most tenderhearted. Do you understand what I am saying?"

"You will avenge your sister if she is not treated with the care she deserves."

His Grace nodded. "And not that I would need their help, but I have four brothers-in-law who will gladly join me in seeking justice."

Drake swallowed hard, the lie about his title coming to mind. "I would never intentionally hurt your sister, Your Grace."

"Intentionally or unintentionally, I will not have my sister hurt." The duke straightened and folded his arms across his chest. "Tread carefully, Wakefield, for I will be watching. Whether or not you court my sister is up to Felicity—unless I am forced to get involved." He resettled his stance. "I do not advise that you get me involved."

No coward, but determined to remain in the duke's good graces, Drake gave a single curt nod. "You have made your position quite clear, Your Grace, and I expected nothing less." If Drake had been blessed with a sister, he would have been just as protective.

"Very well, then." Broadmere motioned toward the door. "Let us see what Felicity says."

"Can you hear anything?" Felicity whispered to Merry. They both had their ears pressed to the library door.

"They are coming!" Merry sprang back, dragging Felicity with her.

Heart pounding, Felicity patted her hair and straightened the folds of her skirt, attempting to look as nonchalant as possible.

The library door opened, and Drake entered the hallway first, his somber expression making Felicity catch her bottom lip between her teeth. What in heaven's name had Chance said to him? But more importantly, what in heaven's name would she say to him if Chance had agreed? Could she be certain he was telling the truth about that *something* that had sparked between them in Lady Atterley's kitchen? A *something* that might grow into so much more? Or was he simply telling her what he knew she wished to hear? She had felt an unmistakable *liking* for him, but had he really felt the same for her?

She held her breath as he approached, the look in his eyes unreadable.

"Lady Felicity?"

"Yes?" Good heavens, could she possibly sound any more like a cornered mouse? She cleared her throat. "Yes, Lord Wakefield?"

"Would you grant me the honor of courting you?"

So many things tumbled through her mind as she sank into the mossy-green depths of his hazel-eyed gaze. Had Chance agreed? Was the decision truly hers? Was she brave enough to risk courting this man who admitted he needed her dowry but also swore he felt something for her? She had always been the mouse. Always the wallflower who hid from every possible interaction with a gentleman. Was this providence's way of nudging her to step away from the wall, to come out of hiding, and risk grabbing hold of the same joy her older sisters had found?

"Lady Felicity?" Drake said, his deep voice as soft and soothing as a tender touch. "I implore you to give us a chance. To give *me* a chance."

And then she saw it—the sincerity in his eyes. She supposed it had always been there, but now it was stronger, the sincerity and caring. "Yes, Lord Wakefield," she whispered back. "I shall grant you permission to court me."

He smiled like a man granted freedom from the gallows. "Your answer pleases me greatly, my lady. I swear I shall not disappoint you."

Without a word, Chance turned around, stepped back inside the library, and closed the door.

"Congratulations, Felli. You actually rendered our brother speechless," Merry said.

"I am quite speechless myself." Unable to resist, Felicity boldly reached out and touched Drake's arm. "But do not underestimate me, my lord," she warned him. "Remember my bitter biscuits."

His smile dimmed the slightest bit, and he tipped a serious nod. "So noted, my lady. So noted."

Chapter Seven

FELICITY TRIED NOT to fumble and accidentally stab Drake in the eye with her parasol as she moved it to her other shoulder. She found breathing at a normal pace extremely difficult as they ambled along the village green's path as an officially courting couple enjoying a summer promenade. The situation was both exciting and frightening. When he placed his hand atop hers where it rested in the crook of his muscular arm, her heart pounded. Merry followed along behind them at a discreet distance. Close enough for proper chaperoning, but far enough back so they could share a private conversation. A private conversation? *Good heavens.*

Felicity swallowed hard, then cleared her throat. "It is a lovely day for a promenade. Is it not?"

He smiled down at her. "I had not noticed. Your loveliness dims all else for me."

She almost laughed but caught it just in time. "Do not try so hard, my lord. We are courting now. It is a time where we may get to know one another better."

"Then tell me why you doubt your beauty."

A bit surprised by the boldness of his question, she wished she could sink deeper into her lace-trimmed bonnet and hide from it.

"Felicity?" He gently patted her hand. "Come now. Tell me why you doubt your beauty."

She twitched a shrug and almost lost her parasol when it tried to slip off her shoulder.

"Felicity?" There was a gentle yet stern insistence in his voice. He was obviously unwilling to let the subject go.

"I suppose because my sisters are all so stunning, both in beauty and personality. I am the shy mouse. Always have been." His slightest squeeze of her gloved hand encouraged her to continue. She shrugged again. "My hair is more of a soft brown than their shimmering gold, and my figure is a great deal more generous." She didn't like this line of conversation, but supposed it was necessary to make him understand. "I do not feel sorry for myself, though. I am simply being honest." She huffed a wry laugh. "And others have reinforced my opinion over the years. Playmates sometimes taunted me for being the timid one until my sisters pummeled them. Modistes clucked their tongues about seams that stretched too quickly. And after I unwillingly stumbled into Society, behind my back, gentlemen mocked me as the cull of the litter—until they had too much drink, and then they mocked me to my face." She fortified herself with a deep breath. "The kitchen is my safe space. My world. There, I am accepted and enjoy creating scrumptious treats to make people happy."

She dared to glance at him, hoping she hadn't shared too much. The look he gave her melted her heart. His hazel eyes had turned more green than brown, and they flashed with a fire she didn't understand.

"I wish I had been there to defend you from every fool who ever caused you pain."

His protectiveness warmed through her like a delicious sip of hot chocolate. "Everyone has pain," she said, "and as you can see, I survived quite well. I have always been blessed with a loving family. Many are not so fortunate."

He shifted against her with a heavy sigh that escaped him as a low growl. "You are stunning, my lady. Perhaps even more so because you do not see it for yourself. You have the soulful eyes of a delicate, watchful creature of the woods, their brilliant sapphire deep and dark, filled with mystery. Your silken curls shimmer like old gold that has been guarded from the light of day by those who know how to treasure it. And your figure…" His words trailed off, and he rumbled with an almost sensuous groan. "It would not be fitting for me to tell you all that I wish to say about your luscious figure."

"Oh my." She wished she had brought her fan. She was suddenly quite warm. "Perhaps we should speak of something else?"

"Indeed, we should." He chuckled. "For both our sakes." He patted her hand again. "What shall we talk about? Ask me anything you wish to know." He glanced down at her with a tensed expression. "I know there is much about me and my situation that is most concerning, not only to you but to your brother."

While she hated to pry or cause him unease, she *was* curious, but didn't exactly know how to go about asking. "Were you close to your uncle?"

"As a child, yes." Drake stared off into the distance, his eyes narrowing. "As an adult saddled with the results of his selfish choices, I wish I had never met the man."

The angry vehemence in his tone made her wish she hadn't inquired. "You have done your best, I am sure."

"The merchants in this village would tell you that my best has not been good enough." He rolled his shoulders as if resetting the weight of his problems to a more bearable position. "The estate fell short of satisfying the entirety of the legal debts, and, fool that I was, I used everything I had to attempt to settle the rest, thereby ruining myself in the process. All that remains is the land I inherited from my father, upon which sits Wakefield Manor."

"Legal debts?" she repeated, feeling slightly confused. "Were their illegal debts as well?"

His strong jaw flexed as though he clenched his teeth. "Yes, my lady. Gambling debts with unscrupulous moneylenders. Moneylenders who would just as readily take what they are owed in blood if coin is not available."

Fear for him filled her. "Are you in danger?" He took longer to answer than she liked. "Drake—are you in danger? Will these moneylenders come for you since your uncle is dead?"

He gave her a smile that seemed a bit too tight and forced. "I am quite safe, my lady. Never fear." He pulled in a deep breath and let it ease out. "What else would you like to know?"

"You were happier before you became an earl, weren't you?" She had noted the way his tone had changed when he spoke about inheriting his father's land. Pride was there, along with the determination to protect it.

"I was content, and life was simpler."

"Simpler is often best," she said, "like cress-and-butter sandwiches. Remember?"

"Indeed." He nodded at an approaching couple who seemed to eye them in disbelief. "They appear to be shocked you deigned to be seen with me. We shall be the gossip of the village."

She couldn't help but laugh. "They could be shocked because you deigned to be seen with *me*."

He grinned. "Perhaps we two *culls* are a proper match after all."

"The *ton* are harsh critics, and dislike to be proven wrong." She idly twirled her parasol on her shoulder, holding her chin higher as another couple ogled them. "I am sure they are surprised to see me promenading with a gentleman. Usually, when my sisters drag me out of the kitchens and force me to take some fresh air, I enjoy the green with them."

"You do not like fresh air?" he teased.

"Not when it comes with the expectations of others." She had another question that she simply had to ask. "Have you enjoyed the green with many other ladies?"

Behind them, Merry was suddenly stricken with a coughing spell, making them pause.

"Are you unwell?" Felicity asked her sister, knowing full well that Merry, with her keen sense of hearing, had overheard her question about Drake's promenade partners.

"I believe I swallowed a bug," Merry said with unconvincing innocence. "I am quite over it now, though. I was able to rid myself of the beastly thing."

"Thank goodness for that." Felicity gave her a pointed look that she knew Merry would understand. When she turned back to Drake, she caught his grin before he could hide it. "What?"

"Are you jealous, my lady?"

She huffed and looked away. "I merely like to know my standing among the gossips."

His self-satisfied chuckle irritated her immensely. "The gossips have no one with whom to compare you. You stand alone, my lady."

"Well, then." Now she didn't know what to say. "Have you any other questions for me?"

"Yes," he said, thoughtfulness ringing in his tone. "What made you decide to take a chance on me even after I admitted I needed your dowry?"

"Your eyes."

"My eyes?"

She didn't know exactly how to explain it. "Some say the eyes are the windows to the soul. When I look into yours"—she sheepishly tipped her head—"I see a good man. A man who has endured a great deal. A man whom I would like to trust and not have him play me for a fool." She dared to lock gazes with him. "Can I trust you, my lord? Do you swear to be honest?"

He stopped walking and turned her to face him. "The answer to both is a resounding yes, and please know I understand that words mean little if they are not backed by actions. While we are courting, I hope to convince you that you can always trust me. I hope to erase all doubts that must surely be there because of my circumstances."

"There is that soul," she whispered, impulsively touching his cheek. "Not that I am an expert, but I find it hard to believe that a ruthless cove could possess such eyes. Eyes that make me feel so safe."

He started to kiss her hand, but Merry scooted between them and shepherded them onward. "Come along now, my naughty children. We must adhere to all proprieties."

Drake grinned. "Yes, Lady Merry. Do forgive me, but your sister makes me forget myself."

"That is why I am here to remind you," Merry said with a smugness that made Felicity roll her eyes. "I am rather enjoying this newfound sense of power. Perhaps I shall offer my services as a chaperone to others."

"That would throw Serendipity and Chance into quite the tizzy," Felicity said as she and Drake resumed their stroll. "It would be quite the chore to find you a proper match if you are chaperoning others."

"Serendipity is the eldest sister, correct?" Drake asked.

"Indeed, she is, something she likes to remind us of every chance she gets." Upon noticing clouds gathering, Felicity closed her parasol. "Chance is the firstborn, then Seri is next."

"Is the eldest not usually the first to secure a match?"

"She promised Mama she would not marry until the rest of us were settled in our own happily-ever-afters. Only then will Seri consider entering the Marriage Mart herself." While Felicity was grateful for her sister's sacrifice, she often wondered if that was Seri's way of hiding from the inevitable, as all the rest of them had tried.

"Chance will get her married off as soon as Felli and I are gone," Merry said from behind them. "He'll not be satisfied until he receives his full inheritance."

At Drake's quizzical look, Felicity explained, "For Chance to inherit full access to the Broadmere accounts, all of us, his seven sisters, must have happily settled down in love matches."

"A love match is a rare thing," Drake said. "Marriages are more like business agreements for many. I assume a sharp-eyed solicitor is watching to ensure those terms are met?"

"You assume correctly. Mr. Sutherland, the elder, has been the Broadmere solicitor for as long as I can remember, and he is training his son, Mr. Sutherland, the younger, to take his place once he retires." Felicity had always liked both solicitors. They seemed to be kind and honest persons, which was not surprising. Mama and Papa would not have bothered with any other sort.

The soft rumbling of distant thunder drew her eyes to the sky once more. "I fear our promenade is soon to be over. Perhaps we should start for home."

Scowling at the clouds that dared to end their visit, Drake nodded. "Allow me to escort you, ladies. With any luck, we should be able to make it to Broadmere Hall before the skies open up."

"That would be very nice," Felicity said, ignoring the smug looks of those traipsing off to the shelter of their carriages. "I find a brisk walk quite refreshing."

Thunder rumbled again, louder this time.

"We had better hurry," Merry said, "or we shall soon find ourselves refreshed by a good dousing."

With her arm still looped through his, Felicity picked up the pace. Hearty laughter bubbled free of her as the three of them scurried down the lane, not quite breaking into a run, but walking a great deal faster than what was considered proper. The clean, fresh scent of the approaching rain rode high on the wind, urging them on. There was something exhilarating about running alongside the man who swore he was interested only in her, and even the threat of a rainstorm didn't dampen his spirits. Her joy in the simple things was contagious. Merry and Drake joined in her laughter as they raced along like three children escaping their daily lessons. She had never imagined courtship could be this lovely.

Lightning flashed, making Merry squeal. "Oh my goodness! Here it comes!"

The sky opened up and kept its promise of a good soaking.

Felicity opened her parasol and tried to shield Drake and herself, but it merely slowed the drenching. Merry added her parasol to the mix as they all huddled together, but their efforts were futile. The silk and cotton of the frilly things filtered the water more than stopped it. The fashion accessory was meant to shield one from the sun, not the rain.

Felicity's bonnet soon drooped so low, she removed it so she could see. "I thought we could at least make it home," she said, speaking loud enough to be heard over the deluge.

"Forgive me for not having a carriage, my lady." Dark hair drenched and plastered to his head, Drake shook the water off his hat and carried it at his side. "This is contemptible."

"It is not," Felicity said, finding his appearance wild and breathtaking. "I like the rain."

"She does," Merry chimed in. "As a child, she was always the last to come inside whenever it rained, and that was only at Mama's insistence."

He removed his coat and draped it around Felicity's shoulders. "If you catch your death, I shall never forgive myself."

His warm scent of sandalwood and citrus surrounded her, making her breathe deeply to savor it. "I am quite hearty, my lord. This wallflower is not a fragile lily." She couldn't help but stare at the way his soaked shirt clung to his muscular chest. My goodness, it was as though he wore no shirt at all. With great reluctance and finding a strength she never knew she had, she tore her eyes away and forced her gaze back to his face.

He gave her that lopsided smile that said he knew exactly what she was thinking.

Her cheeks heated with a furious blush.

"Will you come inside, Lord Wakefield?" Merry shouted as she pushed open the gate to Broadmere Hall. "I am sure Chance would gladly offer you a brandy to help you dry out."

Without pulling his gaze from Felicity's, he slowly shook his head. "I best not, Lady Merry. You and Lady Felicity hurry along now, before this soaking makes you ill."

Hugging his coat around her one last time, Felicity removed it ever so slowly. "Thank you, Drake. I truly enjoyed our time today."

He accepted it with a nod so formal, one would think them in a ballroom. "I enjoyed our time as well, Felicity. More than you will ever know." He bowed over her hand, then grazed a quick kiss to her gloved fingers. "Until our next time, my lady."

"Yes." Felicity tried to remember how to breathe, but it was so difficult with her heart thumping like a herd of galloping horses. "Until our next time."

DRAKE GROANED AS he walked home, ignoring the storm pelting him down the lane. *Gads alive.* The way her porcelain skin had glistened with the rain. She was a voluptuous sculpture of the rarest marble. A sea nymph risen from the waves with her hair in disarray, clinging to her face and sending curling tendrils along her throat, creeping toward her bosom. Felicity was the living embodiment of Botticelli's *The Birth of Venus*. And the way the wet muslin clung to her curves…

He groaned again. What he wouldn't give for the opportunity to worship her as she so deserved. He shook his head at the rakish thought. No, Felicity deserved the very best. While he wouldn't mind stealing a sumptuous kiss or two, the best would be saved for their wedding night.

Their wedding night. He liked the sound of that and wondered how soon he might be able to make that happen. Instinct told him not to push too hard. Such an action could be misread as eagerness to get his hands on her dowry. No, he had to be patient. Courting Felicity with purpose and care was something they both needed.

He lifted his face to the rain and smiled. She loved rain, cress-and-butter sandwiches, and was happiest in her kitchens. A lady of privilege who shunned the chaos of Society for simple things and quiet ways. His shy little mouse was more powerful than she could possibly realize. There was a steeliness within her of which she had no idea. Felicity would weather anything and everything with grace. She possessed him, heart and soul.

Could he be any more fortunate? He stretched out his arms and embraced the deluge, delighting in the revelations the storm had brought. Then his conscience nudged him with a quiet reminder of the very large lie that could ruin it all. He dropped his arms and unleashed a heavy sigh. How would Felicity react to the greatest ruse of all: his very-much-alive uncle?

Chapter Eight

"I THOUGHT A treat of ices would be nice and refreshing before our promenade with Lord Wakefield." Merry led the way to the white wrought-iron chairs at their favorite table in Caruthers Treat Shop. The quaint confectioner in the center of the village of Binnocksbourne had become the place to see and be seen when the *ton* retired to the Lake District for the summer. "Which flavor shall you choose today?"

Felicity smiled and idly twitched a shoulder while watching passersby through the wide front window of the shop. She had no idea what flavor of ice or sorbet she wanted. It was just as sweet and a great deal more pleasant to drift away into lovely imaginings of another promenade with Drake. He was so attentive, so enjoyable to be around, so very kind and caring. That *something* between them had wiggled into her guarded heart and taken over. "You choose, Merry," she said with a contented little sigh. "What did we have last time?"

"Horse manure."

"Sounds delicious," Felicity said, before realizing what her sister had suggested. "Merry! How awful of you to say such a thing."

"Well, what was I to do? You had that glassy-eyed look again, and I knew I had lost you to the imaginings of your handsome suitor."

"I cannot help it." Felicity also couldn't stop smiling. "He makes me happy." And that was an understatement of all that he made her feel. Not only did he steal her breath away with the excitement of his presence, but he was *safe*. Comfortable. Perhaps not the most romantic way to describe a man she might someday marry, but it meant more to her than anyone else could ever understand. Drake cared about her feelings and seeing that she was treated with kindness and care, unlike many of the gentlemen of her acquaintance. The more she was with him, the more she trusted him, and trust won over her heart more quickly than anything else.

"I shall have the maple ice again," she finally said in response to Merry rolling her eyes. "And do not be so insufferable. You encouraged this, and just wait until *you* become smitten. I wager you will be even worse."

Merry snorted. "I have yet to find suitable material with which to become smitten."

Ignoring her sister, Felicity waved over her dear friend, Mrs. Caruthers, from where the rosy-cheeked matron hovered nearby, obviously straining to overhear their conversation. She was a notorious gossip—if the shopkeeper's wife didn't know about it, then it was not worth knowing. "Come and join us, Mrs. Caruthers. I am sure Sarah and Mr. Caruthers can do without you for a little while."

Mrs. Caruthers glanced around the busy shop, then hurried to take a seat. "Well...perhaps just for a moment." She went uncharacteristically serious as she leaned forward and lowered her voice. "There was a matter I wished to speak with you about, Lady Felicity. A matter of grave concern."

"Oh?" Felicity and the shopkeeper's wife had enjoyed many a chat about recipes, and had even gone so far as to create new and innovative treats together in the shop's kitchen. "Grave concern, you say? For whom?"

Lips pursed as if the news was fighting to burst free of her, the woman clasped a hand to her generous bosom and glanced around the shop again. "You, Lady Felicity. It pains me to report that the matter concerns you."

"Do go on, then." Felicity braced herself. One never knew quite what to expect from the tattle-tongued Mrs. Caruthers. What could the woman possibly have heard?

Flattening both hands on the table in front of her, the matron leaned in even closer, like an oversized cat about to pounce. "It is my understanding that you are courting the Earl of Wakefield. Is that understanding correct, my lady?"

"Yes." An ominous dread settled like a rock in the pit of Felicity's stomach. "Lord Wakefield and I are courting. How might that be a grave matter?"

"The poor man, while kind and as good-hearted as can be, inherited nothing with his title but destitution and debt. Why, Mrs. Beatrice told me he even brought in the silver service from his parents' wedding and used it to pay down the credit they had extended to his uncle. It is said he has sold everything except his parents' land. Even the entailed properties are gone. His uncle gambled those away after convincing the current earl to go through a common recovery to do away with the entailments. If not for the housekeeper's brother, they could ill afford something as simple as a sack of flour." The matron clucked her tongue, sounding like a frustrated hen. "He must surely be a dowry hunter, my lady. Pure and simple. Gentle creature that you are, you must find a way to steel yourself against him and his ways."

Teeth clenched, Felicity fisted her hands in her lap, struggling to tamp down her embarrassment and shame for poor Drake. How terrible it must have been for him to part with mementos of his parents. "It is not unheard of for a gentleman to consider a lady's dowry when he begins his search for a wife." She cleared her throat and sat taller. "In fact, it is quite common."

Mrs. Caruthers sat back in her chair. "But it becomes a serious matter when that search endangers a lady whom I consider a dearest friend." She sadly shook her head and resumed her infernal tongue clucking. "None in Binnocksbourne will extend him any additional credit. We will do business with the man only if he is able to pay up front." She perked up like a hound on the scent as the bell on the shop door jangled. "There is Mrs. Beatrice. She will tell you the same." She waved a hand, flagging down the half-owner of the village's mercantile. "Mrs. Beatrice! Do join us!"

Felicity suppressed a groan and looked to Merry for help. Merry's pained expression said it all. She had no idea how to escape this either.

As soon as the portly Mrs. Beatrice settled into a chair, Mrs. Caruthers caught hold of her arm and leaned her closer. "I was just informing our dear Lady Felicity that she must steel herself against the wiles of the Earl of Wakefield."

"Oh yes, do," Mrs. Beatrice agreed, her adamancy unmistakable. She patted the tabletop in time with her words. "The poor man has nothing, Lady Felicity, absolutely nothing. I know he might seem ardent enough, but I fear it's all an act to win you over and gain your dowry. Mr. Herbert and I would have warned you the other day, but we did not realize the situation had become so dire. Courting the man?" The matron of the mercantile shook her head so hard her bonnet nearly went askew. "You must break it off, Lady Felicity. Guard the tenderness of your dear heart with everything possible and send that dowry-hunting earl on his merry way."

"While I appreciate the warning," Felicity said, "I truly believe—"

"There!" Mrs. Caruthers interrupted. "Lady Nedia! Do come over and join us, my dear. Our beloved Lady Felicity so needs to hear the sordid tale you shared with me just the other day."

Again, Felicity stifled a groan and nudged Merry under the table. They needed to escape this well-meaning attack of Mrs. Caruthers and Mrs. Beatrice, especially before the loathsome Nedia joined them. That vain little chit prided herself on being the cruelest debutante of the *ton*, even though her debut was two Seasons ago. She was a spiteful, backbiting liar, and none of the Broadmere sisters liked her.

The ostentatious young woman swept toward them after

pointing for her maid to wait outside the shop. "Lady Felicity. Lady Merry." She suffered a bored nod their way, then turned to Mrs. Caruthers and Mrs. Beatrice. "Sitting with your patrons now? How quaint, but I believe I shall refrain from joining you."

Mrs. Caruthers rose from her seat and offered it to the haughty girl. "It is about Lady Felicity courting Lord Wakefield. We felt she needed to be warned, and providence sent you in here at the exact moment we were speaking with her."

Felicity started to rise but found her escape blocked by the oversized bows and puffy sleeves of Nedia's pretentious gown. She glared at Merry, willing her usually quite forward sister to come up with a means of escape.

Merry jerked a slight nod at the portly Mrs. Beatrice, who had boxed her into the corner beside the window.

"So the rumors are true?" Nedia said to Felicity, sounding entirely too pleased by the news. "Lord Wakefield finally worked his way down to you, did he?"

"Dare I remind you our brother is a duke while your father is but a viscount?" Merry replied with such cutting bluntness that Felicity wanted to cheer. "I daresay Lord Wakefield has not *worked his way down* to my sister."

Nedia snickered, hissing like a snake in the grass. "Oh, that is not what I meant at all, Lady Merry." She flounced down into Mrs. Caruthers's vacated seat and coyly drummed her fingers on the table. Her smile chilled Felicity to the bone. "What I meant," she said, "is that he has already exhausted his field of possible heiresses and dowries. One by one, he has gone down through the line and summarily asked each of us to marry him." She flicked a hand in the air and laughed, revealing a mouth crowded with entirely too many teeth. "Of course, we refused him. A husband who brings nothing to the marriage but a title? Ridiculous!" She hissed her insulting snicker again. "I feel certain you were the last on his list because after all..." She laughed. "You are... For lack of a better way of saying it, you are *you*." She shrugged and offered a simpering grin. "Of course, with the

Broadmere money, one would have expected him to choose you first. Odd, is it not?"

Felicity swallowed hard, determined to remain stoic and not give Nedia the satisfaction of a reaction. "What I find odd, Nedia, is that even though he has not been the Earl of Wakefield for all that long, you say he has proposed to every eligible young lady of the *ton*? That hardly seems possible or realistic."

"Well." Lady Nedia wet her thin lips as if preparing to bite someone. "Perhaps not *all* available ladies, but, including myself, I know of at least a half dozen or more." She haughtily patted at the blonde curls framing her face. "Six or more proposals of marriage, and all refused for the same reason." She reached over and patted Felicity's arm. "Of course, he is handsome, dearest, and quite eloquent, but unless you wish to live off your brother's generosity, I heartily recommend you spurn him and run. Surely, spinsterhood would be a much happier choice." She swept a sneering gaze up and down Felicity's form. "What did he tell you, dearest? That your loveliness mesmerized him, and he wanted you for you and not your money? Do you not realize he said the same to us all?"

Felicity rose, unceremoniously bumping Mrs. Caruthers back a step. "This conversation has reached the end of my patience. Good day, Lady Nedia, Mrs. Caruthers, Mrs. Beatrice." As she charged toward the door, she clenched her teeth against the loud whispers of *poor thing* filling the shop behind her.

Merry hurried to catch up, not taking hold of her arm until they were well out of sight of the treat shop. "You know how Nedia lies. She finds it more natural than breathing."

"That is not the point, and you know it." Felicity rapidly blinked, refusing to cry until safely tucked away in her room. "Everyone in Binnocksbourne believes her, and I am quite certain that evil cow will happily spread the gossip even farther during her next visit to Town."

"If he had proposed to that many women, do you not think we would have heard about it before now?"

Felicity trudged along faster. She couldn't quit the confines of the village fast enough.

"Should we not go to the green?" Merry asked. "We promised to meet Lord Wakefield there."

"I am going home."

"You are not even going to give the man a chance to defend himself?" Merry yanked on her arm. "Stop this very instant. You were so happy, Felli. Are you going to let that lying Nedia destroy that?"

Felicity pulled her arm away and whirled around to face her sister. "If I do confront him, what do you think he will say? Of course, he will deny it."

"You do not know that. What if he denies what she said? What if that is the truth? He might have a perfectly good explanation."

"About how he worked his way *down* to me by process of elimination? Leave it, Merry. Have I not been humiliated enough for one day?"

"You had to know this might happen," Merry said with a gentle firmness that hurt. "You knew his circumstances."

"Which we discovered by spying on his garden." Felicity threw her hands in the air again. "What if we had not done that? Would he have said anything or gone along as if all was in order? He did not *tell* me about his situation, Merry. What else is he hiding?" All Felicity's doubts, all her fears, surfaced with a vengeance.

Merry eyed her, sadly shaking her head. "You have been so happy these past few weeks. He makes you joyous, Felli."

"Then I am an even bigger fool than I feared I was." Felicity charged toward home, almost breaking into a run. It would be a very long time before the village of Binnocksbourne enjoyed her presence again.

"He deserves the opportunity to explain himself," Merry shouted from behind her. "He said you stood alone, remember? The gossips had no one else with whom to compare you. He seemed sincere. Let me help you when you talk to him. You know I am good at spotting lies."

Felicity swiped away an escaped tear and kept loping along. She needed to get home. Home to her kitchens. Home to her room. She needed the safety of her family, who would never hurt her as badly as anyone from the outside ever had. Granted, Serendipity's advice on restraint when it came to food had often stung, but none of her sisters or her brother had ever been mean-spirited, not as mean-spirited and humiliating as this. She was a fool, believing Drake was interested in her for anything other than money.

She veered off the road and cut through the field toward the entrance to the kitchens. The last thing she needed right now was to come across Serendipity and have to explain why she and Merry were home so early from the village.

"My lady?" Cook looked up from the dough she was kneading against the floured table. "Are you unwell?"

"I am most unwell," Felicity said as she ripped off her bonnet and gloves and threw them, her reticule, and her parasol into the corner. "And starving. I know it is not yet teatime, but would you care to join me in eating every biscuit this kitchen possesses?"

"Oh, my lady." Cook's tone dripped with compassion as she dusted the flour off her hands. "Sit yourself down. I shall set the kettle to boiling." She shooed the scullery maids out of the kitchen with a stern jerk of her head. "Chocolate or almond, my lady?" She paused at the door to the pantry.

"Both." Felicity intended to eat herself into oblivion. After all, why shouldn't she? Weren't fat spinsters considered jollier?

By the time Merry and Serendipity joined her in the kitchen, she was dipping her fourth biscuit into her tea.

"Felli?" Serendipity said softly. She gently hugged her and pressed her cheek to her hair. "Merry told me."

"Yes, we had a lovely time at the treat shop," Felicity said with a viciousness that surprised even her. "It appears I am the village's newest amusement—the silly lady whom they all pity."

She finished off the last of the chocolate biscuits and moved on to the plate of almond. "Would you care to join me? I fear all the chocolate ones are gone, but I have yet to eat all the vanilla or almond." She held up a finger as she freshened her tea. "And please, no admonishments regarding my lack of restraint. There really is not a point now, is there?"

"You may eat every biscuit we possess, my dear one." Serendipity gently brushed Felicity's curls back from her face. "Whatever it takes to make you happy again."

"I am empty inside," Felicity whispered, never realizing before how much emptiness hurt. "Stupid heart. All the happiness leaked right out of it. It is well and truly gone."

"Shall I send Chance to thrash him?" Merry offered. "And Thorne, Matthew, Wolfe, and Jansen? Shall I send for them too?"

Her overfilled stomach already aching, Felicity shook her head. "No. My misery is of my own doing. I failed to ask Drake if anyone else had already spurned him." She huffed a pained laugh. "Carelessness on my part. Silly of me, really." If she kept eating, she would soon need a basin to cast up everything her poor stomach struggled to hold.

"Let us go upstairs so you can have a bit of a lie-down." Serendipity firmly led her away from the counter with an arm still around her shoulders. "You have gone a bit green. I fear a chamber pot to be in your near future." She hugged her tighter. "Come along now. You leave this situation to Merry and me. And remember what a liar Nedia has always been."

"The village believes her." That was the crux of it. Yes, Felicity could talk with Drake and listen to whatever he had to say, but how could she overcome the humiliation of the treat shop? And could she really trust Drake to tell her the truth? If he had proposed to all those women, as Nedia had said, why had he failed to mention it so she could make a choice? So she could be better prepared. "Do you intend to force Nedia to hold an assembly in Binnocksbourne Hall and deny what she said?"

Serendipity nodded. "We might. One never knows the levels

of creativity that Merry and I can achieve." She patted Felicity's shoulder as they climbed the stairs. "And I shall also be having a word with Madame Couire. She has become much too bold with her opinions regarding seams and their repair. Apparently, she needs some reminding about the appropriate ways to communicate with those who purchase a great many gowns from her. Were she to lose the Broadmere account, I feel certain many others would soon follow."

"What has come over you, Seri?" Felicity hiccupped and held her poor, sloshing stomach. Even as miserable as she was, she couldn't help but be touched by the sincerity in her sister's tone.

"Many have treated you poorly. Some because they are simply mean-spirited and others because they thought themselves to be helpful." She bowed her head as she opened the door to Felicity's bedchamber. "I am sorry, Felli. So very sorry for my part in it, and I promise it will never happen again. You have been so happy these past few weeks, all because a man chose to make you the center of his existence and treat you the way you should always be treated. It breaks my heart to see that end."

Felicity clapped a hand over her mouth. The ache in her stomach had churned itself into a fury that refused to be denied.

"Chamber pot!" Merry sang out to the maids. "Bring extras!"

"Cool water and rags as well!" Serendipity said as she lifted the lid to the commode and stepped out of the way. She held Felicity's hair back while she heaved, just as Mama had always done whenever one of them fell ill.

After emptying herself of what she hoped was *all* the biscuits, Felicity dropped into a heap across her bed. It had been a long time since she had eaten herself sick. It had been at a party when she overheard several gentlemen taunting one another about who might be unfortunate enough to have to sit beside the Broadmere cull at dinner. As she recalled, she had sworn never to eat herself sick ever again. So much for that oath.

A cool cloth was pressed across her eyes, and someone plucked the jabbing hairpins from her hair. Heartbroken and her stomach sore, at least she still had her caring sisters.

DRAKE STROLLED ALONG the lane toward the village, happier and more content than he had been since allowing Uncle George to drag him into what he had come to label life as *the Wakefield mess*. And it was all because of Felicity. She was the sunshine to his dark and dreary soul. Soon—very soon, he hoped, he would ask her to marry him. The banns could be read, and within a month, they would be married.

As for their courting, he couldn't have hoped for better. Well…perhaps a little bit better. He ached for a taste of what he was certain would be the sublime sweetness of her lips. Her loveliness drew him in, transfixing him, mainly because she was so unaware of her beauty. How anyone couldn't see her delightful radiance was beyond comprehension. He shook his head. The fools had to be blind.

He lifted his face to the sun, thankful that the rain had subsided so their promenade would not be missed. Their strolls around the village green were his second favorite of their chaperoned meetings. Sitting at the kitchen worktable and watching Felicity cook was his favorite above all. She was an artist with ingredients, and the kitchen her canvas, her eyes sparkling brighter whenever she was creating something delicious—well…mostly delicious. He grinned, relieved that they could now laugh over the hideous batch of bitter biscuits.

As he neared the green, he scanned the area for his bonneted beauty, frowning when he failed to find her. Checking his pocket watch to ensure he wasn't too early or terribly late, he meandered along the path the villagers had constructed to be an almost exact copy of Rotten Row in Hyde Park. A shame, really. As time passed, the village increasingly modeled itself after London to cater to the elite, and in doing so, it became less quaint and friendly. The longer he walked, nodding to those he met along the way, the more he felt as though he was being watched. Not by any one person in particular, but by everyone. What the bloody hell was going on here? He stopped in the shade of a sprawling oak and rechecked his watch, noting it was now half past the agreed-upon hour they were to meet. Had something happened? Had some ill befallen his lady love?

He crossed the green and hurried into Mettlestone's. If anyone knew everything going on in Binnocksbourne, it was the Mettlestones, either them or Mrs. Caruthers from the treat shop. In his opinion, the Mettlestones were the lesser of the two evils.

"Good day to you, Lord Wakefield," Mr. Herbert called out from behind the counter. "I did not expect to see you today."

Drake forced himself not to react to the shopkeeper's insinuation that if he hadn't come on the usual day to pay on his accounts, he knew better than to darken the shop's door. "Perchance, have you seen Lady Felicity today? She and I were to meet for a promenade."

The shopkeeper shook his head as he continued dusting the shelves behind the counter. "I have not seen her, my lord, but I believe my Beatrice mentioned seeing her earlier at Caruthers."

"I see," Drake said, not really seeing at all. It appeared Felicity had been at the village at some point in time that day, but now she was nowhere to be found. "Was she accompanied by her sister, Lady Merry?"

Mr. Herbert offered a solemn nod. "Yes. My Beatrice mentioned seeing Lady Merry as well."

Drake could tell by the way the shopkeeper acted that Mrs. Beatrice had mentioned a great deal more, but Mr. Herbert simply wasn't sharing it. There was naught to be done but hurry to the Broadmere residence to ensure Felicity was all right.

"Good day to you, sir," he told the shopkeeper, and dashed out the door. With long, ground-eating strides, he left the village behind him, all the while wishing he had ridden into the small town. But it couldn't be helped. It would take far too long to fetch his horse to ride over to the Broadmeres'.

By the time he reached their front door, the exertion had him slightly out of breath. He banged the brass door knocker, willing the portal to swing open and let him inside.

And swing open it did, just wide enough for a pale, watery eye to peer at him. "Yes?"

"Walters, please let me inside. Lady Felicity failed to meet me at the park today, and I am concerned about her welfare." Surely, the ancient butler remembered him from his visits before.

The crack in the door did not widen. The old codger simply glared at him.

"Walters? It is I, Lord Wakefield. I am calling upon Lady Felicity."

"She is not receiving." The door shut with a harsh bang.

"What the bloody hell?" Drake clacked the brass door knocker again, slamming it harder this time.

The door opened wider this time, revealing the younger butler, Fipps. "Good afternoon, Lord Wakefield." With a polite nod, he ushered Drake inside. "How may I help you?"

"Lady Felicity. Is she receiving today? Walters quite abruptly informed me that she was not."

The butler's expression revealed nothing. Fipps was the epitome of a staid servant. "It is my understanding that Lady Felicity is indeed not receiving today, my lord."

"But she is here...and well?"

Still expressionless, Fipps gave a single nod. "She is in residence, my lord. Would you care to leave your card?"

"No, I do not care to leave my bloody card." Drake ran a hand through his hair, staring deeper into the house and fighting the urge to run through the halls calling her until she came out. "Her sisters. Lady Merry. Lady Serendipity. Are they receiving?"

"They are not, my lord."

"And you are going to just stand there and tell me nothing when you know damn well what is going on." Servants knew everything. They were the *ton*'s most valuable lines of communication.

Fipps returned to the door and opened it. "Good day, my lord."

"No, it is not, Fipps, and no one will tell me why." Drake stormed out of the place, racking his brain for what could have possibly gone wrong. Felicity knew everything about him.

Well, almost everything.

He came up short, halting in the middle of the road. Had she somehow discovered the truth about Uncle George? He slowly shook his head. No. There was no way. And even if she had, would she not have asked him? They'd endured several long discussions about his state of affairs, and she had admired him for attempting to restore honor to the Wakefield name.

But if not the truth about his uncle, then what? That was the only secret left between them. What had caused everything to suddenly turn sour?

Chapter Nine

DETERMINED TO SEE Felicity if he had to sit on her doorstep each day from dawn to dusk, Drake banged the brass door knocker that he had come to hate. He likened it to a death knell on the precious moments he had shared with his beloved Felicity. Beloved? Yes, most definitely. He loved her and needed whatever had come between them to be resolved.

The door opened. Thankfully, it was Fipps. "Good day, my lord. Do come in."

"Thank you, Fipps. Is my lady receiving today?" Drake was in no mood to dance around with niceties. He needed to see Felicity. Speak with her. Find out what had gone so terribly wrong.

Expressionless as always, Fipps paused and eyed him for a long moment before proffering a polite nod. "A moment, my lord. I shall confirm whether or not Lady Felicity is receiving."

Drake resettled his footing, struggling to maintain a calm demeanor even though he didn't feel calm at all. He wanted to bellow Felicity's name until his lady love answered.

Fipps reappeared, ambling down the hallway and giving nothing away with his stoic mien. *Damn his eyes.* The butler could at least give a glimmer of hope. He halted and bowed. "Lady Felicity will see you in the garden, my lord. If you would be good enough to follow me."

Drake would follow the man straight into the jaws of hell if it led him to Felicity. "Lead on, Fipps."

Felicity was seated at the garden table where she had locked his jaws with her infamous bitter biscuits. She stared off into the distance, not even bothering to look his way as he approached. He glanced all around, searching for either Lady Merry or Lady Serendipity, but didn't see them. Surely, they had to be nearby. Never would they allow Felicity the impropriety of being alone with him.

"Felicity?" He waited for her to acknowledge his presence before he dared to take a seat.

Ever so slowly, she tore her gaze away from the garden and leveled it on him. The hurt and hunger for retribution in her expression shocked him.

"Have a seat, my lord," she said with a coldness that sent a shiver through him. When he started to sit in the chair beside her, she stopped him. "No. Over there, if you please." She nodded at the seat across the table.

"Felicity, please..." He settled into the chair she had indicated. "What is wrong? What have I done?"

Unsmiling and slightly pale, she barely narrowed her eyes, glaring at him with such intensity that it burned. "The scrapings you found at the bottom of the barrel deserve better, my lord. You might not think so. But I do." Her delicate fist trembled as she thumped the table. "I deserve better."

He slowly shook his head, utterly confused. "I fear you have me at a loss, my lady. I do not understand."

"Did you have a list that you went through? Did you check off each name when it failed?"

"A list? What names? Felicity—" He reached across the table for her hand, but she yanked it away before he could take it. "Pray tell me what I have done that has angered you so?"

"I am not angry," she said, her tone eerily calm. "I am enraged. Humiliated. Hurt. Heartbroken." She jutted her chin higher. "Job well done, my lord. You obliterated my soul in flames, but like the phoenix, I have risen from the ashes. Thanks to my sisters."

"What did I do, my darling? Please tell me so I might set things right between us."

"You do not have permission to address me so intimately. Either observe common decency or leave."

Heart sinking like a lead stone, Drake swallowed hard. A grievous wrong had been done here, but he had no idea what or how. "Forgive me, Lady Felicity. But again, I must ask what I did to fall from your impeccable graces."

"Lady Nedia Stranserton," she said, spitting the name as though it was poison.

Drake frowned, trying to match the woman with the name. "I seem to recall meeting a Lady Nedia Stranserton, but I am not certain. The name is familiar, but the face…" He shook his head. "I cannot bring her to memory."

"So, you proposed to so many well-dowried ladies of the *ton*, you can hardly keep track. Is that what you are telling me?"

"Proposed?" This was madness. He hadn't proposed to anyone. He had discreetly sniffed out information about dowries, but that was the extent of his efforts on the Marriage Mart.

Eyes glistening, Felicity blinked hard and fast, obviously struggling to maintain her unnaturally cold demeanor. "No? You do not recall her? Then what about her friends, Lady Margaret Feathersby and Lady Delphia Morgbrouton? Both assured me you proposed to them as well after Lady Nedia spurned you, because you brought nothing to the union but a title and destitution."

"I do not know what cruel game this is, my lady, but I swear to you upon my father's grave, I have proposed to no one." He leaned forward. "I have not even proposed to you, my lady, because you wished us to court for a while."

"I do not believe you."

He thumped the table. "Then bring those women here. I want the right to confront my accusers, whose faces I cannot even remember." This was utter madness. Why would those women say such a thing? "Who told you this? Why in heaven's name would they tell such lies?"

"Mrs. Caruthers and Mrs. Beatrice were warning me away from courting you when Lady Nedia came into the shop and swore you had proposed to every eligible woman of the *ton* possessing an ample dowry. She found it quite amusing that you had finally worked your way down to me."

He leaned back in the chair, scrubbing his face with both hands. "I have not proposed to anyone, my lady, and will swear that is the truth until my dying day. I did make discreet inquiries regarding dowries. Yes. I am guilty of that, and you are very well aware of why, but there was no list of women for me to *work my way down*." With a heavy sigh, he let his hands drop to his lap. "I do not even remember those women. Could you describe them?"

"Three waspish harpies," Merry said as she emerged from the depths of the maze of roses, "none of them aging well as they approach their third Season."

"Blonde, tall, and striking," Serendipity said as she came out from behind the ivy arbor. "However, Lady Nedia does look remarkably like a goose with her overly long neck. Lady Margaret wears entirely too much rouge on her cheeks and lips, and Lady Delphia laughs like a braying donkey."

Drake thought long and hard about the parties he had intended. Indeed, he had come across three women fitting those descriptions, but as far as he could recall, he had steered clear of them. Dowries or not, he couldn't imagine marriage to any of them. The very idea had made him shudder. "I do not believe I have ever spoken to those three. Why in heaven's name would they claim I proposed to them?"

The Broadmere sisters remained silent, all of them staring at him as if tearing into his soul.

"I think he is telling the truth," Merry said, her eyes narrowing to critical squints.

"Perhaps," Serendipity said while slowing drumming her fingers atop the table. She turned to Felicity. "Nedia is known to be the cruelest sort of liar."

"And Margaret and Delphia are known to follow wherever she leads." Merry arched a brow at Felicity. "It could be they are jealous of you."

"Jealous of me, why?" Felicity kept her glare locked on Drake. He prayed she wouldn't find him lacking.

"You said they are approaching their third Season out," he said. "Perhaps they are jealous you have a man who adores you."

"A man who adores my dowry. You know that is what everyone in Binnocksbourne believes." She folded her hands on the table, clenching them so tightly her knuckles whitened. She huffed a humorless laugh. "Apparently, I am so utterly unmatchable that no one could want me for any other reason than my dowry."

"You are not unmatchable." What in heaven's name had this poor, gentle creature been told? "The only way you might be unmatchable, Lady Felicity, is that no one deserves you. I, especially, do not deserve you, but providence granted me the opportunity to meet you and give you my heart."

"Pretty words," she said, but the coldness in her eyes seemed less icy. She flinched as though battling pain. "I want to believe you."

"Then do," he said, debating whether to drop to his knees and beg. Then the most obvious answer of all came to him. "Keep your dowry." He almost choked on the words, knowing how badly he needed the money. "If the dowry is all you think I want, then keep it."

She sat back and frowned in disbelief. "The Wakefield estate cannot survive without it."

"Oh, we can survive, but it will be just that," he said, feeling the hope of their future slipping away with every word he uttered. "It will take years and years to undo the damage my uncle left behind, and I have nearly ruined myself attempting to remedy it in a faster manner. I should have left it all alone and tended to what I knew best, taken care of my own land and holdings rather than risk them all because of a title that grows more meaningless each day."

She stared at him, reminding him of a skittish deer, afraid and unsure whether to trust. Just as she seemed about to speak, Fipps hurried into the garden, clearing his throat to announce his presence. "Forgive me for interrupting, but there is a messenger at the door who appears quite agitated." He bowed to Drake. "He has come to fetch you, my lord. It would appear there is a dire matter at Wakefield Manor that requires your immediate presence."

Torn at ignoring the runner and staying to beg Felicity to believe his love for her, Drake held up a hand, waving Fipps away. "There is a dire matter here that requires my presence. Even if Wakefield is on fire, there is nothing I care about there as much as I care about Felicity."

"The messenger said you might say that and asked that I tell you his name is John. He most heartily begs your forgiveness for the interruption, but it is quite necessary. He said the situation could be most dire for even more than those who reside at Wakefield." For the first time since Drake had met the butler, the man looked pained.

"You said it was John?"

"Yes, my lord."

"Damn and blast," Drake muttered, then jerked back to his senses. "Forgive my coarseness, ladies."

"Go," Felicity said with a tip of her head at the door.

"It would seem best that you do so," Serendipity added.

"We are not done here," he told Felicity. "I refuse to lose you."

Her bottom lip trembling and her eyes glimmering with the sheen of tears, she nodded again. "Go."

More disheartened than he had ever been in his life, Drake rose and bowed to the three of them. "Good afternoon, ladies." Then he hurried out, damning the ill timing of whatever his fool uncle had done this time.

As soon as the front door closed behind him, he confronted John. "What the bloody hell has he done now?"

Striding alongside him, the loyal stable keeper gave a sad shake of his head. "Himself got a letter. A rough-looking sort delivered it. Yateston said soon as himself read it, he sent for you. Said you had to come quick. Life or death, he said."

I should have left him on his own and let him stew in the mess he created. Drake didn't say the words aloud, knowing that the three remaining staff of Wakefield Manor as much as worshipped the ground his uncle walked upon. Why they did so, he would never fathom, but their loyalty was unshakable.

He arrived at his uncle sitting in the entry hall, head bowed, and the letter in his hands.

"I am so very sorry," Uncle George whispered as he handed it over.

There were only seven words written in large, bold letters on the paper bearing the name of Rum and Catherty Counting House preprinted across the bottom: *We know, and you both will pay.*

Drake went cold as death. Those words could mean only one thing. "How do they know, Uncle? What have you not told me?"

"They beat it out of me," Uncle George said, keeping his head bowed. "That day in the garden."

"You said they asked nothing. You said you told them nothing."

"I lied."

"And now you have damned us both straight to hell." Drake threw down the paper and turned away before he lost his temper and struck the old man. "You realize the power you gave them? Not only do you still owe them money, but you handed them my neck in a noose for impersonating a peer to save your sorry arse from the death threats." Drake hit the wall with his fist, cracking the plaster. "They will blackmail us now, you ignorant bastard. You do realize that, do you not?"

"What the hell was I supposed to do?" his uncle shouted.

"Taken the beating and remained silent?"

"That is what an honorable man would have done. A reformed man trying for a second chance."

"Well, we both know I have never been an honorable man. Nor am I reformed. I simply ran out of options."

"You selfish bastard. I should have let them kill you." Drake shook his head. "But in honor of my father and the image of the man I once thought you were, I risked everything to save you, and now I am just as ruined."

"Not if you marry that girl," Uncle George argued. "With that dowry, you can pay them off."

"They will bleed us all dry! There will never be a way to *pay them off*. Are you that great of a fool?" Drake shook his fist, aching to slam it into his uncle's jaw. "As long as you live, they have this lie to hold over my head." He grabbed hold of the bath chair's armrests and went nose to nose with the sniveling man. "They own us both now, you old bastard. Our lives are not our own."

His uncle bared his teeth. "Then kill me. Bring us both some relief."

"Do not tempt me," Drake said with a low, throaty growl, then pushed himself away before he did the old man damage. He paced in a tight circle, raking his hands through his hair. "I do not see a way out of this. We have no money. No credit. All I have is this land, and I will not part with my father's land." He glared at his uncle. "*He* was a man of honor. Unlike you."

"Then what do we do?" Uncle George asked with a weary flip of his hands.

"I do not know." Backed against the wall, Drake slumped to the floor with his head in his hands. He had as much as lost his precious Felicity, and now this. He had half a mind to take his uncle to Rum and Catherty and hand him over.

"You could sell part of the land," Uncle George quietly suggested. "Your father often bemoaned having so much to watch over."

"I will *not* sell my father's land." Drake drew in a ragged breath and blew it out. "This house and that land are all I have left of him, and I have dishonored that memory enough. You squandered all of yours. Keep your bloody hands off mine."

"Well, it probably would not be enough, anyway."

"We will never have enough to satisfy them. Have you not realized that by now?"

His uncle blew out a dismal huff and folded his gnarled hands in his lap. "I suppose all we can do now is wait."

"Wait?"

Uncle George nodded. "They will send their demands in a few days. They wish to give us time to stew about what they intend to do with us. Much like cats, Rum and Catherty enjoy toying with their prey before they go in for the kill."

"We are already dead," Drake said, holding his head in his hands. "And this is hell."

"He renounced your dowry," Merry quietly reminded Felicity as they strolled among the roses. "That has to count for something."

"I want to believe him," Felicity said, more to herself than her sister. "He seemed sincere."

"He did indeed, and we know Nedia and the rest of those cows are consummate liars."

"What I do not understand is why." Felicity paused and cradled a velvety red rose in her hand, breathing in the sweetness of its scent. "What have I ever done to them?"

"Cruelty needs no reason. It merely needs a target." Merry continued to the yellow roses a few steps up ahead. "They were probably bored and thought it entertaining to make themselves a part of the gossip already surrounding you and Lord Wakefield. Boredom can be a dangerous thing."

"I wonder what ill befell Wakefield Manor that dragged him

away in such a hurry." He had not wanted to leave. That was clear enough, and yet another reason for Felicity to believe he was telling the truth.

"I do not believe he was going to go until Fipps gave him the messenger's name. That *John* person must be one of the few servants remaining at the estate." Merry waited for Felicity to join her, and they continued along the path. "This truly does not seem to be his fault. What do you think you will do?"

"I do not know." Felicity had still been made such a fool over the entire ordeal, and those whom she thought were her trusted friends had unknowingly joined in and hurt her even more. It would be exceedingly difficult for her to look at Mrs. Caruthers and Mrs. Beatrice the same way ever again. "I never thought to be the talk of the *ton*. I have always been invisible."

"You must decide which is more important to *you*," Serendipity said as she caught up with them. "Lord Wakefield or gossip."

"But gossip is so cruel, and difficult to ignore." Felicity ran a finger along the ruby-red bloom's stem and barely tapped on the first thorn. Such sweet beauty and also such pain. She huffed a soft laugh. Love was much the same. It could be so beautiful until it drew blood. "Do you think Lord Wakefield and I would ever escape the gossip swirling around us?"

"Of course you would," Merry said. "As soon as they become bored with you and move on to the next poor soul. The best thing you can do is live your life as you see fit. Face the fools head-on and refuse to allow them to steal your happiness." She held her head higher. "You do not need them. You have your wonderful sisters."

"Indeed, I do." Felicity readily admitted that she would be lost without her family, even though they sometimes drove her to the brink of madness itself.

"Speaking of which," Serendipity said, "we shall be going to Winterswick for a few days. Our Joy is having a garden party, and all the family is invited."

The delight of seeing her precocious nieces and nephews did

little to ease the worry of setting aside the absolute mess of her courting and leaving it unresolved. "When?" Felicity currently felt more like running and hiding rather than mingling with her large family.

"In a fortnight." Serendipity produced the letter, scanning the contents. "She apologizes for the short notice, but it appears our dear nephew, Lion, has learned to run rather than walk. Since Joy does not trust leading strings, the entire household is in a constant state of disarray, helping Nanny to catch him." She looked up from the page and smiled. "With Lion, Ross, Rorie, Quill, Remy, Gwynnie, Connor, and Sissy, this visit should be just the thing."

While Felicity adored her lively nieces and nephews and dearly loved Wolfe's younger siblings, Connor and Sissy, the entire affair would soon devolve into barely controlled chaos that would surely give the *ton* even more to gossip about the Broadmeres. And currently, she would much rather crawl into a hole and hide, rather than deal with her prying siblings and their spouses. "It will be just the thing for what?" She squared her shoulders. "I feel I should remain here and attend to the tattered fabric of my courtship."

Serendipity gave her a slightly damning look. "One must always support family, and Joy needs our assistance. Would you deny your own sister your help?" She tapped the letter again. "She specifically requested your help with the menus. You know how much you enjoy that. Come now. Would you truly wish to miss it? Miss time visiting with the children?"

Felicity threw up her hands and turned away. "Do not badger me, Seri. Has today not been trying enough already? For heaven's sake, I need a bit of quiet to reflect and consider how to move forward."

Serendipity eyed her for a long moment, then nodded as she refolded the letter. "Indeed, it has. Forgive me, Felli." She motioned for Merry to follow her. "Call for us if you need us. The garden is the perfect place to sort your thoughts. Mama's roses always seem to help me."

"They help me too," Felicity admitted with a sad smile. "Thank you."

She watched them go, her heart not only heavy but confused. Drake had seemed so sincere. She had believed him even before he had told her to keep her dowry, but had she believed him because she couldn't bear the thought of life without him, or because he had convinced her that they were victims of malicious gossip? She wanted to think it was the latter, but she simply didn't know anymore. She was somewhat ashamed at how quickly she had believed the worst about him. Did that mean that, deep down, she didn't truly believe he was more interested in her than her money? That revelation was worrisome.

She forged deeper into the roses, coming upon the bush that Papa had planted right after Mama had died. Its flowers were supposed to blossom with snowy whiteness to symbolize the purity of their love, but it had never bloomed. While it was healthy and its leaves a vibrant, glossy green, no one could discover why the precious bush, placed in the garden three days after the funeral, never flourished enough to produce any roses. But no one had the heart to order it removed. They all decided that the bush refused to flower because Mama and, six months later, Papa were gone.

"How do I stop being the timid mouse?" Felicity asked the plant as she seated herself on the bench beside it. "Drake has worked his way into my heart, but I cannot seem to shake free of all my doubts. Why? Why can I not have the confidence of my sisters? Forge ahead and grab hold of life. Take risks. At least try to be more…courageous?"

Chance and the girls would never allow harm to come to her. Even if she tried and failed, her family would always be her safe haven. And Merry was right. Once the gossips grew bored with her and Drake, they would move on to some other poor soul— possibly even one of themselves. One never knew when the tongue-tattlers might turn on each other.

"I need to be brave." She fisted her hands in her lap. "It does not matter what the gossips say. I am the one to live my life by my terms, not theirs."

And when Drake had said she could keep her dowry, he had meant it. She had seen it in his eyes, and Merry had seen it as well. That amounted to something. The more she remembered the rundown state of Wakefield Manor, the more she realized that his forfeiting that money mattered a great deal.

Nervously chewing on her bottom lip, she concluded with a firm nod, "We will continue to court, and move past this as best we can—and the next time I see Nedia, I shall spit on her shoes."

Chapter Ten

"SISTERS!" JOY HURRIED toward them as they disembarked from the carriage, her slight limp and bejeweled cane not slowing her in the least. "It is so good to see you all."

Felicity hung back as Serendipity and Merry rushed to embrace their sister. She so admired Joy. Even though her sister had suffered an attack of apoplexy when she gave birth to little Lion, she had fought to regain her health and mobility and now only walked with a cane. Such courage, she had.

"I wish I had such courage," Felicity said under her breath.

"Felli!" Joy called out with her arms open wide. "No hug for your favorite sister?"

Joy's husband, Jansen, stood beside her, grinning as he attempted to hold fast to their son, whose given name was actually Richard Wager Lionheart Winterstone. "Shall I loose the Lion upon you? You know how silly he is about his Auntie Felli."

After hugging Joy, Felicity held out her hands to Lion. "Come here, beastie. You only love me because Auntie always brings you treats."

"Tweats!" the toddler crowed as he dove into her arms, then started twisting in search of her reticule. "Tweats!"

"I must set you down to fetch them from my bag," she told the squirming lad. "Will you promise to stay right here and not run away?"

With sincerity born from his love for biscuits and his big blue eyes flashing with mischief, Lion nodded.

As soon as the child had a biscuit in each hand, he took off, but Nanny was at the ready and intercepted him. "Oh no, Master Lion. We shall be having a cup of milk with our biscuits, and then off we go for a nap," she said.

Lion shook his head hard and fast. "No nap!"

"Yes, nap."

The two argued all the way out of sight.

"I have a surprise," Joy said, her eyes as sparkling with mischief as her son's.

Felicity braced herself. One never knew what Joy might have in store for the family. Even though she was married and a mother now, she still adored a good game of chance or a dare. Rather than rise to the bait, Felicity withdrew a note from her reticule and handed it over. "Before you dazzle us with whatever you have planned, here are several more menu suggestions for the party in addition to the recipes I already sent over."

Joy took the notes and brazenly tucked them inside her bodice between her bosoms. "Thank you. I shall hand these over to Cook. I am sure she will be most grateful, as am I." She stamped her cane while excitedly looking at her sisters one by one. "Well? Do you not wish to know my surprise?"

Felicity backed up a step and shook her head. "Not I. The last time I saw you this excited about a *surprise* was when you helped Blessing replace the pillows on Chance's bed with sacks of stones."

"Where is our darling brother?" Joy asked. "Is he so foolish as to shun my party?"

"He had several appointments he swore he could not possibly miss. Once through them, he shall be here." Serendipity pulled Felicity forward. "What is your surprise, Joy?"

"Lord Wakefield is coming to the party. In fact, he has already arrived."

Felicity went cold and lightheaded, feeling as though all her blood had drained away. Over the past two weeks, she had refused to see Drake whenever he called after deciding they both needed a bit of time away from one another. She had decided their courtship would be the better for it if they both stepped back and took a breath, considering how easily a bit of malicious gossip had very nearly torn them apart. She had to conquer her insecurities about him and needed time to do so.

Of course, this tactic was a double-edged sword. It gave Serendipity's exemplary contacts time to watch him and see how he reacted. Those results would give Felicity either the reassurance or the resolve to stop not only doubting him but also stop doubting her instincts. To his credit, the man had never left Wakefield Manor unless it was to stand on Broadmere Hall's doorstep and bang on the door. Felicity had planned to move forward with their *fresh start* upon her return from Winterswick.

"Felli! Are you unwell?" Joy took hold of her arm. "You have gone terribly pale."

"She and Lord Wakefield are presently at odds," Serendipity said in a hissing whisper. "Did you not receive my letter?"

"I wrote to you as well," Merry said as she took Felicity's other arm. "Do you still allow your correspondence to lie unread for days? I thought you were doing better about that."

"Lion keeps me very busy," Joy said. "Oh, Felli, please forgive me."

Blessing joined them, holding her youngest son, Ross, on her hip. "What have you done to her? She's gone as white as fresh cream."

"I should not have invited Lord Wakefield," Joy said as she wrapped an arm around Felicity's shoulders and hugged her. "I am so sorry, dearest, but fear not, we can fix this."

"Not if he has already arrived."

"Did you not say you were ready to resume your courting?" Merry asked. "Simply do it here. Problem solved."

"Yes," Serendipity said, "or torture him a bit longer by flirting with other available gentlemen."

"I do not flirt." Felicity pulled away from all of them, went to the bench alongside the circular drive, and plopped down upon it. She picked at a seam on her glove. "Besides, he might have a change of heart and leave. I may have already missed my opportunity."

"You have not missed your opportunity," Blessing said. "He arrived an hour ago and appears quite determined to stay."

"Take hold of the situation," Grace said as she strolled up to join them. "Besides, do you not think you possibly overreacted? After all, the misunderstanding turned out to be nothing but lies that were not of Lord Wakefield's doing. Seri's spy network is busily sowing the truth throughout the village. A version of it even made it back to Wolfebourne Manor."

"Everything my sources say is quite positive," Fortuity said as she swooped in from another direction.

"Lovely," Felicity muttered. "A conversion of the Broadmere sisters."

"You make us sound like witches," Merry said.

"Sometimes you are." Felicity hugged herself, grudgingly admitting that everything her sisters had said was correct. Even she had second-guessed herself, wondering if she wasn't being a little silly about the whole affair. "I will speak to him." She glared at Serendipity. "But I will not be a party to ridiculous games that will only make matters worse. I do not flirt."

Serendipity threw up her hands. "Fine. It was merely a suggestion." She glanced around, then tipped a nod at the mansion. "Are we to stand in the drive all day, or might we go inside and refresh ourselves so we can help Joy with last-minute touches?"

Felicity pushed up from the bench and flounced up the steps. "Since I have been so sorely put upon by the lot of you, I am taking the corner room at the top of the stairs." Serendipity and Merry usually fought over that room whenever they visited Joy. This time, it was Felicity's turn. The nicest room of all, it looked out over the garden with a balcony perfect for spying on those below. It never hurt to be aware of one's surroundings and those who shared them.

Before any of her sisters could protest, she breezed into the house, hurried upstairs, and took refuge in that room until the footmen and Daisy, her maid, brought her things. Tossing her reticule and gloves onto the bed, she immediately eased out onto the balcony and crouched down, hiding behind the thick columns of its stone balustrade. From this viewpoint, she could watch anyone below, and they would never be the wiser.

Her heart leapt to her throat as Drake meandered into view. Hands fisted at his sides and his shoulders held at a tensed level, he wandered through the garden like a lost soul in search of everlasting peace. Good gracious, he looked so haunted. A darkness emanated from him, a heart-wrenching sadness.

She caught a hand to her throat, shocked at the sight of him. She had done this. All because she was too cowardly to believe him or trust her instincts. "I am so ashamed. What a ridiculous ninny I am, for putting us both through this." It was time to set her insecurities aside, believe in herself, and believe in him. Hang the gossips.

After Daisy had helped her freshen up from the overly warm carriage ride, she would go downstairs and seek him out. It was time to clear the air once and for all. The brief *delay* in their courting was now at an end.

REFRESHED AND WEARING her favorite sprigged muslin with its pale-pink roses embroidered on the white background, Felicity eased down the stairs while scanning the wide entry area for Drake. Earlier, he had been in the garden, but it had taken her longer than planned to put herself back together after cleaning up from the overly warm ride from Broadmere Hall to Winterstone. Once finished, she had crept out onto the balcony again and peeped down into the garden, but he was no longer there.

The place was a beehive of activity, with servants rushing

around to ensure every guest had whatever they required. Surprisingly, none of her sisters were in sight. Joy was probably still greeting guests, Merry was more than likely enjoying a visit with the children, and Serendipity and the rest were no doubt plotting some sort of foolery that would involve eligible gentlemen meeting eligible sisters.

"Well," Felicity muttered, "I am no longer available. Merry best take care, for she will be their next target." When she reached the main floor, she pondered whether to meander into the parlor or retreat to the safety of the kitchens. *He will not be in the kitchens. Stop being a coward.* She squared her shoulders and marched into the parlor, determined to cast aside her mousy ways.

"Lady Felicity, how lovely to see you again," said a smiling gentleman she couldn't recall ever meeting.

Drat it all. She was such a horror when it came to remembering names and, in this case, faces as well. Returning the man's smile, she curtsied. "I only just arrived. How are you finding this lovely summer gathering?" Maybe if she kept him talking long enough, it would trigger her memory.

"Lady Joy and Sir Jansen's hospitality is always exemplary." The gentleman, comely enough with his dark hair and winning smile, offered his arm. "Would you do me the honor of joining me for a stroll outside? Refreshments abound, and a cool breeze has set in that many of the guests are enjoying."

Oh dear. How on earth could she search for Drake whilst on the arm of another man? What the devil was this person's name, and where in heaven's name had they met? Unable to think of a polite way to decline, she took his arm and fell in step alongside him. "A cool breeze will be most welcome. The carriage ride over grew quite warm."

"I would imagine so," he said. "I rode rather than bothering with a carriage. After all, Tinslow is but the next estate over."

Lord Tinslow! Joy and Jansen's neighbor. *Now* she remembered him. He had been quite nice at a dinner or something of that sort that Joy had hosted. Felicity relaxed somewhat, but the problem of her arm linked with his remained. She needed to remove herself and find Drake.

"Are your crops doing well, Lord Tinslow? My brother was saying there has not been nearly enough rain this year." She had no idea what else to say to the man. From what Joy had told her, he was much like her. He kept to himself and rarely left his country estate for Town.

"Barley and wheat thrive so far, but I agree with His Grace. We could use more rain." He snorted in amusement. "Something not often said here in England. Do you not agree?"

"Oh, indeed." Good heavens, could either of them possibly be more boring? As they stepped outside, she furtively glanced all around, not only in search of Drake but also one of her sisters to rescue her. She had no idea how to make small talk without sounding like a complete fool, and also didn't wish to encourage the very nice viscount.

"Would you care for some lemonade?" Lord Tinslow asked. "I would be most happy to fetch it."

"That would be lovely," she hurried to say. Not only would it release her from his arm but give her a moment to think of a way to excuse herself from his company once he returned.

As he headed for the refreshment table, she stretched up on tiptoe in a most unladylike manner, searching more for one of her sisters at this point than Drake. Where was Serendipity when she needed her?

"Who on earth are you looking for?" Grace asked as she joined her in the shade of one of the white tents dotting the grounds next to the gardens. "As if I didn't know."

"I need an escape."

"You are not going to the kitchens."

"I do not wish to go to the kitchens." Well, she did, but Felicity had already decided that wouldn't possibly do this time. "Lord Tinslow is paying attention to me."

Grace wrinkled her nose. "Lord Tinslow? I do not recall

meeting a Lord Tinslow."

"Neither did I, but all of us met him at one of Joy's dinner parties. He is her neighbor. A viscount." Felicity forced a smile. "And he is coming my way with lemonade. Whatever shall I do?"

"I suggest you drink it. It is quite warm today."

"You are a troll."

"That did not bother me when we were children, and it bothers me even less now." Grace eyed the crowd. "Where is your Lord Wakefield? I thought you meant to find him and mend your fences?"

"I have yet to locate him," Felicity said, then cleared her throat as Lord Tinslow joined them. "Grace, you remember Lord Tinslow?"

Grace smiled and curtsied. "Of course, how could I not?"

The gentleman bowed. "A pleasure to see you again, Lady Grace. Would you care for some lemonade?" He offered her the second glass that had obviously been meant for himself. But then his pleasant demeanor melted into a disapproving scowl. "Lord Wakefield. I am surprised *he* is here."

Felicity bristled, and Grace's eyes narrowed, but she remained silent. Felicity appreciated her sister allowing her to take control of the conversation. "Why would Lord Wakefield's presence surprise you?" Felicity asked, struggling to keep her tone even.

"The man's uncle was a despicable cove, my lady." He snorted like a bull about to charge. "Forgive me for speaking so strongly in your presence."

"You condemn Lord Wakefield for his uncle's behavior?" She wasn't about to play the innocent maiden and let it go. "The child should pay for the sins of the father? Is that how you truly feel, my lord?"

"Well, I—"

"Have you ever *met* Lord Wakefield?" She handed her untouched lemonade off to a passing servant, observing with some glee that her action did not go unnoticed by Lord Tinslow.

The gentleman offered her an apologetic tip of his head. "I do beg your pardon, Lady Felicity. Please excuse me." Then he turned on his heel and hurried away.

Grace giggled. "Oh my goodness. Our little mouse has finally found her claws." She hugged Felicity, then nudged her away. "I am proud of you. Now, go talk to your Lord Wakefield and set things right."

Felicity turned and found Drake staring at her with such pain and loss that it broke her heart. Rather than run to him as she wanted, she forced herself to meander as though doing her part to mingle with her sister's guests. She didn't want to attract anyone's attention in their direction.

Within an arm's length of him, she curtsied. "I am glad you are here," she said ever so softly. The grounds were so crowded. They would surely be overheard. He remained silent, then his gaze slowly tore away and shifted to something or someone behind her. She turned and discovered that Lord Tinslow had returned to speak with Grace. Their conversation appeared to be very animated.

"Drake?" She shifted in front of him, attempting to block his view. "Might we stroll around the grounds? Joy is quite proud of the view of their lake."

"What about your viscount?" he asked with such bitterness that it backed her up a step.

She jutted her chin higher. She understood how things had appeared, but this sullenness would not do at all. "I do not possess a viscount. In fact, I struggled to remember the man's name when he approached me."

"I see." Jealousy flashed in Drake's narrowed eyes. "Why am I here, Felicity? Punishment before you dismiss me permanently?"

"Joy was unaware that our courtship was in the midst of a brief recess." Try as she might to remain calm and understanding, Felicity did not like this side of him. "Stop being so surly, or I shall leave you to yourself until you can behave in a more civil manner. We have much to resolve."

"How am I supposed to behave when you refuse to see me

for a fortnight, then lift my hopes with this invitation only to show me that a more acceptable suitor is showering you with attention?" He bared his teeth like an enraged beast. "You are not the wallflower you claim to be, my lady." He shook his head. "Oh no, I would say you are well on your way to a much more acceptable proposal than mine before this party is over."

She clenched her fists at her sides, struggling not to shake them at him. "You may go, sir, until you are better behaved. I am sick to death of males who act like rude children. Either I am snubbed because the lot of you believe I am the cull of the litter, or I am treated like a broodmare with a mouthful of money to hand over as soon as the marriage contract is signed. Well, no, sir! Not anymore. If you cannot treat me with the respect I deserve, you shall take your leave of me." She stamped her foot. "Good day to you, Lord Wakefield."

So angry she was about to cry, she whirled about and headed inside, ignoring the stares of those who had witnessed her outburst. How dare he! Granted, she had made him wait overly long, and she could understand how the Lord Tinslow situation might appear, but where was her calm, understanding Drake?

She turned to the archway that led to the kitchens and found it blocked by a pair of sheepish-looking footmen. "Excuse me. I should like to pass."

The younger one on the left wrinkled his freckled nose. "Lady Joy said we was to keep you out of the kitchens, my lady." He gave her an apologetic bow. "Begging your pardon, but she was most firm about that."

"Was she now?" Felicity glared at them, but they didn't step aside. They stood there, uncomfortably fidgeting in place. "Well, fine." She couldn't retire to her room without feigning illness, and her sisters would know that was a lie. Grace had witnessed her tidy little scene with Drake, and Felicity felt sure that information was currently traveling at an alarming speed to each of her sisters. There had to be somewhere she could take refuge to think through this irritating development. For the life of her, she couldn't understand what had come over Drake. She understood how he might be a little jealous, and she found that quite flattering. But his surliness? She huffed. That was most unwelcome.

"Joy's private conservatory. Surely, I could take refuge there." She hurried down the hallway to the left of the stairs, thankful her sister had taken up an interest in painting while temporarily confined to a bath chair after the trauma of Lion's birth.

As soon as she entered and closed the door behind her, she understood completely how this sanctuary had assisted in Joy's healing. Even though it had a gabled glass roof and two walls of nothing but windows, the place possessed a privacy to it because of its location on the far side of the house, away from the gardens and festivities.

"This is exactly what I needed." Felicity headed to the corner farthest from the door and windows and flounced down onto the settee covered in an abundance of pillows upholstered in vibrant floral prints. She hugged one of them like a child clutching her teddy. Calm enough that she no longer felt like crying, she tried her best to see things from Drake's perspective. Granted, she had expected him to be rather upset and maybe a *little* jealous, but he had all but stood there and accused her of lying about being a wallflower.

She huffed and squeezed the pillow harder. "I mean, really." He had made it quite clear that at that moment in time, there would be no reasoning with him. "Now, how am I supposed to sort things through with him?"

LADY JOY STORMED toward him, flanked by Lady Serendipity and the Abarough sister who had appeared engaged in quite a robust conversation with that damnable Lord Tinslow.

Drake braced himself. This could not possibly bode well. The women were probably coming to cast him out and order him never to allow his shadow to cross anything remotely related to a member of the Broadmere empire ever again. He nervously raked a hand through his hair, wishing he had not allowed his bloody temper and jealousy to overcome him. He should not have spoken to his precious Felicity the way that he had.

"Are you that great of a fool?" Joy demanded as she and her sisters surrounded him. "What the devil did you say to my sister?"

He bowed his head, unable to look any of them in the eyes. "In answer to your first question: yes, I am that great of a fool." A heavy sigh escaped him, and he kept his gaze locked on the tips of his boots that were in dire need of polishing. "I made it clear that I did not believe her to be a wallflower as she had claimed, and that Lord Tinslow would propose to her if she bloody well allowed it." Rage pounded through him all over again at the image of *his* Felicity walking arm in arm with a viscount who was known to possess the wit of a sack of rocks.

"You called our sister a liar?" Serendipity stepped forward, looking ready to strike him. "How dare you!"

"Let me set my dogs on him," said the sister he had never met. "I brought only three, but I am sure they are up to the task."

"I should beat you with my cane." Joy squeezed her bejeweled weapon of choice, then stamped the ground with it. "You and I have only just met, but know this—my sister does not lie."

"Why do you think you met her in Lady Atterley's kitchen?" Serendipity asked. "She hides away after growing tired of watching everyone else's joy at every ball and party. You know better. You know Felli never lies."

He nodded. "I know." He shrugged and forced himself to meet their anger like a man. "I was enraged when I saw her on Tinslow's arm. My jealousy took control, shoving what little sense I ever possessed out of my head." He risked glancing across the grounds at the viscount in question. "He is a better match for her than I ever could be. After the past fortnight of being rebuffed, I felt sure I had lost her, and she was sending me on my way."

"She was coming to sort things out with you, you thick-skulled fool." The unknown sister nudged Serendipity. "Let me set the dogs on him. Please."

"Grace, no." Serendipity barely shook her head, studying him as though he were a bug she was about to crush. "What are your intentions *now*, Lord Wakefield?"

"Leave and never trouble her with my presence ever again."

Grace snorted, and Joy rolled her eyes.

"The two of you have had the most difficult times, and yet it is all of your own doing," Serendipity said. "Neither of you has learned to trust and speak openly with the other. Your squabbles always stem from misunderstandings, gossip, and things that should have been shared, yet were left unsaid. Have you learned nothing?"

Felicity's sisters had no idea about his greatest lie of all, the lie that was about to end him. "You are quite correct, Lady Serendipity."

"Then how do you expect to be married and not only coexist but ever find any semblance of happiness?" Joy slowly shook her head. "Felicity is smitten with you, but at this rate, you will lose her forever."

More defeated than he had ever felt before, he hung his head. "As I said, I shall take my leave and trouble her no more." Felicity would be better off without him, especially with the latest development in the Rum and Catherty debacle.

Grace threw up her hands. "So, you are simply giving up, then? Just like that? You do not intend to make things right? Fight for her?" She jabbed a finger at him, pointing. "You do not deserve our sister."

Joy turned and nodded at the house behind them. "Go in there and find her. Talk to her. *Listen* with your heart, you fool. Not your head." Then she lifted her cane and shook it at him. "If you hurt our Felicity any more than you already have, you will not only have us to deal with, but the other three as well. Am I clear, Lord Wakefield?"

"Yes, Lady Joy. Quite clear." Yet he stood there, uncertain where to begin in his search for Felicity and a bit uneasy about being told to search the hostess's home.

With an almost feral growl, Joy took his arm and tugged him to fall in step alongside her. "Come. I will help you search."

"We are coming too," Serendipity said.

"I shall catch up with you after I fetch the dogs," Grace grumbled. "They might yet be needed."

Drake trudged along between the two women, feeling like a cowardly fool who had shirked the opportunity to be a better man. But if they knew the latest risks that had befallen him, the sisters would surely understand. They would also forbid him from going anywhere near their sister. He could not tell them. He couldn't even tell Felicity. If he weren't such a selfish bastard, he would leave now to save his dearest from even more heartache. But he couldn't. Damned if he didn't love her and need her more than anything else in the world. He couldn't imagine a life without her, even though he'd told the sisters he would leave and never darken Felicity's door ever again. He'd known it was a lie when he said it.

"Shall we go to the kitchens?" he asked. "She told me once the kitchens were her *safe* space."

Joy paused in front of a pair of footmen blocking the entrance to a hall off to the right. "Did Lady Felicity come past here?"

The ruddy-haired lad with the freckles nodded. "Yes, my lady, but we nay let her pass."

"She weren't none too pleased with us either," the other footman added.

"I am sure she was not." Joy tapped the floor with her cane. "Well done, gentlemen. Did you happen to see where she went after that?"

"Down the hall to the left of the stairs, my lady," said the one with the freckles. "Mumbling to herself the whole time."

"Either the library or the conservatory," Serendipity said.

"Which shall we try first?"

"The conservatory, I'd wager." Joy led the way, determined to tug Drake along by the arm. He didn't fight her. The woman's cane looked capable of leaving quite a knot wherever it struck.

She halted again outside a closed door at the end of the long hallway. "This is your last opportunity." She thumped his chest with the bejeweled knob of her cane. "Do not waste it." As he opened the door and went to step inside, she caught him by the sleeve. "And you will not compromise my sister. Serendipity and I shall be right here, guarding the door as well as eavesdropping."

Serendipity shoved him onward. "Honesty is best. Remember that!" She closed the door behind him with a soft but final click.

Tense, he stood just inside the doorway, taking in the room's splendor. The main part was open and full of light streaming in through the glass, while the back corners, with walls of reddish-brown mahogany and rosewood paneling, were filled with enough shadows to hide one from prying eyes.

"Felicity?"

"Has your temperament improved?" asked a quiet voice from behind an arrangement of potted palms and ferns.

"Yes. I have come to apologize." He remained rooted to the spot, waiting for permission to approach her. "Forgive me for implying you had lied about being a wallflower." He flexed his hands, nervously opening and closing his fists. "I know you are incapable of such."

Hugging a pillow, she rose from the settee and started toward him, then paused and tossed the pillow back to it. "I am capable of lying," she said as she faced him, her chin set to a defiant tilt. "I simply do not do it."

"I was angry." He didn't know how to explain the explosive rage he had felt. So many things had gone wrong for him, been ripped away and lost forever. When he had seen her with that viscount, he feared her slipping away, too. "When I saw you on Tinslow's arm…" He still did not possess the strength to finish that sentence in a gentlemanly fashion.

"He caught me by surprise as soon as I came down from my room," she said, coming within an arm's length of him, but then warily stopping. "I was merely being polite."

"You deserve better than him." He swallowed hard. "You deserve better than *me*."

She stared at him for a long moment, the shadows in her eyes gathering like storm clouds. "I deserve a man who will cherish my heart."

"And is he that man?"

Her frustrated expression turned to one of disbelief. "Are all men's heads so thick?" She took a step closer and poked him in the chest. "My heart has chosen you. Or were your words about caring for me and not my dowry a lie?"

"I love you," he said, then added a pained growl to the confession. "Gads alive, I love you, Felicity. Is there any possible way you might love me, too? Someday? Can we ever get past our misunderstandings?"

She wet her lips, making him hungry for a taste of them. "Perhaps."

"What would it take to change *perhaps* to a *yes*?"

"I fear it might already be a yes."

He closed the distance between them and took hold of her hands, his heart and soul rejoicing at her touch. "Mightn't it truly be a *yes*?"

"Yes," she said, her whisper soft and sultry.

"May I kiss you, my lady?"

She caught her bottom lip between her teeth, almost making him groan. "I have never been kissed before, my lord."

"Good." He pulled her into his arms and covered her luscious mouth with his. Gads alive, never had he tasted such sweetness. He tightened his embrace, silently swearing never to let her go again.

She pressed closer, the perfect warmth of her softness in his arms, making him groan.

Before the kiss grew even more heated, he broke the connection and pressed his forehead to hers. "You are exquisiteness itself, my lady," he whispered, struggling for control.

With an innocent hesitancy, she reached up and touched his cheek. "You are quite fine yourself." Her cheeks flushed a delightful red, and her eyes brightened. She searched his face, frowning ever so slightly. "But we must do better with one another. We must stop assuming things and listening to what everyone else says."

He almost choked on the gentle scolding. If she only knew, but he daren't tell her. Not yet. Not when the battered bridge between them had just risen from the ashes. Soon. Soon, he would find the courage to tell her. Somehow. Someway.

$$— \sim\!\text{\textcurrency}\!\sim —$$

Chapter Eleven

FELICITY COULD STAY like this forever, in his arms, still tingling from the kiss that had left her breathless. She kept her hand pressed to his cheek, sinking into his eyes that churned with so many emotions. "I am sorry about keeping you away for so long. This shy little mouse had much soul searching to do to find my courage."

Drake tipped her chin higher and brushed a tender, heart-stopping kiss across her mouth. "I am sorry for everything," he whispered, seeming as though he wished to say more.

"What is it, Drake? Please tell me."

"The honorable thing for me to do would be to release you until I get my life in order."

Catching her breath, she went to deny it, but he pressed a finger across her lips to stop her. The sadness in his eyes made her ache to find a way to console him.

He slowly shook his head. "But I am neither an honorable nor a self-sacrificing man. I am selfish, Felicity. As selfish as my uncle. I cannot let you go. You are my haven, my bright star of hope in my life's angry storm." He bowed his head and again pressed his forehead to hers. "Please forgive me for being too weak to deny the wants of my heart."

His words stirred her as much as his touch. She framed his face with her hands and made him look her in the eyes. "We shall ride out the storm together. I know how to swim." Snuggling in to rest her cheek on his chest, she closed her eyes and breathed him in. This felt oh so right. "Do you think we might hide in here for the remainder of the party?"

His soft chuckle rumbled against her cheek. "Doubtful. Two of your sisters are outside the door at this very moment. They know we are here."

"I wondered how you found me."

"Lady Joy. My first inclination was to look in the kitchens."

"Those dratted footmen blocked my way, or I *would* have gone to the kitchens." She fully intended to speak to Joy about that. Of course, they had allowed her the luxury of this exquisite privacy with Drake. She hugged him tighter, enjoying the impropriety while she could. "This is quite scandalous, you know."

"Shall we join your sisters, then?"

"We shall not." She toyed with the folds of his cravat, which was tucked neatly beneath the lapels of his waistcoat. Then a thought occurred to her. Fortuity had once said that such situations caused men a great deal of physical stress because it *teased* their amorous inclinations. Come to think of it, her own insistent yearning had grown increasingly uncomfortable. She wanted more kisses, more…well, she wanted a taste of what she had read in some of her sister's books. "Uhm…do you think we *should* join them?"

He trailed his hands down her back, squeezing her closer, molding her against him. "We will have to join them soon, lest we get carried away." His low groan thrilled her. "After all, my dearest lady, we are courting…not engaged."

"We could be engaged," she said before she lost the courage to say it. Her heart pounded so hard, there was no possible way he could not hear it.

He eased back a step, dropped to one knee, and took hold of both her hands. "I have nothing to offer but myself, my lady. But if you could find it in your heart to accept me, I shall spend the rest of my life doing my best to make you happy."

Tears sprang to her eyes. "I will accept you, my lord, and we shall be happy. I just know it."

He pressed a kiss to each of her hands, then hugged them to his cheek. "I love you, Felicity."

Before she could answer, the door burst open, and Joy and Serendipity poured into the room.

"Well done." Joy excitedly bounced the tip of her cane harder against the marble floor. "Well done, indeed."

Serendipity hugged Felicity and whispered, "You are certain?"

"I am certain." And she was. Something within her had clicked into place as if this were what she had needed all this time to make her whole. "We shall have the vicar announce the first of the banns this Sunday."

"Then we have but a month to plan the wedding and the breakfast." Serendipity hugged her again, then turned to Drake. "Chance should arrive sometime this afternoon. You may speak to him then, although I cannot imagine his refusing Felicity's wishes."

"I am of age," Felicity said, wanting to make that clear. This was her decision. Not Chance's.

"Still," Joy said, "Chance deserves that common courtesy. I know he can be a lout at times, but we must humor him. You know how fractious he gets when we ignore him."

"Indeed." Men could be as petulant as toddlers. "Where are the rest of the girls? If I don't share my news with them before anyone else hears it, they will be most displeased."

"Lady Grace was fetching her dogs," Drake said, his expression unreadable.

"How many did she bring?" Felicity asked Joy. Grace had as many hounds at Wolfebourne Lodge as their sister Blessing had cats.

Joy counted off on her fingers. "Gastric, of course. He is her favorite. Connor and Sissy's dog Hector, and I believe Lucy, the foxhound."

Felicity turned back to Drake. "Why was she fetching them?

She usually sees them settled in a side garden somewhere away from the festivities until it is safe to allow them back into the house."

Drake rolled his shoulders as if shrugging on an uncomfortable jacket. "She was going to set them on me for upsetting you."

Felicity laughed. "Gastric is so round that he waddles. Hector is a terrier who would barely reach your knees, and Lucy's favorite activity is stretching out in a sunny patch and napping. I daresay you would be quite safe."

With a leery shake of his head, he nodded at the far wall of windows. Beyond the span of panes, Grace could be seen marching along with the dogs in tow. "With your sister goading them on, I have no doubt they would rise to the occasion."

"I shall tell her all is well." Joy hurried to the window, tapped it with her cane, and drew Grace's attention. Then she smiled and tapped her ring finger on her left hand.

Grace grinned and herded the trio of canines back in the direction from which they came.

"That leaves Blessing, Fortuity, and Merry—most especially Merry." Felicity looped her arm through his and tugged. "We must tell them before you speak with Chance."

Drake gave her a bemused look. "Should I not speak with your brother first?"

"Oh, no. Sisters first." Felicity couldn't help but smile. "Chance likes to think himself the head of the household, but we are the neck."

"I see," he said, the wariness in his tone becoming more pronounced.

"I will protect you," Felicity promised, then tugged again. "You already know Merry will be thrilled. I am sure Blessing and Fortuity will be too."

"Everyone will be thrilled as long as our Felicity is happy." Serendipity leveled a pointed look at Drake.

"I assure you, I will do my best to keep her happy."

"See that you do." Joy moved to the door and held it open.

"Onward. I know Merry is in the nursery. I am unsure where Blessing and Fortuity got off to, but we shall find them."

Felicity hugged closer against Drake's side and patted his arm. His hesitancy concerned her. Did he fear they might reject him? She knew he struggled with bruised pride from all that had gone wrong since he inherited the title. "It will be all right," she whispered.

"I hope so," he said just as softly, then cleared his throat and stood taller. "We shall make it all right, shall we not?"

Joyous excitement bubbled through her. "Indeed, we shall."

AFTER SHARING THEIR happy news with the rest of the sisters and receiving their blessings, they returned outside in search of refreshments. Drake kept Felicity on his arm, determined that one and all would see that she belonged to him. If not for the nagging worry about Rum and Catherty, his joy would be complete. But the threat of blackmail and possibly worse hung over him like a black cloud, following him everywhere.

"Where are your thoughts?" Felicity playfully tugged his arm. "You are scowling."

"Forgive me, dearest." Shoving the unpleasantness to the back of his mind, he patted her hand where it rested in the crook of his arm. "Would you like some lemonade or tea, perhaps?" He escorted her to one of the tables beneath the shade of a white, open-sided tent billowing with the summer breeze.

"Let us sit for a while, and then perhaps I will enjoy something." Her sparkling smile lit her up as she looked at all the partygoers. "Joy is so pleased. Everything is splendid. Lady Constance will be green with envy."

"Lady Constance?" The name sounded vaguely familiar, but he wasn't certain.

"A one-time friendship of Joy's that turned sour." Felicity

folded her hands on the table, then flattened them on the white tablecloth, smoothing away wrinkles only she could see.

"Felicity?" He waited, holding his breath. Something dire was troubling her. "We promised to share our worries. Remember?" Could he possibly be a larger hypocrite? He ignored his conscience, shunting it away.

"I know you said you would relinquish my dowry, but I prefer you don't." Her quietness was laced with steely resolve. "There is much work to be done at Wakefield Manor, and that money could be put to good use."

While he heartily agreed, his pride would not allow it. He had told her to keep her dowry, and he meant it. "It could indeed be put to good use, but I fear that is not possible. I will not go back on my word."

"You would not be going back on your word. I would be insisting."

"Felicity."

"Do not say my name like that."

"Like what?"

"Like I am a child, trying to wheedle you into giving me my way."

He couldn't help but smile. If today's kisses were any indication, once they were married, she would always get her way. "I cannot go back on my word." He waved down a passing servant carrying a silver tray of beverages. "Lemonades?"

The footman bowed. "Yes, my lord." He set a glass in front of each of them. "Will that be all?"

"Yes, thank you." Drake braved a sip of the pale-yellow liquid, which he usually let pass, and was pleasantly surprised. "Sweet but tart. I believe this is the best lemonade I have ever sampled."

"It will not work, you know." Felicity took a drink of her own.

"What will not work?"

"You are trying to change the subject. My dowry will more

than cover all the repairs needed for the manor, and there will be plenty to spare."

"If you insist upon a dowry, it will be held in your name to provide for you and our children should you become widowed. I will not make your future any more uncertain than it already is since you agreed to marry me. I am sure your brother will agree when he and I discuss it." Drake licked his lips, discovering that the lemonade he had thought was good left a mawkish aftertaste that was not at all pleasant. "Is that drink supposed to linger with such strength?"

Felicity puckered her lovely lips into a sour-faced pout. "Joy's cook refuses to add any salt to balance the sugar. It is the unbridled sweetness that causes the lemon and lime to leave behind that cloying trail. Salt is as important to a recipe as sugar." She braved another sip, then set her goblet back on the table. "You could still use part of the dowry to hire more servants. Poor Yateston and Mrs. Pepperhill must surely be struggling to keep up."

Everyone at Wakefield Manor was struggling, but that was neither here nor there. He released a heavy sigh that turned into a groan. They had only just mended their fences from their last misunderstandings, and here they were fussing again—about money. Gads alive, but he hated the problems that financials caused.

"I love you," he said, determined to keep the conversation on solid footing. "But I need you to allow me to work this out with your brother in *your* best interest." He would not ask her to leave him some small bit of pride. Now was not the time for surliness. He had learned that much from his earlier outburst.

She eyed him for a long moment as though contemplating his fate. "I love you as well," she finally said, "and once we are married, I hope you come to realize we are partners to help one another through anything. That is the way it was with my mama and papa."

He idly ran his thumb up and down the stem of the lemonade

goblet, unable to keep from smiling as a long-ago memory of his own parents came to mind. "I believe that was the way of it with my parents, as well." He slowly shook his head. "It's difficult to remember for certain. I was very young when a fever took my mother."

"I am sorry." She reached across the table and rested her hand on his. "I am discovering that no matter how many years pass, we still miss them."

"Excuse me. Lady Felicity?"

Drake jerked and faced the man who dared to interrupt this private moment. "Lord Tinslow. How may we be of service?"

The viscount drew himself up and hiked his sharp nose higher in the air. "Excuse me, Lord Wakefield, but I need to speak with Lady Felicity."

The man actually sounded as if he expected Drake to scurry off with his tail tucked between his legs. Instead, Drake rose from his seat and squared off in front of the lordling, struggling to hold tight to his temper. "Lady Felicity and I do not wish to be interrupted." He turned to Felicity. "Do we, my love?"

The endearment sent a renewed blush to her cheeks, and she smiled. "Might we speak some other time, Lord Tinslow? You see, Lord Wakefield and I just became engaged."

"Engaged?" The man's shock was borderline insulting.

Felicity nervously shifted in her chair, and her smile became forced. "Yes. Engaged. The banns are to be announced this Sunday."

Tinslow aimed a damning glare at Drake. "You have nothing to offer this delightful creature. Have you no honor?"

"Have you no manners?" Drake widened his stance, ready to pummel the man, but only if forced. He would not be the ruination of Lady Joy's party. That would not sit well with his future in-laws. "This delightful gathering is not the place for this conversation. In fact, there is no place for this conversation, because my engagement to the lovely Lady Felicity is none of your affair."

Tinslow puffed up even more. "I intended to ask for her hand."

"It is not my hand that chooses whom I marry, my lord," Felicity said. "It is my heart."

The viscount snorted. "Your heart will not keep you clothed and fed, my lady. This man has nothing but his land and tenant farmers who struggle under his poor management. I cannot believe you would willingly condemn yourself to such a life."

Raging inside, Drake stepped forward, caught the man up by his poorly tied cravat, and forcibly walked him back until they were well behind the tent. "Your conversation with my intended is quite finished, Lord Tinslow. On your way now, my good man." Then he punched him in the jaw. Hard.

The viscount tumbled back into the bushes and went still.

"Oh, dear heavens, Drake, did you kill the fool?"

"No, my dearest." He waved Felicity back while glancing around to ensure he had not attracted any unwanted spectators. "He is merely having a bit of a nap. I am sure he will be quite all right in a little while." He tucked her arm through his and ushered her away. "Come. Let us enjoy your sister's party."

She grinned up at him. "You handled that quite nicely. You are my knight in shining armor."

"I am not so certain about that, but I did not like the way he spoke to you. He had no right." The viscount might've been correct about their life not being filled with the luxuries Felicity was accustomed to, but it was not that bastard's place to chide her for her choice.

Drake pulled up short. "You know there will be many who share Lord Tinslow's feelings?"

"That is their problem. Not mine." Felicity gave a curt nod as if proud of herself for taking such a stance. "I cannot live my life by everyone else's expectations. I know that now. I might still prefer a quiet corner rather than the center of the party, but I am determined to no longer be a cowering little mouse."

After stealing a glance at the other guests, he hurried to kiss her hand. "You are not a cowering mouse, but a gem of the first water." He glanced back at the bushes where the viscount had landed, then placed her hand on his arm. "Come. Let us find another place to sit and enjoy each other's company." Unable to stop himself, he grinned. "This area is entirely too crowded."

Felicity laughed. "We should probably warn Joy that Lord Tinslow is napping in her boxwoods."

"Is she overly fond of the man?" Drake hoped he hadn't erred in bettering the viscount's manners.

Felicity grew thoughtful. "I do not think so. He is her closest neighbor to the north. I believe she is simply kind to him because…" She frowned. "The last time I met Lord Tinslow, he was married. I remember his wife now. Seems as though I recall Joy saying the poor woman died just this past winter." She snorted. "He has no young children in need of a mother to explain his wish to remarry so soon. The man should still be in mourning. How despicable!"

"And sad."

"Indeed. It makes one wonder how he treated her while she lived." She squeezed Drake's arm. "No matter. I chose the better man."

Hearing her say that both thrilled and saddened him. "I am glad you chose me, my lady. I would be lost without you." And as soon as he returned to Binnocksbourne, he would be visiting the inn and calling upon Rum and Catherty. Yateston had discovered the moneylenders had taken up residence there like vultures circling a dying animal. Well, he was determined to live, and just as determined to thwart them.

$$\text{Chapter Twelve}$$

Chapter Twelve

THE ENTIRE RIDE home from Winterstone, Drake ran through every possible situation that might successfully oust Rum and Catherty from his life. He still hadn't come up with a plausible solution other than dumping his uncle on their doorstep. He doubted that cruel tactic would work. They didn't want Uncle George. They wanted their money plus their exorbitantly compounded interest. Their blackmail demand for their first payment, which they had so generously agreed to accept, was still on his desk.

If he went to the Bow Street Runners about the blackmail, he might very well be brought up on charges of fraud and imprisoned. But he had only impersonated a peer to save his despicable uncle's life, and then very nearly ruined himself by attempting to pay off all the old man's debts—at least, the legal ones—with his own funds. He was unsure whether that would make a difference to the courts or not. After all, once Uncle died, Drake was the legal heir to the title. Would that sway them in his favor? The uncertainty of it all made deciding what to do even more difficult. The courts might be friendly, but then again, they very well might not. Many despised the Wakefield name because his uncle had cleaned out their pockets in the gaming hells. When Uncle George won, he won big. Unfortunately, when Lady Luck's pendulum swung the other way, he lost even bigger.

"I have no idea what the devil to do," Drake told his horse as they neared Wakefield Manor. But he had to decide something. Tomorrow was the last day the scoundrels had given him to pay up. If he threatened to turn them over to the Bow Street Runners and acted as if he didn't care if his poorly carried-out plan was revealed, what would they do? As much as he dreamed about them throwing up their hands and giving up, he doubted very much if it would be that easy. After all, Uncle George owed them a great deal of money, and they had a reputation for always collecting what was fully due to them. In their letter of demands, they had mentioned his property, knowing that was all he had left.

Drake shook his head. Social standing meant nothing compared to the land that had been in his family for more lifetimes than he could count. And deep down, he knew they would never be satisfied. No amount of money, no amount of land, would ever pry him free of their clutches.

There was no choice. He would tell Rum and Catherty of his plan to go to the Bow Street Runners, and then he would tell Felicity everything before he went to London to speak to the proper authorities. He would lose her over this. She would never forgive him for hiding such a terrible lie.

Gut-wrenching anguish filled him, making him throw back his head and roar. His horse startled and took off, nearly throwing him from the saddle. He got the poor beast under control just as they reached the front gate of the manor. Halting the mount, he stared at the once-stately home that had deteriorated so quickly over the months of neglect. He could almost hear his parents' wails rising from their graves.

"I will fix this," he told them, his voice breaking. "I swear I will make this right." Hang the title. No one in Society respected him as it was. He had heard their whispers. Everyone knew his mistakes, all in the name of making things right. The best he could hope for was ostracism from the *ton*. The worst? Imprisonment, and both would cost him the woman he loved.

He snorted. She deserved better than him anyway.

He turned his horse toward town and urged it to a gallop. Better to start the end of his life today rather than wait for tomorrow.

When he reached the inn, he handed off his mount to the lad who hoped to be paid for watching patrons' horses. Drake had a coin or two in his pocket for the boy, but decided to wait until his business was finished to pay him. He held up the money to reassure the lad. "I'll not be long. When I return, these are yours."

The boy brightened and led the horse to a grassier spot beside the inn.

Drake climbed the steps and went to the counter, nodding at the innkeeper. "Good afternoon, Mr. Thomassan. Are Mr. Rum and Mr. Catherty holding court in the parlor today or in one of their rooms?"

Concern filled the older man's eyes as he jerked a nod toward the parlor. "In there, my lord. Mind your back, aye? Them two bear watching."

Drake smiled. He had always liked Mr. Thomassan. "Thank you, sir. I appreciate the warning." He removed his hat and tugged off his gloves as he entered the small, private parlor reserved for a select few who patronized the inn.

The businessmen had seated themselves at the far side of the room with their backs to the wall, facing the doorway. Since no one trusted them, they trusted no one either.

"Lord Wakefield. Well done. Our clients are rarely a day early in making their payments." The tallest of the pair, the pale Mr. Rum, dressed all in black and resembling an undertaker with the beak of a buzzard, didn't bother to rise from his chair. He merely puffed harder on his cigar, then waved it toward the empty settee beside them. "Come, my lord. Have a seat. Would you care for some refreshment?"

"I would not."

"Now, now," said Mr. Catherty, the slovenly other half of the moneylenders' partnership, "that came out rather curt. Are we fractious today, Lord Wakefield?" He snorted and made a wheezing sound that Drake took to be a laugh. "Or should we say Mr. Pemberton? That would be more accurate, would it not?"

Drake squared his shoulders and resettled his stance. "Indeed, it would. Just as I intend to tell the Bow Street Runners when I report your blackmail scheme as soon as I reach London."

Both men went deadly quiet, their eyes narrowing.

"You would risk prison?" Catherty asked.

"Banishment from Society?" Rum added. Each of them snuffed out their cigars and leaned forward as if about to launch themselves at him.

"I am already imprisoned by the two of you, and Society shuns me because of my destitution." Drake shrugged, assuming an air of bitter nonchalance. "What would be the difference?"

Pursing his lips, Rum rubbed his hands together. "Difference is, you would lose that young Broadmere hen."

"Yes," Catherty said, chiming in with another wheezing snicker. "Fine, plump bit of skirt, that one, and we heard tell you like her for more than just her dowry."

Their hired jackals had to have gotten that information from Uncle George. Drake would deal with the careless old man once he returned home. He jutted his chin higher. "Lady Felicity deserves better than me, anyway. Honor demands I step away from her until my problems are resolved."

Rum hooted and slapped his knee. "Till your problems are resolved?"

Catherty chuckled and relit his cigar. "What makes you think your problems will *ever* be resolved?"

"As I said, I intend to go to the authorities. While moneylending is quite legal, extortion is not."

Both men relaxed back in their chairs and exchanged disturbing glances. Rum stretched out his long, spindly legs and crossed them at the ankles, while Catherty adjusted the cushions around his wide girth.

It was Catherty who spoke first, pointing the chewed tip of his cigar at Drake. "You care about that fine, plump hen. Don't think we don't know that."

Rum grinned, revealing large, yellowed teeth that made him resemble a laughing mule. "We got it on good authority that you are quite smitten with that one."

"Lady Felicity will know the truth of everything before I ride to London to speak with the authorities."

Catherty shrugged. "Do you think we care if she knows the truth or not? That's between you and her."

Rum slowly tamped out his cigar again, then shoved it into the plate so hard that it split. "But we know you would care should anything *happen to her.*" He snorted again. "So would that family of hers, and those Broadmeres are rich as Croesus."

Drake lunged forward, only to be caught by powerful hands and dragged back a few steps. A pair of men who rivaled the size of bears, dressed all in black like their employers, stood on either side of him, clutching him by the arms. He fought them to no avail. "If you attempt to harm Felicity, I will hunt you down and make you rue the day you were born."

Rum and Catherty widened their eyes in feigned shock, each of them gasping before they broke down into laughter. "Did we say any harm was to come to her? From us?" Rum clutched his chest as if he couldn't imagine such a thing.

Catherty shook his head. "We merely said we knew you would be most upset should anything ever happen to her." He huffed yet another wheezy snort. "That weren't no lie or insinuation."

"You will stay away from her." Drake stomped the instep of the man to his left, ripped his arm free, and gut-punched the man to his right. Before he could do them further damage, they recovered and dragged him even farther back from Rum and Catherty. "You will stay away from her," Drake repeated through clenched teeth.

"Your payment is due, Lord Wakefield," Rum said with icy calmness.

"Should you default on your payment," Catherty said, "any

and all repercussions will be no one's fault but your own." He smacked his sausage-like lips, then set his cigar between his yellowed teeth. "Think hard on that, old chum." He nodded at the door. "Gentlemen, do be good enough to show Lord Wakefield out."

The pair of ruffians dragged Drake out of the parlor, through the inn's reception area, and out the door, before shoving him free and returning to their unscrupulous employers. No small man himself, Drake was tempted to go after them and do as much damage as he could.

"I wouldn't be doing that, my lord," said the youngling tending his horse. "There be four more just like them two. They just went 'round back, but I seen'm all talking together afore. Them blackguards all be cut from the same cloth, as my mam always says."

The lad was right. The best thing Drake could do was hie himself to Broadmere Hall and warn the duke and his sisters. He dug every coin he had out of his pocket and gave them to the boy. "Thank you."

With a hearty nod and a grin, the lad handed him the reins. "Thank you, my lord."

Drake launched himself into the saddle and spurred the mount onward to the Broadmeres'. Heart pounding and gut churning, an ominous sense of doom nagged at him, whispering, *You are too late.* He clenched his teeth and pushed the horse harder. He could not be too late. His precious Felicity had to be safe.

As soon as he neared the entrance, he leapt from the saddle, ran to the door, and hammered on it. He almost shouted, *"You must let me in!"* But he caught himself in time.

Thankfully, Fipps answered the door and swung it open wide. "Good afternoon, Lord Wakefield. Do come in."

"Thank you, Fipps. Is Lady Felicity available? It is most urgent."

The butler puckered the slightest frown, which was unusual

for the stoic servant. "Lady Felicity has gone to the village with her sister, my lord. Would you care to leave your card so she will know you called?"

"No. That might be too late." Drake debated going after her, then glanced at the closed door of the library. "Is His Grace available? I promise it is most urgent. Lady Felicity could be in danger."

"One moment, my lord." As Drake had hoped, Fipps quietly knocked on the library door, then entered after a muffled command bade him to. It was but a moment before he reemerged and motioned Drake forward. "His Grace and Lady Serendipity will see you now."

"Thank you, Fipps." Drake swallowed hard. This would not go well. How could it possibly?

"How is our Felli in danger?" Serendipity asked before he was fully into the room and had closed the door behind him.

Broadmere came out from behind his desk, looking ready to do battle. "What have you done?"

"My uncle owes Rum and Catherty a large sum of money from his days in the gambling hells. They are willing to do anything to him"—Drake thumped a fist to his chest—"and to me to collect what they are owed and then some."

Broadmere's eyes narrowed as he moved closer. "You speak as if your uncle still lives."

"He does."

"What?" Serendipity shot up from her seat and charged toward him. "What do you mean?"

"Rum and Catherty's cutthroats caused the carriage accident that supposedly killed Uncle George. He did not die. We made it look as though he did to keep them from trying again and succeeding."

Slowly shaking her head, Serendipity turned to her brother, but they both remained silent.

"We faked the funeral, the burial, everything," Drake said. From the look on the duke's face, he would be lucky if

Broadmere didn't kill him. "The old man bound to the bath chair at Wakefield Manor is not Mr. Charles Pembroke, but the sixth Earl of Wakefield."

"That makes you…" Broadmere stared at him.

"A fraud. An impostor. Nothing more than a once-proud member of the landed gentry." Drake kept his hands fisted at his sides, digging his fingernails into his palms. "I did not do it for the title, but to save my uncle. Just as my father often saved his brother up until the time he died." He stared down at the floor, shaking his head. "And I used up every possible resource I possessed to try to pay my uncle's debts and restore some honor to the Wakefield name. All for naught, because Rum and Catherty unraveled our poorly established farce and are now not only demanding payment for what they are owed but blackmailing me for impersonating a peer."

"They will never be satisfied," the duke said. "You do realize that?"

With a heavy sigh, Drake forced himself to look the man in the eye. "I do."

"And you think they will harm Felli?" Serendipity eased closer, her hands tightening into fists.

Drake braced himself. She was surely about to strike him, and she had every right. "They are aware of my love for Felicity. Their spies are quite thorough, it seems. I feel certain my spineless uncle also told them anything they wanted to hear."

"Your uncle is not the only one who is spineless," Broadmere said, his tone blazing with rising fury. "When did you intend to tell my sister of this inconceivable lie?" The enraged duke bared his teeth like the caged lion he resembled.

"I do not know." And he didn't. Drake had hoped against hope for a miracle. Perhaps his cantankerous uncle might die or something. Anything that would enable him never to have to tell Felicity about this despicable secret.

Broadmere drew back and punched him in the face, backing him up several steps. Drake stumbled, but regained his footing before he hit the floor. With the back of his hand, he wiped the blood streaming from his throbbing nose, but he didn't fight back. He simply stood there and took it. He deserved every bit of their rage, but nothing they could possibly do would equal the fury he wished he could visit upon himself for being such a damned, trusting fool when it came to trying to save his worthless uncle.

"You realize your marriage would have been invalid if you had not told her before the wedding?" Murder in her eyes, Serendipity shook a fist at him.

"I had not thought of that," he admitted, his soul crumbling even more.

"It seems to me you have not thought of a great many things," the duke said, then punched him again, this time hitting him in the eye and knocking him to the floor. "You not only mismanaged your ridiculous attempt to save the most manipulative, selfish bastard known to haunt the streets of London, but you mishandled every other resource placed at your disposal." Broadmere slowly shook his head, then turned away. "You are a damned fool, Wakefield." He barked a bitter laugh. "No. Not Wakefield. What the bloody hell is your real name?"

"Pemberton." Drake gingerly touched his eye as he rose from the floor. "The name my father gave me. A name of honor."

"Well, I would say the last thing you did was honor it," Serendipity said before spitting on him. "And now you have endangered my sister's life. Not only that, but when she learns of this latest lie, you will have ripped out her heart."

"When did she and Merry leave for the village?" the duke asked Serendipity.

She shook her head. "It has been a while. They should be back anytime."

"All I want is for her to be safe," Drake said. "Even though I love her, I shall sever all ties with her. I swear it."

"And that will not only break her heart but ruin her as well," Broadmere said. "Even though the banns have not officially been read, word of your ridiculous engagement to my overly trusting sister has already spread across the entire Lake District." He threw up his hands. "Knowing the speed at which the *ton's* gossip travels, all of England has probably heard." He dropped into his chair behind his desk and held his head. "What a bloody mess."

Shouts echoed out in the hallway, but Drake couldn't make out who it was or what was said.

Serendipity ran to the door and yanked it open just in time for a sobbing Merry to tumble into her arms.

"She is gone, Seri!" Eyes wild, face red and shining with tears, Merry clutched her sister by the shoulders and shook her. "They made off with her. They stole our Felli!"

Drake sprang forward. "Who? Did you see who took her?"

"Three men," Merry said, breathless with her sobbing. "A black carriage I have never seen before. They jumped out and knocked her senseless, then grabbed her and dragged her into that carriage." Screeching with a keening wail, she clutched her fists to her chest. "I fear they did her grave harm. I tried to stop them, but they threw me into the ditch. By the time I climbed out, they were gone."

"Are you hurt?" Serendipity caught hold of Merry and led her to the settee.

"Just scrapes and scratches." Merry pierced the air with another yowling sob. "Nothing like our poor Felli. Why would anyone do this? Who would wish to harm our sweet, gentle soul?"

"I will kill them." Drake started for the door. "Which direction did they take?"

"North, I think." Merry hugged herself and rocked in place. "But I failed to see which lane they took at the fork."

"I am coming with you." Broadmere rounded his desk. "You can take one fork, and I shall take the other." Then he caught hold of Drake's shoulder and held it with a bone-crushing grip. "If anything happens to my sister, I will kill you myself."

Drake accepted the oath with a curt nod. It was nothing less than he deserved.

DRAKE HEADED UP the fork to the right as the duke took the fork to the left. Even though they had hurried to arm themselves, so much time had passed since the abduction that the roadway's dust had settled, refusing to give any clues. Where the devil would they take her? How far would they carry her to keep her hidden?

Why had he not told her sooner?

He snorted, already knowing the answer. Because he was a selfish, cowardly bastard. He clenched his teeth until his jaws ached. He was no better than his worthless uncle. If he had told her straight away, and she had sent him packing, at least she would now be safe instead of stolen away in broad daylight.

He slowed his mount. If he kept up at the breakneck pace, the horse would surely fail in the heat of the overly warm afternoon. Raking his gaze across the horizon, he prayed for a cloud of dust or some other sign of the runaway carriage. Even though the blackguards had a head start, they couldn't have gotten that far ahead. That left him to wonder if they were hiding her somewhere close. But where? Everyone in Binnocksbourne knew and loved Lady Felicity. Surely no one would provide a place for the ruffians to keep her.

He scrubbed a hand across his face, wincing when he hit his bruised, swollen flesh. That pain was nothing compared to the ache in his heart. And Merry had said those heartless bastards had hit Felicity, rendering her unconscious. His poor, dear one would be terrified when she awakened to discover her circumstances. Not only terrified, but confused as to why this had happened. Knowing Rum and Catherty, they would delight in telling her all the sordid details.

He shook his head. None of that mattered now. All that mattered was her safety and getting her home to her family.

A bit of dust farther down the way made his heart stutter.

Once again, he urged his mount to a hard gallop, but his hopes were quickly dashed. It was merely a farmer with a wagon loaded down with hay.

"Excuse me, good sir," Drake said as he came up alongside the man. "Did a black carriage pass through here recently? Within the last few hours?"

The farmer shook his head. "Been hauling hay on this road most of the afternoon. Nothing along here but me and some sheep today." He nodded at Drake. "And now yourself."

"Thank you." Drake shifted in the saddle, squinting as he scanned the countryside. If the carriage had come this way, the farmer surely would have seen it. They had to have taken the fork to the left. He prayed that Felicity's brother had caught up with them and shot the bastards.

He turned his mount and headed back the way he had come. If the duke were to encounter the carriage, he would need assistance. Drake knew the enraged man could very well fire upon him, but he didn't care. If Felicity's brother shot him, he hoped the bullet traveled straight and true to his heart.

Chapter Thirteen

FELICITY AWOKE IN a crumpled heap on what had to be a carriage floor. The deafening rattle and grinding crunch of the thing bouncing along the hard-packed dirt road could be nothing else. Terror filled her, freezing her in place like a frightened hare. What had happened? Vaguely, she remembered a dark coach rolling along beside her and Merry as they returned from the village, then everything went dark. No, it didn't go dark until after those horrifying men had jumped out of the vehicle and lunged for her.

She clenched her teeth to keep from sobbing aloud. This had to be a mistake. Some horrible, awful mistake. The bump and sway of the vehicle as it careened along threatened to be her undoing. Head throbbing, stomach churning, shoulders aching, she tried to pull her arms out from behind her back, only to discover her wrists lashed together with a rough rope that sawed into her flesh.

"The hen's awake," said a man whose voice was gruff and grating as the gravel beneath the carriage wheels.

"She ain't goin' nowhere, trussed up as she is." A boot nudged her, roughly shoving against her rump. "Are you, hen?"

"Could I please sit in the seat?" She tried her best to sound calm, but her voice cracked with terror. "Please?"

"Please?" the man with the gravelly voice mocked her, and no one moved to help her.

"Her ladyship ain't used to such a fine conveyance," the other man said.

"Get her into the seat," ordered a deeper-voiced man. "I'm tired of her feckin' head hittin' me foot."

"If old Rum had got us a bigger carriage, 'twould have been a damn sight better," Gravelly Voice retorted.

All she could see was the black kickboard under the seat in front of her and her captors' filthy boots, which smelled distinctly of manure. She gagged and fought the rising bile burning at the back of her throat.

"Pull her up," repeated the deep-voiced man, his words tinged with impatience. "Now."

Rough hands caught hold of her and yanked her up onto the bench.

"There, your ladyship," said the large man with a wicked scar running across his face.

"Thank you." She swallowed hard then took deep breaths through her nose and blew them out her mouth. The coach was sweltering with its black shades drawn, trapping her inside with the stench of manure and men who hadn't bathed in a while…if ever. She gagged again and turned her head to press her mouth against her shoulder.

"How much farther?" The deep voice belonged to the grubby man sitting across from her. "She looks ready to shit through her teeth."

"Leastwise she's aimed at you," said the mountain of flesh beside him.

The grubby man turned and glared at him. "How much farther?"

"Nearly there," said the man with the scar after squinting through a crack in the shade.

"Why are you doing this?" Felicity fought not to vomit all over herself and everyone else.

"Because we can." The grubby man sneered at her as if she were the most contemptible creature on earth. "And old Rum turned loose a fair bit of blunt to see it done."

She had no idea who *old Rum* was, and it really didn't matter. At the moment, she was scared witless and only wanted to go home. "My brother is the Duke of Broadmere. He'll give you even more blunt to take me back home."

All the men laughed. The two across from her elbowed each other, grinning at her obvious stupidity. "It ain't wise to cross old Rum, and even worse to go against Catherty."

"Who are Rum and Catherty? What have they against me?" Never had she heard those names before.

"You?" The fleshy man beside the grubby man snorted. "They ain't got nothin' against you. 'Tis the company you keep." He shook a chunky finger at her. "You chose poorly, your ladyship, when you took up with the likes of Lord Wakefield."

All the men laughed again, their hooting louder this time. "Lord Wakefield, my hairy arse," the mountain of flesh said. He nudged her foot with his. "You done engaged yourself to a man of the gentry, hen. Marry him, and your name will be Mrs. Pemberton."

Head throbbing harder, Felicity struggled to focus. "My intended is the seventh Earl of Wakefield."

The ruffians laughed even harder.

"Ain't no *seventh* earl till the sixth one dies, hen," said the man with the scar.

Felicity closed her eyes and prayed for her head to stop hurting. "The sixth one did die. In a carriage accident."

"That be a lie, your ladyship. Your Mr. Pemberton done lied to you about acting like the seventh earl so old Rum and Catherty would stop huntin' down the sixth earl 'cause of all the money he owed them. Even faked the funeral and set up a fine headstone for the old bastard, though he was still alive." Scarface caught hold of her arm and yanked her straighter in the seat. "But they found them out. Thanks to us. We beat the fool till he admitted it. Ole Rum and Catherty will get what's theirs now. Plus some, I reckon."

That couldn't possibly be true. Felicity wanted to shake her head, but knew it would hurt too badly. "I do not believe you. Drake would never hide such a thing from me."

The men huffed and snorted, waving her words away.

"You go on thinking that, your ladyship." The grubby man shook his head. "You was foolish enough to engage yourself to a pauper. 'Pears to me you'll believe 'bout anything. Ain't my place to convince you."

She closed her eyes, praying harder than she had ever prayed before. *Please send someone to save me. Please.* Her head ached so horridly, it was hard to think, hard to make sense of much else. But what they had said about Drake *pretending* to be the Earl of Wakefield stayed at the forefront of her thoughts.

She clamped her lips tighter shut. It couldn't be. It could not possibly be true.

But the trio of ghouls had said Drake had done it to stop the determined Rum and Catherty from continuing their hunt for his uncle. Had they been trying to do the man bodily harm to extract payment for the money he owed them? Did such a thing truly happen?

The carriage hit a rut and shook her with such a hard bump that she whacked the side of her head against the wall. She bit her lip harder to keep from crying out, preferring not to call any more attention to herself than she already had. She wanted so very badly to cry, but she didn't dare. Something deep inside warned her that tears would only make the situation worse.

Her stomach churned even harder, making the nausea almost impossible to bear. Her head hurt so badly, it was surely about to split in two. The man who had said their destination was not much farther had lied. Just as she gave up all hope, the carriage jerked to a stop.

"Keep her here whilst I check," the grubby man said as he kicked open the door to the carriage and stepped out.

The gust of fresh air from the open door hit her in the face, coaxing her to open her eyes. Sunshine streamed into the carriage, but it was cooler now, much later in the day. She squinted against the brightness as it made the pounding in her skull worse.

Grubby Man reappeared in the open doorway, grabbed hold of her arm, and pulled. "Come on, your ladyship. Your accommodations await."

The scar-faced man and the mountain-of-flesh ruffian snorted with laughter.

She stumbled out of the coach and vomited as soon as she hit the ground, retching so hard that she felt as though she was turning herself inside out. When she finally finished, she stumbled to one side, nearly sagging to the ground, but one of the men roughly yanked her to her feet.

"Walk, woman. I ain't carryin' you. You ain't no light filly." The scarred man shoved her along the dirt path leading to a ramshackle cottage that appeared to be built into the hillside. The whitewashed wood of the place was in dire need of refreshing and one of the only window's shutters hung off to the side, one of the hinges broken. Smaller structures, two of them, stood off to the side. One appeared to be a stable of sorts, while the other's purpose was questionable. Felicity prayed that small, windowless box was not to be her prison.

Chickens meandered all around, pecking at the ground in search of bugs. An overgrown field of wildflowers surrounded the clearing, effectively hiding the place from view until you were nearly upon it. The door to the cottage was open. Just outside it stood a bent, older woman, clutching a cane of twisted wood, her graying hair haphazardly stuffed into a dingy white cap. Beside her was a much younger, hulking man with his eyes squinted into a scowl.

"This here be your keeper," the scarred man said as he yanked Felicity to a stop in front of the old woman. "Mrs. Bean here knows to keep you alive and to use that stick of hers to keep you cooperating. Understand?"

Felicity didn't answer. Her head was spinning so badly, black spots swam through her vision. Her blood roared in her ears, and it was all she could do to keep from dropping to her knees. Heaven help her. Was she dying?

The blackguard yanked her straight and spoke louder. "Understand?"

"Yes," she hissed, wishing the earth would swallow the man alive, then spit out his bones.

"Got some fire to you after all." He laughed and shoved her forward, letting go of her arm.

She went to the ground, landing on her knees in front of the old woman.

"Where be the rest of my coin?" Mrs. Bean asked him.

"You get the rest when it be done. Keep her alive and none the worse for wear. If a beatin' be needed, hit her where the bruises won't show. Understand?"

The old woman scowled at him, then answered with a single nod.

Felicity sagged over onto her side, unable to remain upright any longer. She lay there on the ground with her eyes closed, praying for her head to stop tormenting her so she could run away at her first opportunity. A breeze washed across her, and all she could hear were the grasses rustling in the wind and the chickens softly clucking, almost purring like cats. It occurred to her that it had gone quiet for a while.

She opened her eyes to Mrs. Bean and the old woman's young giant standing there, staring down at her.

The ancient matron leaned on her cane and jutted her chin forward. "Hit you in the head pretty good, did they?"

"Yes," Felicity said, keeping her voice soft and low so it wouldn't make the pounding between her ears worse.

Mrs. Bean nodded, her puckered face wrinkling with a thoughtful scowl. "Cut that rope off'n her arms, Edmund, but put the shackles on her so's she can't be running when her pate stops hurting."

Edmund nodded, then lumbered off. Presumably to fetch the

shackles.

Shackles? "I'll not run." Felicity fixed the woman with a pleading look, praying for some compassion.

Mrs. Bean laughed and gimped closer, leaning heavily on her cane. "Course you would, gal. I would if'n I was you." She peered down at her, her bushy gray brows almost knotting over her dark eyes. "Pretty little thing, you are. What did you do to get mixed up with the likes of them?"

Felicity gingerly pushed herself up to a sitting position and swallowed hard, determined not to cry. "Fell in love with the wrong man, I think."

Mrs. Bean gave her a sad shake of her head. "Aye, that'll do it every time." She patted her chest with a gnarled hand. "As old Mort told you, I be Mrs. Bean." She nodded at the man approaching with the shackles rattling in his hands. "That there be my Edmund. He's my son and be a quiet one, but just because he be quiet don't mean he ain't sharp as a well-honed knife. Us two will be kind to you as long as you do as you're told. Not because we be kind or generous but because old Mort and his brothers will burn us out and make us beg to be dead should anything go wrong." She tipped a curt nod. "You understand my meanin'?"

"Yes." Felicity understood completely. Mrs. Bean and her son were prisoners just as much as she was. "I am sorry."

The old woman looked surprised. "Sorry? What for?"

"Those men. Their threats."

"Ain't no threats, gal. They be promises. That bunch there don't do it just for the blunt. They do it 'cause they be the cruel sort. Full of meanness all the way to their bones, they are." She nodded at Felicity's legs. "Give my Edmund your ankles. He won't fasten them so tight as to chafe you."

"I promise I won't run."

Mrs. Bean chuckled. "I heard you, gal, now hold still for them shackles. My Edmund won't cause you harm lest you give him reason to."

Too nauseated to argue the point, Felicity held still while the man locked the shackles around her ankles. Then, true to his mother's orders, he cut the rope off her wrists. Without a word, he walked away, heading for the lean-to to the left of the cottage.

"Come along now, gal." Mrs. Bean stamped her cane. "Pull yourself up and brush that dirt off'n that fine gown of yours. It be all you have to wear till Mort and them come to fetch you. I got supper to fix." She pointed at Felicity. "Today and today only, I'll be lettin' you sit and rest whilst I work. I reckon that head of yours ain't none too good right now." She stamped her cane again. "Come along now. I can't be standing out here all day. There be work to be done."

After a deep breath and a hard swallow, Felicity slowly pushed herself to her feet, keeping them spread as far apart as the shackles would allow so she wouldn't lose her balance. The world spun like a child's toy, threatening to send her back to the ground. Staggering like a drunkard, she made it inside, scuffling her feet along the dirt floor until she reached the bench against the far wall. There she sat and even debated lying upon it and covering her aching head with her arms. How in heaven's name had she come to this?

Because of Drake. The accusation played through her mind like a resounding chorus. How could he have done this to her? Endangered her in such a manner? Apparently, his uncle's well-being meant everything while hers meant nothing.

Momentary guilt about so quickly believing the worst about her future husband filled her, but then she angrily shoved it aside. No, he deserved her rage. How many times had he hidden the truth from her before? Not by telling outright lies, but by not telling her the entire truth. Lies of omission. Mama and Papa had always taught that a lie of omission was still a lie. Just because you didn't say something that should have been said did not mean you didn't lie.

She sagged to the side and buried her head in her arms, her shackles rattling as she tucked her feet up under her. Now here she was, tethered in irons like an animal, a prisoner of total strangers for who knew how long.

"It ain't too good, is it?" Mrs. Bean chucked more wood into the hearth, stoking the fire beneath the grating balanced on the stonework.

"No. It is not," Felicity agreed without uncovering her eyes.

The old woman clicked her tongue. "Get through this and you be havin' a fine tale to tell your children."

Felicity wished Mrs. Bean would leave her alone in her misery. She couldn't decide which hurt worse, her head or her heart. "At this point in my life, I doubt I ever have children, since I have decided never to marry."

AS THE SUN sank on this terrible day, Felicity forced down a few bites of bread at Mrs. Bean's insistence, but she passed on the boiled potatoes. Despondency filled her, leaving no room for food. It was just as well that she hadn't eaten. Edmund finished off everything left on the fire and still looked hungry for more. Poor man. He needed a good joint of beef or an entire chicken or two. But he didn't complain. Just kept his head down and did whatever his mother asked of him. Even though he never spoke, Mrs. Bean understood him as though she read his mind, carrying on long conversations with his side of the discussion consisting of only nods or shaking his head. It was more than obvious the two were inseparable.

At least it is them watching me and not Mort and his brothers. Felicity gingerly rubbed her wrists, chafed from the rope being lashed so tightly around them.

A crock of some sort of balm was thrust into her hands. She lifted her head to find Edmund glowering at her. He dipped a curt nod at her wrists, then turned and walked away as silently as he had approached. He was an odd young man, but for some reason, she didn't feel threatened by him. Even in the few hours since her arrival, she had concluded that the Bean family was much like her—victims of their circumstances. The pair was doing their best to get by.

A victim of their circumstances. She almost snorted aloud at the thought but stopped herself because she knew it would increase the pounding ache in her head. After a hesitant sniff of the crock's contents, which turned out to have a delicate, sweet scent, she dabbed a little on her wrists and massaged it into her skin. She hesitated to use very much. The Beans had so little of everything; she didn't want to strain their already meager resources. Once finished, she carefully covered the contents once more with its square of oiled linen and lashed it tight with a worn ribbon.

Mrs. Bean lit a twisted cloth wick in what appeared to be a bowl of tallow placed in the center of the table. It sputtered and smoked until the flame settled well in place, providing much-needed light as night ended the day. With a weary groan, the old woman seated herself in the only chair the Beans possessed and took up her basket of mending. The rest of the seating in the cottage consisted of Felicity's rickety bench and a pair of wooden stools. According to Mrs. Bean, she and her son had little time for sitting, so they simply didn't see the need for more chairs.

"What be your name?" Mrs. Bean asked as she angled herself to catch more light on her sewing.

"Felicity."

The matron nodded. "Pretty name. Suits you." Silence settled across the room, only interrupted by the wood popping in the hearth, even though the night was warm. "How come Mort and his brothers stole you like they did?"

"Money, I suppose." Felicity hugged herself. "I trusted the wrong people."

"Wagered some money and lost it?"

"No. I wagered my heart, and he lost it."

Mrs. Bean rocked in her creaking chair, squinting closer at the seam she was sewing. "They mean to punish him that you lost your heart to by stealing you away and holding you for ransom?"

"It would seem so."

"You in love with a rich man, then?"

"No. He has nothing. But my family would pay well to see me returned safely." What good would it do to lie about it? "My brother is a duke. But those horrid men don't want the money from him. They want it from the man I promised to marry."

"Thought you said he had nothing?"

"He doesn't." Felicity blew out a heavy sigh and rubbed her tired and gritty eyes. "I feel certain he shall need to get the money from my brother."

Mrs. Bean slowly shook her head while frowning down at her mending. "You trusted poorly."

"I did indeed."

The elderly lady set down her needlework and frowned at the fire. "Daren't be feeling bad about it. 'Tis easy to trust poorly. The good-hearted are often taken in by the bad."

"I just want to go home." Felicity folded her arms on the table and cradled her head atop them. She couldn't stress enough how badly she wished to go home. Eyes closed, she willed herself not to cry, knowing that if she ever started, she would never be able to stop.

"Tomorrow will be better, gal."

"I very much doubt that."

"Me and my Edmund will take good care of you long as it takes for that brother of yours to pay your way back." Mrs. Bean shook her head as she selected another garment to mend. "You be better off with us than old Mort and his brothers."

"I am sure you are quite correct on that count," Felicity said, wishing the old woman would be quiet.

"Kind of nice having someone to talk to other than my Edmund." Mrs. Bean gave her son a loving smile. "Him is a good man but ain't much for conversation. Much like his father was."

Felicity bit the inside of her cheek to keep from commenting that Mrs. Bean seemed quite capable of carrying on a robust conversation all by herself. "I appreciate your kindness," she said, instead of what was really on her mind.

The old woman chuckled. "Ain't kindness, gal. Me and my Edmund need the coin somethin' fierce." She blew out a heavy sigh and stared into the crackling fire. "Last winter was hardest we ever had. There for a while, I wondered if we would make it. Need that money for stores for the coming winter, since we lost everything 'cept this here place."

Even in the depths of her misery, Felicity saw a tiny ray of hope. "Help me get back to my brother, and I shall see that you are paid triple what Mort and his men promised you. They don't seem all that trustworthy to me. What's to keep them from not paying you the other half of what you are owed?"

Mrs. Bean shook her head. "A fine idea, gal, and you do speak true about Mort and his lying ways, but me and my Edmund can't be crossing him. To do so would cost us our lives. Old Mort gots himself a terrible temper. Gave his own brother that scar that runs across his face." She offered Felicity a sad smile. "Sorry, gal. We just can't be doing it. They would burn us out, and leave us to starve to death. The risk be too great."

Felicity's hopes crumbled along with her ability to hold back her tears. "I understand," she whispered, then buried her face in her arms.

Chapter Fourteen

DRAKE'S HOPES FELL as he spotted the duke returning to the fork in the road just as he arrived at the juncture. "I found no sign of them," he told the stormy-faced man. "And the farmer I spoke with had not seen anyone all day."

Broadmere shook his head. "If they came this way, it is as though the earth opened up and swallowed them. I went as far as the end of the lane. In her terror, I fear Merry was confused about the direction they took. We have lost precious time."

Drake headed his horse off the road, cutting across the meadow toward the village. "To the inn, then, to confront the devils responsible."

"Lead on." Broadmere rode alongside him.

By the time they reached the inn, its patrons were coming down from their rooms to enjoy tea in the dining room. The door to the private parlor was closed.

Drake charged up to the counter. "Rum and Catherty. Still in there?" he asked the wide-eyed Mr. Thomassan.

The innkeeper nodded as if afraid to speak and be overheard.

Drake kicked in the door and stormed in with the duke on his heels.

Rum and Catherty floundered up from their seats, and their pair of meaty guards stepped in front of them.

Drake drew both of his pistols. "Two of you will die in short order if you do not tell me where she is."

"The remaining two will die by my hand," Broadmere said. "Who would like to meet the Almighty first?"

"If you kill us, you will never find her," Catherty sputtered, edging behind the tallest guard.

"And upon our deaths, our other men know to dispose of her," Rum said, baring his teeth like a cornered dog.

Drake shrugged. "That simplifies things. We kill the guards and simply shoot the pair of you in the knees. With a proper tourniquet, you will not die until we will it."

"And we most assuredly will it," Broadmere added.

"Ten thousand pounds," Catherty said with a belligerent growl. "Pay us what your uncle owes, and we will lead you to her."

Snorting a humorless laugh, Drake shook his head. "My being a trusting fool got my beloved Felicity into this horrid mess. You will take us to her. Now."

Rum just jutted his chin higher. "We will bring her to you. Here. Tomorrow. Have the money ready."

"No." Drake aimed one of his pistols at the nearest guard's forehead. "You will take us to her. Now. She has suffered enough."

"It appears we are at a standoff," Catherty said with a roll of his fleshy shoulders. "Kill the guards. They are nothing to us."

"Your Grace," said a voice from behind them. "Lord Wakefield. Can my men and I offer some assistance?"

Drake didn't dare turn and face the man, even though the voice sounded familiar. "And you are?"

"The magistrate," Broadmere told him before the man could identify himself. "The esteemed Mr. Osbourne."

"How may I be of service?" Mr. Osbourne asked.

"These gentlemen, and I use that term loosely," Drake said while keeping his pistols trained on the men, "abducted Lady Felicity this very day. They did her bodily harm and carried her off. If they do not lead me to her, I intend to kill the two guards and cripple Mr. Rum and Mr. Catherty to convince them to be more cooperative."

"That man is an impostor." Rum pointed a shaking finger at Drake. "The sixth Earl of Wakefield is still alive and owes us ten thousand pounds. That man there, his nephew, faked his uncle's death and assumed the title to keep us from collecting what we are owed."

"My misguided transgressions do not excuse your abduction of Lady Felicity." Drake noted that Rum and Catherty's guards had sweat streaming down their faces. "She is not an impostor, but an innocent young woman caught up in your dastardly plan."

"I agree, Lord Wakefield." Mr. Osbourne stepped up beside Drake, drew his pistol, and leveled it at Catherty. "I am quite familiar with these two and their practices. My cousin is a Bow Street Runner and has noted on many occasions the slipperiness of this pair and their London ways. Well, Binnocksbourne is my jurisdiction, and the abduction of His Grace's sister is my primary concern. I strongly recommend you take us to her."

When the men remained silent, the magistrate tossed a glance back over his shoulder. "Come fetch them, lads. Take all four to the roundhouse. They can stay there until they feel more helpful."

"I would rather kill and cripple them," Drake said, struggling to keep his frustration and rage in check. He kept his pistols raised.

"As would I," Broadmere added, stepping closer and leveling the aim of both his pistols.

"I am sure you would, Your Grace and my lord." Mr. Osbourne lowered his pistol as his men took custody of Rum and Catherty and their guards. "And we may yet allow it if they do not tell us of Lady Felicity's whereabouts."

"He is not a lord!" Catherty spat, his face turning a dangerous red. "He is an impostor. His name is Pemberton."

"And his father was an honorable man beloved by this village," Mr. Osbourne said. "Take them to the roundhouse and place extra guards. If they refuse to talk, we will gather volunteers and find Lady Felicity for ourselves."

"You will never find her without us." Rum sneered at Drake as the magistrate's men dragged him out. "Never."

Unable to hold himself back any longer, Drake shot the man in the foot. "Good heavens, my pistol accidentally went off. How dreadful."

Amidst Rum's howls, Mr. Osbourne cleared his throat. "Yes. Dreadful when that happens. Perhaps you should have its mechanism checked."

Drake tipped a nod while noting with no small amount of satisfaction that Catherty had started frothing at the mouth like a rabid animal. "Yes, Mr. Osbourne. I shall have it checked at my first opportunity." He stepped forward and shoved the barrel of his unspent gun against the side of Catherty's head. "I need only one of you alive to find her."

Catherty paled considerably. "West of here. Between Grange in Borrowdale and Derwentwater."

"You lie." Broadmere shoved his pistol to the other side of Catherty's head. "How could they possibly get that far in such a short amount of time?"

"That is where they were to go," Catherty said through clenched teeth while holding his head extremely still. "Ask for the Beans. The locals can guide you there."

"If she is not there," Drake said, "I shall return and kill you...slowly."

"Your Grace." Mr. Osbourne cleared his throat again. "Lord Wakefield. We shall keep these four in the roundhouse until we return from Grange."

Reluctantly, Drake stepped back and slowly lowered his weapon. Broadmere did the same.

Reloading his pistol, Drake noticed the magistrate stayed behind as his men dragged the injured Rum from the room along with Catherty and the two guards. "Once Lady Felicity is safely returned, I shall answer whatever questions you might have regarding my assumption of the title to Wakefield."

"I shall have no questions, my lord," Mr. Osbourne said, his expression grim. "I was in search of you when I was directed here to the inn."

"In search of me?" Drake finished loading his pistol and tucked it back into his belt. "You had already become aware of my fraud?"

"You are not a fraud, my lord. The sixth Earl of Wakefield was found dead in your garden earlier today. Your butler, Yateston, heard gunfire. When he investigated, he discovered the earl with a self-inflicted wound that proved most fatal. I was fetched to the scene immediately and can confirm without a doubt your uncle ended himself, since witnesses here at the inn and also Broadmere Hall provided us with a most reliable alibi for your whereabouts." He dug in his pocket for a moment, then pulled out a note. "And then there is this. It was pried out of his hand when we examined him."

Try as he might to feel *something* about his uncle's death, Drake felt nothing at all. Not anger. Nor relief. His uncle's suicide was but one more facet of a man Drake realized that he had never known at all. He opened the parchment to find four words written in the center of the page: *Now you are real.* He crumpled it and threw it into the hearth, where enough smoldering coals remained to catch it afire. As far as he was concerned, it was too little, too late. He would never be real, and nothing as insignificant as the title would ever excuse how he had hidden the truth from Felicity and put her in harm's way.

"Thank you, Mr. Osbourne." He offered the man a polite bow, then turned to Felicity's brother. "Shall we leave now?"

His expression unreadable, Broadmere nodded. "Definitely."

"I shall come with you," the magistrate said with finality. "They have surely left people there to guard her, and who is to say how many scoundrels you shall face?" As he escorted them from the parlor, he nodded as though speaking his thoughts aloud. "We shall bring a few of my men as well."

"We are leaving immediately," Drake said. There was no

time for niceties. "And you must not deplete the forces guarding Rum and Catherty." Even after Felicity was safe, he still had grim business to finish with those men.

"Our forces will not be depleted," the magistrate reassured him. "Binnocksbourne will not go lightly on those who would harm a daughter of the Broadmere family."

Drake wasn't surprised at the sentiment, especially when it came to Felicity. A kinder, more caring woman could never be found. He swallowed hard and lengthened his stride. He had to save her. Not only so he could apologize but also assure her he would never trouble her again.

"We will not reach her by nightfall," Broadmere said as they took to their saddles.

Drake spurred his mount onward. "Then darkness shall be our cloak."

CURLED ON A pallet in the corner, Felicity stared out into the darkened room lit only by the remaining coals still glowing red in the hearth. Both Edmund and Mrs. Bean's snores drowned out the gentle chirp of the crickets outside the door and window. Both had been left open to coax inside some of the cool night air and dispel the oppressive warmth still coming off the stone fireplace that not only heated the cottage but also served to cook all the meals.

She tried not to move too much and cause her chains to rattle. It was silly, she supposed, to worry about disturbing her captors' sleep. But the Beans were not bad people. They were merely trying to survive and had been as kind to her as the current situation allowed. Their fear of the vile Mort and his brothers was palpable, and Felicity completely understood. She harbored no doubts whatsoever that those men were capable of any cruelty.

A heavy sigh left her, and for what seemed like the hundredth time, she tried to wad the thin pillow to a more comfortable angle under her aching head. Mrs. Bean had cleared away the blood and promised that the split and the large knot left behind by the terrible blow would soon heal. Felicity's fear now was what had happened to Merry. She knew her sister and could just imagine an enraged Merry giving no thought to her own safety as she jumped into the fray to save her.

Please let Merry be safe.

She tried to close her eyes and think of happier thoughts, but at the moment, she hadn't the strength or the mood to bring any to mind. She was a prisoner, her sister could be wounded or worse in a ditch, and this was all because of the man she had trusted with her heart. A choking lump of emotions knotted in her throat, making her squeeze her eyes shut tighter. She had always sensed there was something more he wasn't telling her, other than he was penniless and in dire need of a wife with a dowry, but never had she imagined such a grandiose lie as impersonating a peer. It was inconceivable.

But he said he loved me. It had seemed so real when he had said it, and their first kiss. She pinched the bridge of her nose and pressed the corners of her closed eyes, determined not to cry. She had to be the greatest fool that ever walked the face of the earth. Had he been lying about his love for her, too? *He rejected the dowry.* But had that been merely a gesture? Grand talk to impress her and her family? Would he have eventually accepted it after *allowing* his resolve to be worn down?

In truth, the only lie of omission of which she had previously been aware was that of his financial state. Would he have told her if she and Merry had not peeked into his garden that day? His supposedly proposing to countless women according to their dowries had been a cruel lie cooked up by the mean-spirited Nedia and her gaggle of friends. Felicity couldn't very well blame Drake for that misunderstanding.

But *this* horrid situation was undeniably his fault. If she ever—no, not *if* but *when*—returned to where she belonged... What? What would she do? Did she have the courage to send him away? Most definitely. Besides, what else had he not told her? Perhaps he already had a wife somewhere. Or a mistress. Perhaps he was behind this kidnapping to get even more money beyond her dowry.

She continued rubbing the corners of her eyes, refusing to allow herself to cry. *You are being ridiculous. Stop letting your mind reel.* Deep in her heart, she knew he had no wife or mistress. That would have most certainly been shoved into her face by the gossips, and while he might be many things, Drake was not cruel. How many times had she seen a longing to be loved and accepted shining in the depths of his hazel eyes?

She shifted again, flinching as she hurt her poor, wounded head. *Be still, fool.* But she couldn't. Not with her mind churning like a maelstrom. At least she knew for certain that Chance would come for her. While her brother could be as irritating as an itch you couldn't reach to scratch, he possessed a raging temper and an endearing protectiveness of his sisters. Chance would come. He wouldn't simply hand over any amount of money and wait for her to be delivered. No, he would come with his pistols, Papa's sword, and the daggers Mama had gifted him one year for his birthday. Chance would come.

But will Drake? She released another heavy sigh. Drake might come, but only if Chance hadn't killed him. What then? What would she do?

"I do not know," she whispered into the darkness. Her heart ached even worse than her head.

※

Chapter Fifteen

IT TOOK FELICITY a moment to realize that the loud, obnoxious crowing of a rooster was not part of some strange dream. She opened her eyes to the rising sun streaming in through the doorway along with the rooster, who behaved as if the cottage were his. He strutted halfway across the room, then stopped and unleashed another earsplitting crow.

"Out with you, Ferdinand." Mrs. Bean encouraged him toward the door with a nudge of her broom. "I'll not have you shattin' in here again. Just because the floor be dirt, doesn't mean it's for the likes of you. Out!" As she turned to set her broom back in the corner, she glanced at Felicity. "Good morning to you."

"Good morning." Felicity sat up, thankful that the pain in her skull had eased to a much more bearable level.

"How be your head?"

"Better, I believe."

"Good." Mrs. Bean nodded at the door. "Tend to your needs. There be a creek for washing just to the other side of the house, but hear me well when I say if you be gone longer than I deem you should, I be sending Edmund to fetch you back."

"I understand." Gingerly, Felicity pushed herself up from the pallet and was relieved to discover her balance much improved as well. She made it to the door without issue, having to adjust her stride to accommodate the length of the chain connecting her ankles.

Ferdinand met her just outside the doorway, eyeing her as though ready to give her a taste of his spurs.

"I am in no mood, rooster," she told the fowl, who seemed to take her at her word. He turned the other way and strutted off as though he were royalty.

She found the water as Mrs. Bean had said and washed her hands and face as best she could after attending to her other needs. At some point between yesterday and today, her gloves, parasol, and reticule had gone missing. She assumed those ghouls had taken them as proof they had captured her. None of that mattered now. Her greatest worry, besides getting herself back home, was Merry's safety. Each time Drake came to mind, she did her best to think of something else.

Drying her hands on her gown, she shuffled back to the cottage. "Thank you," she told Mrs. Bean as she stepped back inside.

"For what?" The old woman didn't bother looking up from the gurgling pot she was stirring over the fire.

"Allowing me some privacy to take care of things."

"Me and my Edmund wish you no harm, gal. Truly, we don't." Mrs. Bean hazarded a taste of the creamy contents of the pot and shook her head. "Porridge be a while longer. Just as well; Edmund still be chopping wood." Wiping her forehead with the back of her hand, she turned and studied Felicity. "You know how to mend, or you one of those that does nothing but fancy sewing? If'n you can mend, that there will be easier on your head than crawling all over creation looking for where them hens of mine hid their eggs."

"I can sew." Felicity bent and picked up the basket overflowing with clothing in need of restoration. As she straightened, a pain shot through her head, and she nearly lost her balance.

"Aye, egg hunting ain't for you just yet." Mrs. Bean tipped her head toward the door. "The light's better out there on the bench. Cooler too. You can go out there to do the sewing, if'n you want."

"Thank you." Felicity gratefully left the overpowering heat of the cottage and seated herself outside. Poor Mrs. Bean. The woman needed an outdoor kitchen, but she and her son barely had the means to maintain the one-room structure they already possessed. No wonder they had made a deal with the devil named Mort.

Felicity selected an item from the basket, found the needle and thread Mrs. Bean had left stuck in the handle, and started sewing. Mending rips and tears was easy. Mending her heart? Not so much.

She became aware of the steady, rhythmic thunk and crackle of wood being chopped and then split off in the distance. If not for her circumstances, she might even consider the warm summer morning on the bench in front of the cottage a calming respite. But her rough treatment from yesterday and the chains around her ankles were reminders enough that her ridiculous trust in Drake had led her to this ruinous hell.

"Them stitches of yours be fine," Mrs. Bean said from the doorway. "Should hold up real well."

"Thank you."

"You said your brother be a duke?"

"I did." Felicity selected another item from the basket, trimmed away the tear's ratty threads, then started closing the seam. "He is the Duke of Broadmere." For a change, the memory of Chance's temper and hardheadedness made her smile. "It has only been six years since my papa died and passed the title to him, but he is growing into the role quite well."

"He be a generous man? Kind like you?"

Felicity smiled again and stared off into the distance. "Yes. He is. Papa and Mama raised us all to be kind and generous."

"There be more of you, then?" Mrs. Bean cast a glance back inside the cottage. "Them grains ain't never going to soften."

"At home, Cook always added more salt and left a silver spoon in the pot while they cooked." Felicity couldn't help but give a soft laugh. "She swore that made the grains soften faster whenever she boiled them." Remembering that Mrs. Bean had asked if there were more in her family other than Chance, she continued, "And I am one of seven sisters. My brother has no choice but to be kind and generous, since we outnumber him."

Mrs. Bean chuckled, sounding like one of the hens scratching in the yard. "He'll be the better for having all you sisters. Makes him a finer man."

"I hope we do." Felicity bit off the thread and moved on to the next item in need of repair. As she started stitching the tear, she decided to repeat the offer she had made last night, even sweeten it some. "Help me get back to my family, Mrs. Bean, and I promise there will be a place for you and Edmund at Broadmere Hall. No more struggling through harsh winters ever again. When Mort's coin runs out…what happens to you and Edmund the winter after next? But if you help me get home—and your chickens can come too if you like—you and your Edmund would be set for life. I promise you my brother would see to it. *I* would see to it."

Mrs. Bean stared off into the distance, squinting as though trying to focus on something far away. She slowly shook her head. "If Mort and his brothers caught us afore we made it back your brother…" She unleashed a heavy sigh. "'Twouldn't be good at all, gal. Not good at all."

"Where exactly are we?"

The old woman nodded at a point in the distance. "Grange in Borrowdale is a good stretch of the legs that way." She turned and pointed in the opposite direction. "Derwentwater lies not too far over there. My Edmund can be there and back with a fine creel of fish in a day."

Felicity's heart fell. That seemed so far from Binnocksbourne. "Broadmere Hall is near the village of Binnocksbourne. Do you know that place?"

Mrs. Bean gave Felicity a sad shake of her head. "That village be a good ways from here, gal. 'Specially since me and my Edmund got nothing but our feet for traveling. Mort and them would surely catch us were we to start out for your Broadmere Hall."

Felicity had no doubt about that, and the journey would be even more challenging for Mrs. Bean with her cane. "Are there any neighbors nearby who might allow us to borrow a wagon? My brother would happily pay them for their troubles."

"Let me think on it whilst I stir the porridge." Mrs. Bean disappeared back inside, then soon reappeared. She grinned at Felicity. "I added more salt. Ain't got no silver spoon for it, though. Maybe it will still work."

"I am sure it will." Feeling much the same as she had last night, Felicity really didn't care whether or not she ever ate again. Never known for her patience, she struggled to come up with a rescue plan that didn't involve sitting here and waiting for someone to save her. If only she could come up with a few resources, she would bloody well save herself. And she didn't feel a bit guilty about the coarseness of her inner dialogue. Considering the circumstances, it was warranted.

She finished stitching the shirt, snapped the thread free, and then moved on to the next garment in the basket.

"There be an Irish family not too far from here," Mrs. Bean said. "Believe they got more than one wagon, and I know for a fact they got at least two mules and maybe a horse. Always seemed friendly enough. Good folk, though there be a lot of them. Large family, they are. They might help us."

"Might they, truly?" Felicity was almost afraid to hope.

"All we can do is ask'm, gal." Mrs. Bean pushed up from the bench with a soft groan. "I know I couldn't walk to your Broadmere Hall, but I could ride."

"Might we go talk to them?" Felicity was ready to jump up and leave immediately.

Mrs. Bean leaned against her cane, her brow wrinkling with her thoughts. "I need to be the one to go. If Mort were to come back today and discover you gone, we would be ended afore we ever started. You can stay here with my Edmund just in case."

While Felicity didn't much care for that option, she saw the sense in it. It also occurred to her that the family might need some reassurance that they would not only get their wagon back but also receive the payment she promised.

Setting the mending aside, she glanced all around to ensure Edmund was not on the way back from chopping wood, then reached inside the neckline of her gown and unpinned the locket she always wore attached to her stays. The gold heart was the keepsake that had often consoled her whenever life proved difficult. Mama and Papa had gifted it to her years ago, and it kept their portraits close to her heart.

"Here." She held it out to Mrs. Bean. "Give this to the family. Tell them it is my dearest possession in all the world, because that is my mama and papa inside. When we bring back their wagon and mule, I will pay them fifty pounds for the return of my locket."

Compassion filled Mrs. Bean's face as she opened the heart-shaped locket and stared down at the images. With a slow nod, she carefully tucked it into the pocket of her apron. "I will convince them to give us the wagon, gal. I swear it." Hobbling over to the end of the house, she shouted around the corner, "Edmund! I be off to the Hogans' for a bit. Our guest is minding the porridge. You watch everything close in case old Mort comes to call. Understand?"

Apparently, the silent Edmund nodded, then resumed chopping the wood. Mrs. Bean returned to Felicity and pointed at the door. "Once it finishes, you and Edmund eat. There be bread on the table too. I can wait to eat after I return."

"Be careful, Mrs. Bean." Felicity set the mending basket aside and rose to her feet. "What will you say if you meet Mort?"

"That I was gone to borrow some herbs 'cause you be unwell." The sly old matron winked. "If'n he shows up, you take to that pallet and act sickly in case he comes across me afore he comes here. Understand?"

"I understand." Felicity couldn't resist giving the woman a hug. "Be careful. Surely, Mort won't return so soon."

"You never know, gal. He be as unpredictable as a wounded

beast."

That was what Felicity feared most. She couldn't bear to think what he might do to poor Mrs. Bean if he suspected the true meaning of her visit to her neighbor. As the old woman hobbled away, she prayed for her safety as she went inside to stir the porridge.

DRAKE TRIED IN vain to roll the weariness from his tensed shoulders, determined not to stop until they reached Felicity. They were nearing Grange in Borrowdale and would stop there in search of someone who knew where the Beans lived. All the while they rode, he, the Duke of Broadmere, the magistrate, and two of the magistrate's men kept watch for the black coach and the demons who had stolen her away. But they never came across them. Either the blackguards had hidden themselves locally, or they had taken an alternate route back to Binnocksbourne.

They needed to find Felicity before the devils discovered their employers were no longer in any position to pay them. Dawn bathed the land with its gentle, golden glow as they thundered into the sleepy village. The first soul they came upon was a yawning lad filling one of the watering troughs in front of the livery stable.

"Boy!" Drake called as all of them dismounted to give their mounts a brief rest and a moment to drink.

The boy squinted at him, pausing with his buckets at his sides. "Aye?"

"Do you know the Bean family who lives near here?" Drake reached into his pocket, drew out a coin, and held it up for the lad to see.

"Bean?"

"Yes. They live between here and Derwentwater."

After dragging his sleeve across his runny nose, the boy shook his head. "Don't know no Bean family, but the vicar might. He knows everyone."

"Where is the vicarage?" Broadmere asked.

The boy pointed across the village square. "Over there. That place with the white fence that goes to the back of the kirk."

Drake tossed the coin to the boy and noticed that Broadmere gave the child another.

"We shall stay here with the horses," Mr. Osbourne said with a nod to his men. "Hopefully, the vicar may be of some help."

Without waiting for the duke, Drake took off across the village square with a long, hurried stride. Urgency pounded through him, along with fear. Time was of the essence. He banged on the door, willing someone to answer with haste. Not a sound came from inside the tidy dwelling, so he banged again. Surely a vicar wouldn't still be abed.

"Here, there," a man called out from the garden area between the vicarage and the small church. "May I be of service?"

"The Bean family," Drake said. "Do you know where they live?"

"Martha Bean and her son, Edmund?" An older man with his sleeves rolled above his elbows leaned against his spade. He nodded to the north. "Their cottage is a good stretch of the legs in that direction." Then he frowned and jutted his chin higher. "Mrs. Bean and Edmund are good people. What do you want with them?"

They couldn't be all that good if they were in business with Rum and Catherty's ruffians, but Drake didn't say that aloud. "My intended, Lady Felicity of the Broadmeres, has been kidnapped, and they were named as the people holding her until the ransom was paid."

The man frowned and exited his garden through the small gate next to the church. "The Beans? Caught up in such terrible wickedness?" He shook his head. "I cannot believe that."

"People will do anything when they need money."

Broadmere fixed Drake with a pointed glare. "Will they not, Lord Wakefield?"

The words stung, but he could hardly deny their truth. "Indeed, they will, Your Grace."

The man with the spade drew a handkerchief out of his back pocket and mopped his brow. "They have endured a rough few years since Mr. Bean died." Again, he pointed to the north. "On foot, it would take you several hours to reach their place. On horseback, you should be there in no time. It's hard to find, though. Built into a hillside and set back off the road a ways beside a creek. This time of year, the grasses are so tall, it is nearly hidden from view."

"Sounds like the perfect place to hide her," Drake said, and Broadmere nodded. "Thank you, good sir." Drake tipped his hat and headed back to the horses. He wished he had enough money to donate to the church, but it couldn't be helped. "The Bean residence is not far from here," he told Mr. Osbourne as he reached the horses. "Think they can go a bit longer?"

Osbourne shook his head. "Better to let them rest a while, my lord, or they'll have no strength to spare once we reach our destination."

"Time is of the essence," Drake argued. "We have no idea of her state."

"We also have no idea how many men might guard her," the magistrate said, "and if they see us descending upon them, they could do her harm. You know we saw none of them on the ride here. They must still be in this area waiting for further instructions from Rum and Catherty."

As much as he hated to admit it, Drake realized Mr. Osbourne was right, and he had already endangered Felicity enough. "What do you suggest we do?"

"Wait a few hours. Give the horses a brief respite, and ourselves as well." The magistrate gave him a hard up-and-down look. "From what I have gathered about you, and also observed, you need time to compose yourself, my lord, so innocent people are not harmed." He offered a knowing smile. "I also extended this same advice to His Grace."

"While I agree it is wise advice, it is difficult to follow when my mind reels with the horrors Lady Felicity could be experiencing at this very moment."

Mr. Osbourne's face fell. "I understand, my lord, but we mustn't endanger her or any other innocent any further."

"The vicar swears the Beans are good people," Broadmere said as he joined them. "We can only hope he knows them well."

"But how much protection can a woman and her son provide against the men that Merry described?" That was Drake's greatest fear, that the cruel demons had visited unspeakable acts upon her. If they had, he would never forgive himself. "Two hours," he told the magistrate. "The horses have two hours to rest. I cannot bear to wait a moment longer than that to resume our search."

"Understood."

It was obvious Mr. Osbourne disagreed, but Drake didn't care. He had to get to Felicity. He would not rest until he saw her safely returned to her family. No hope remained within him that she would return to him. He knew that was not a possibility. Not after the pain, terror, and who knew what else he had caused her. No, she would never be his wife, and he didn't blame her. At present, he couldn't even stand himself.

Chapter Sixteen

WITH A TOOTHLESS but no-less-heartwarming smile, Mrs. Bean pressed the gold locket back into Felicity's hand. "Them Hogans be good people. They felt your word be good enough. They refused to take it."

Swallowing hard at the sudden knot of emotions caught in her throat, Felicity clutched it to her chest. "I will see that they are paid for their kindness. You have my word."

"I know, gal." Mrs. Bean gently patted her arm. "I told them you be a kindhearted soul."

"Thank you, Mrs. Bean." Felicity turned and eyed the mule harnessed to the old farm wagon. It was the loveliest sight she had ever seen. "Do we have everything? Where is Edmund?"

"Me and my Edmund don't lay claim to too much, and he done put it in the back of the wagon. We need to be leaving now." The matron frowned as she looked all around the yard. "I told him to make haste crating up them chickens. Old Ferdinand must be giving him trouble." She shook her cane and hobbled across the yard. "We daren't be dilly-dallying, Edmund!" she said. "If'n that old rooster don't want to come, leave him."

A loud squawk and a harried thumping of flapping wings could be heard off in the distance. Either Edmund had caught the rooster and stuffed him into the last crate, or the bird had met his demise. While Felicity was usually generous in her feelings toward any animal, she didn't care what had happened to the irritating bird as long as it meant they would be leaving soon. Deep in her heart, she feared that Mort and his brothers would return when they least expected it.

Edmund came out from behind the shed with an indignant Ferdinand still fussing and flapping his wings as much as he could inside the wooden crate.

"You be lucky, Ferdinand," Mrs. Bean told the bird. "My Edmund was ready to wring your neck for you."

Edmund grunted and set the crate in the back of the wagon.

Mrs. Bean turned to Felicity. "'Tis best you ride back there on your pallet, gal. If'n me and my Edmund see any folks along the way, you be sure and get down real low when we say so."

"I will happily do so." With Edmund's assistance, Felicity climbed up into the wagon. She appreciated being able to move freely once more with the removal of her shackles. Once seated, she wrapped a dingy, worn scarf around her head and tied it under her chin. No one passing them during their travels would think her anything other than part of the Bean family.

As the wagon bounced into motion, she glanced back at the little cottage that seemed almost sad to see them go. It wouldn't take long for the grass and weeds to reclaim it and hide it forever.

Mrs. Bean turned in her seat and called back over the din of the wheels against the packed dirt of the roadway, "My Edmund thinks we be needing to go through Grange first. Just in case some of your people have come to fetch you."

Felicity wasn't too sure about that idea. "What if Mort and his men are in town? Will that not risk our discovery?"

The matron squinted against the brightness of the day, then leaned close to her son and appeared to ask. Edmund shook his head and leaned forward to rest his elbows on his knees, apparently settling in for the journey.

"'Twill be all right, gal," Mrs. Bean told her.

I hope so. Hugging her knees with one arm and hanging on to the wagon with the other, Felicity watched the Bean homeplace slowly disappear. She wished they could travel faster, but would leave that to Edmund, since she was no expert when it came to mules.

They had traveled long enough to make Felicity wish that the pallet under her bum were a little thicker when Mrs. Bean turned and motioned for her to stay down.

Felicity curled into a ball, wondering if she should have put her pallet on the other side of the chicken crates and covered herself with a ratty old blanket. It was too late now, though. All she could do was hope whoever passed them either didn't notice her at all or merely thought her ill in the back of the wagon. Unfortunately, all she could hear was the creaking rattle and thump of the decrepit farm vehicle as it maintained its slow, steady pace.

But then it slowed even more and came to a full stop.

Felicity cowered deeper into the scarf she had wrapped around her head, closing her eyes and doing her best to sink into the pallet and chicken crates. Then her heart leapt. She knew that voice.

Popping upright, she tore the scarf away. "Chance!"

"Felli!" Her brother leapt from his horse, charged to the wagon, and snatched her down into his arms. "Gads alive, Felli." He crushed her to his chest. "I feared I would never see you again."

She clung to him, sobbing, "I feared the same, my sweet brother. I feared the same." When she opened her eyes and saw Drake, she froze and drew back. Her heart fell to her stomach with a sickly gurgle. "What is *he* doing here?"

"He came to warn us about Rum and Catherty threatening to do you harm." Chance steadied her. "He was there when Merry returned to tell us you had been taken."

"Merry." The fickle, lying Drake could wait. Felicity caught hold of her brother. "Is she all right? Did they harm her?"

"Nothing worse than a few scrapes and scratches from where they tossed her into the ditch." He offered a lopsided smile. "You know our Merry. A more courageous fighter was never born."

"Thank heavens. I was so worried about her."

All humor left Chance as he leveled a narrow-eyed gaze on her. "And you, my dear Felli?" he asked barely above a whisper. "Are you…whole and unharmed?"

She knew what he feared, and adored him even more. "I have a bump on the back of my head. Other than that, I am quite well." She nodded at Edmund and Mrs. Bean. "Thankfully, the *jailers* those terrible men chose are the kindest folk and took good care of me. I have promised them lifetime employment at Broadmere Hall. They risked their lives trying to return me. That is why we borrowed this mule and wagon from the Hogan family. By the way, I owe the Hogans fifty pounds, but would like to pay them more. They risked their well-being too. I believe those horrible ruffians terrorize this area."

"We shall pay them three times that." Chance offered Mrs. Bean and Edmund a gracious bow. "You have my eternal gratitude and the safety of Broadmere Hall for taking such good care of my sister."

Mrs. Bean's weathered face wrinkled even more with her teary-eyed smile. "Thank you, Your Grace. Thank you ever so much." She nodded at Felicity. "Her ladyship is a kind soul. We could do no less for her."

Movement out of the corner of her eye drew Felicity's attention back to Drake. He had dismounted and was easing toward her. "Felicity?" he asked, his voice ragged. "Are you well?"

She charged over to him and slapped him so hard that it turned his head and made her hand sting. "You have no right to ask me that."

He bowed his head. "I agree. I do not."

"I hate you," she said, the words coming out in a sob. "You lied to me and risked my sister's life."

He nodded. "I know there is no excuse, but I lived in terror of losing you if I told you my uncle still lived."

"Well, your terrors are now realized." She wanted to scream, wanted to cry, but instead, she slapped him again. "I trusted you with my heart, and you crushed it."

"I am sorry," he whispered.

"You will never be sorry enough, and I will never forgive you." She turned away from him, facing Chance once again. "Help me back into the wagon, brother dear. It is a long ride home."

"No!" Drake roared, and threw her to the ground just as a shot rang out.

The magistrate and his men returned fire, then took off after the remaining villain, riding away. Two lay writhing where they had fallen, bleeding from their chests. Felicity recognized the scar-faced man and the mountain of flesh, Mort's two brothers. It didn't take long for them to go still.

"Felli." Chance helped her up and turned her toward Drake. He lay on his side, a dark, wet stain spreading across the back of his jacket.

"Help me down, Edmund," Mrs. Bean commanded, banging her cane against the wagon's buckboard. She pointed a bent finger at Felicity. "Press on that wound, gal. Got to slow that bleeding lest he die."

"She is right." Chance cut away Drake's jacket and split the back of his shirt open wide.

Fighting against a surge of nausea and her spinning head, Felicity knelt beside Drake and pressed the wadded rags of his shirt against the wound.

"Hard, gal," Mrs. Bean ordered her. "If'n he bleeds too much, he'll be gone."

Even in all her anger and heartbreak, Felicity had never wished Drake dead. She had wanted him to suffer as she had, but nothing like this. "Don't you dare die," she said with a growl that surprised even her.

"Check his front, gal," Mrs. Bean said. "With any luck, it passed through. He'll be better for it if'n it did."

"I shall check," Chance said, crouching on Drake's other side. He shook his head. It had not passed through. "We must get him back to town and find a surgeon."

Hands bloodied, Felicity blinked against the black dots swimming through her vision. She could not swoon. There was no time. She had to stay focused and give Drake the help he needed, even though she felt like shaking him.

The thunder of galloping horses made her look up. It was Mr. Osbourne and his men returning alone. Her heart fell. That had to mean the worst. Mort had escaped.

When the magistrate and his men reached them, they alighted and took over Drake's care.

"Fear not, my lady." Mr. Osbourne offered Felicity a formal bow. "Our bullets found purchase in the third man as well. Those three are now standing before the greatest judge of all."

"Them three will be found wantin'," Edmund said.

Felicity stared at him in shock.

Old Mrs. Bean laughed. "I never said he couldn't talk, gal. My Edmund just ain't much for speaking." She nodded at Drake. "Think you might want to speak with him whilst you still have a chance?"

While she still had a chance? Felicity went to her knees and rested his head in her lap. "Don't you dare die," she repeated, meaning it more as a challenge than anything else. He needed to live so she could spurn him as many times as it took to be rid of him, but she didn't wish him dead.

"I am so sorry," he whispered, grimacing against the pain. "So very sorry."

"You should be."

"I am. More than you will ever know."

"A lie of omission is still a lie." She used a corner of her gown to wipe the dirt and sweat from his face. "A lie is a lie."

"I know." He sounded weaker. "I will never forgive myself for being such a fool and throwing you away. You—the best thing that ever happened to me in my entire life."

She wouldn't say *good* and agree that she wouldn't forgive him either. Not now, when he lay knocking at death's door. She swallowed hard, her throat aching because her heart had lodged in it sideways. Hot tears streamed down her face, making her angrier still.

Chance took hold of her by the shoulders. "Let us get him into the wagon, Felli. We have to get him to the village. With any luck, they have someone there who can help him."

Drake didn't make a sound as the men lifted him, even though he had to be in agony.

"Help me up there," Felicity told her brother. "I need to hold the rag to his wound. The ride will be rough." It wasn't that she loved him still. No, that foolishness was over. It was merely her Christian duty to do what she could to help him.

Without argument, Chance lifted her into the wagon. Once again, she pillowed Drake's head in her lap while pressing hard against the wound that was not in the center of his back but nearer to his shoulder. The fact that he had pushed her to the ground and taken the shot meant for her didn't escape her. It didn't matter. She would still be rid of him as soon as he was well.

Because he *would* be well. She wouldn't contemplate otherwise.

The wagon lurched into motion, making Drake bare his teeth and dig his fingers into the pallet until the material ripped. But he didn't make a sound, simply took his punishment as if it were his due.

"I am sorry," he said again, barely loud enough to be heard over the rattling of the wagon. "So very sorry."

"So you said earlier." She wiped his face again, trying to keep him as steady as possible as they thundered across the rough terrain. "Save your strength. I refuse to have your death on my conscience."

He caught hold of her hand and pressed it to his mouth, tenderly kissing it. "Forgive me so I might die in peace."

"I do not forgive you. Therefore, you best not die."

"Felli...please."

"Do not call me that. We are no longer that familiar." She frowned at the wad of rags she held pressed to his back. The bleeding was worse. They needed to hurry so they could stop shaking him and stanch the flow. "Now, stop talking and save your strength."

He became almost peaceful, frightening her even more. "You thought you were a shy wallflower, yet you sound like a fierce general on the battlefield."

"If I have learned anything since meeting you, it is that I have many strengths of which I was unaware." Good heavens, would they never get to Grange? "It is time for you to look within yourself now and draw upon your own strengths."

He didn't answer, and his lips were barely parted. Panicking, she pressed her hand to the middle of his chest. A sob escaped her when she felt nothing. No, it had to be because of the rough ride. He was not dead. She bent forward and kissed his forehead, willing him to live. "I told you not to die," she said through gritted teeth.

Relief filled her when the heat of his breath barely brushed across her fingers as she held them close to his face. *Thank the Almighty.* Drake was breathing. The pain and loss of blood must have finally rendered him unconscious.

"How much farther?" she called out to Mrs. Bean.

The old woman turned and cast a worried look at Drake. "Soon, gal. I know it feels like forever, but we be there soon enough."

Felicity held tight to Drake as the wagon swayed and bumped over a particularly rough patch of road. At this rate, soon enough might not suffice.

THE GRANGE IN Borrowdale Inn wasn't much, but it was clean, and the nearest place they could find Drake the care he needed. It just so happened that the innkeeper's husband was also an experienced surgeon who had learned his trade on the battlefield.

Binnocksbourne's magistrate didn't stay in Grange with Chance, Felicity, and the Beans. He bade them farewell and returned to deal with the criminals awaiting their punishment in the roundhouse. Rum and Catherty's moneylending business was now closed. Permanently.

With Mrs. Bean's help, Felicity kept Drake as comfortable as possible when he wasn't so wild with fever as to knock them away. When those demons overtook him, Edmund came forward and kept Drake still so he wouldn't harm himself and rip open Mr. Warner's handiwork. The surgeon had removed the bullet, cleaned and stitched the wound as much as he could, and then offered little hope. Drake's recovery depended on the Almighty.

Someone squeezing her shoulder startled Felicity into opening her eyes, which she had risked closing for just a second. She jerked to complete wakefulness. "Yes? What is it?"

"It be all right, gal," Mrs. Bean said quietly. "I be goin' downstairs for a while. You need me to fetch anything for you?"

Felicity rolled her shoulders and rubbed her neck, trying to work out the stiffness. "No, thank you, Mrs. Bean. Nothing for me. Get yourself some rest. I am fine here."

The old woman shook her head. "You be far from fine, gal, but you be doing the best you can. That be all you can do when things come to this." She cast a concerned glance at Drake. "Leastwise he seems quieter today. A quiet day is a good day."

Felicity rubbed the weary grittiness from her eyes. "Indeed, it is. We can only hope that is a good sign."

Mrs. Bean nodded as she ambled over to the door, the tip of her cane softly clicking against the hardwood floors. "I be back soon, gal."

"Thank you, Mrs. Bean." Felicity rose and went to the washbowl on the table beside the bed, emptied the old water into the bucket on the floor, and filled it with clean water from one of the pitchers beside a stack of freshly boiled and dried bandages, crocks of balm, and three brown bottles of laudanum. She sometimes wondered if the vile laudanum made Drake worse.

Mama had always hated the stuff. Said it made her dream of frightening and unbelievable things.

Felicity wet a cloth, then dabbed its coolness across Drake's forehead, throat, and the part of his chest not covered by the bedsheet or bandages. His state made her softly snort with a sad laugh. If she wasn't ruined before, she was surely ruined now, tending to a man in such a state of undress. But it no longer mattered. Mrs. Bean was in no condition to handle his care all alone; the innkeeper had her business to run, and Felicity just didn't feel right about Chance hiring a maid for the job. No, family took care of their own. Strangers didn't.

Her hand froze in place as she passed the cloth across Drake's bare shoulders. *Family.* Drake was not family. He was the disgraced man she had intended to marry. Chance had told her about Drake's uncle taking his life, making Drake the real Earl of Wakefield and removing that worry from the equation.

She clenched her teeth. The title was not the issue and never had been, as far as she was concerned. It was Drake's inability to be honest that was the problem. She soaked the cloth again, squeezed out the water, and washed his arms and hands, then draped the wet rag on a peg on the table. Edmund and Mrs. Bean would wash the rest of him. It was not at all proper for her to do as much as she had already done. She dared not do any more.

"Felicity?"

Uncertain whether he had actually spoken or she had dreamed it, she turned back to him and leaned closer. "I am here."

"I am sorry."

He sounded lucid. She girded herself against anything he might say. "Are you going to apologize every time you speak to me?"

Without opening his eyes, he barely nodded. "I will spend the rest of my life apologizing to you, if you see fit to allow it."

She repressed a sigh and swallowed hard. "How is your pain? Are you in need of more laudanum? Mr. Warner said you may have more if you wish."

"No more laudanum." He opened his eyes and barely shifted, quickly halting with a grimace. "I can bear the pain in my shoulder. That is not the agony that troubles me."

She wasn't about to question him further. Instead, she filled a cup with fresh water, lifted his head, and held it to his lips. "Drink—Mr. Warner said it is most important that you drink. We added honey to this water. Mrs. Bean said it would help you."

He sipped the tiniest bit, then slightly turned his head away. "Who is Mrs. Bean? The owner of this place?"

"No, Mrs. Bean and her son, Edmund, were my *caretakers* for a while."

He flinched again. "The ones Rum and Catherty hired?"

"Yes."

"I am sorry."

"Do not be. They are good and kind people who will soon live at Broadmere Hall. I am a better person for meeting them."

Closing his eyes, he went quiet for so long that she thought he had once more drifted off to sleep. "Why did you stay?" he asked, his voice weak and raspy. "Why did you stay to care for me?"

What could she say when she had no idea herself? They had simply stayed because they were supposed to stay. They couldn't very well toss him onto the inn's porch like a sack of potatoes. She shrugged. "We stayed because it was the right thing to do."

"The right thing to do," he repeated, his smile faint and trembling. "I have much to learn about *the right thing to do*."

"Once you heal, perhaps you will find someone who might teach you."

He turned to face her and locked eyes with her. "There will never be another. There is only you."

Determined to escape his gaze, she busied herself around the already tidy room. "Do not say such things."

"I have finally learned to speak nothing but the truth." When she didn't respond, he continued, "I hate what I did to you, to us.

Hate it more than you will ever know."

She went to the window and stared at nothing, holding her head high and fighting to show no emotion at all. "We all have regrets. Make poor choices. I believe they call that *living*." She pulled in a deep breath and held it. Mama had always told her to hold her breath whenever she was angry to keep her from saying something she might regret. She wondered if holding her breath would keep her heart from shattering even more. "Sleep now. You need your rest."

"No," he said. "I need you."

"Well, you cannot have me," she said, even though her heart screamed for her to relent and return to her ridiculous ways of trusting him. "Rest. If you rest now, you might be able to eat a bit of gruel this afternoon."

"That is no way to entice me."

She turned and glared at him. "I do not care to entice you. Do what you need to do to heal, so we might both escape this cruel prison in which we find ourselves." She managed a stiff curtsy. "Mrs. Bean will return shortly. I shall inform her you are awake, so she and Edmund can finish bathing you and change your dressing."

"Felicity?"

She stared down at her hand on the door latch, her knuckles whitening as she tightened her grip. "What, my lord?"

"I am sorry."

"So am I, my lord. So am I." Then she charged from the room in search of her brother. She needed to leave this place as soon as possible. Since Drake no longer appeared to be at death's door, someone else could be paid to take over his care until he became well enough to care for himself. Perhaps Mrs. Bean and Edmund could do so before starting their employment at Broadmere Hall.

She found Chance downstairs in a corner of the dining room, sipping tea as he read a London paper that had to be old news by now. "I want to return home," she said, flopping down into an empty chair at his table. "Immediately."

Chance eyed her over the top of the paper, reminding her so much of Papa that she had to blink hard and fast to beat back the threat of tears. Drawing in a deep breath, then releasing it with a heavy sigh, he folded the *Times* and placed it on the table. "What has happened now?"

"Lord Wakefield is much improved and well on his way to recovery. With his fever gone, someone could be hired to care for him until he is strong enough to return to his home. We could hire the Beans. They could stay here and care for him until they are no longer needed. Then they could write to us, and we could fetch them to Broadmere Hall." She jutted her chin higher, daring her brother to argue. "I need to go home. I am done here."

"Are you?"

"What is that supposed to mean?"

"I have watched you these many days, Felli." Chance paused for another sip of his tea, then lowered his cup back to its saucer, staring down at it with a thoughtful, narrow-eyed glare. "The once-shy mouse turned into a protective lioness." He looked up at her. "A lioness protecting the one she loves."

"I do not love him."

"You also do not lie well." Chance shifted with another heavy sigh. "His uncle manipulated him, Felli. Not a soul in Binnocksbourne despised the man for himself—they didn't trust him because of his scoundrel of an uncle and all the debts the estate fell short of covering."

She clenched her fists in her lap. This was not how this conversation was supposed to go. Chance should be fetching a carriage or renting her a horse or something. "How would you know? We have not been back to Binnocksbourne for days and days."

He tapped on a leather pouch on the table. One she had failed to notice. "Along with my newspapers, Mr. Osbourne forwarded several letters from the villagers, the merchants to whom Wakefield owes the most money."

"Are they so bold as to mock me at this low point in my life?"

"They are not mocking you." Chance drew out one of the letters and slid it over to her. "They are speaking on Lord Wakefield's behalf, stating how very hard he tried to repay all his uncle's debts rather than avoid them or flee the country. In fact, most, if not all, have forgiven the remainder of what he owes. Your earl is debt free."

"He is not my earl, and it is not a matter of the money or the title. Why can no one understand that?" She thumped the table with her fist, uncaring that she sounded like a fractious toddler denied a treat. "He lied to me."

"He swore he was going to tell you at the proper time. Yes, it was a lie of omission—but not a bold, malicious lie in and of itself." Chance motioned to the maid tending the dining room. "More tea, please."

"I want to go home. Now. I should have gone rather than send for more dresses."

"And what exactly do you intend to do? Hide?" He leaned closer, his eyes filled with compassion and a hefty gleam of brotherly stubbornness. "This will not go away, Felli. Your heart will not allow it. Are you too young to remember how Mama and Papa sometimes were?"

Doing her best not to melt into a sniveling puddle, she straightened her spine. "What the blazes are you talking about?"

"That is not proper language for a lady, Felicity. Do not make me regret telling Serendipity to remain at home with Merry." He paused as the maid brought a fresh pot of tea and poured a cup for Felicity. Once she left them, he continued, "Mama and Papa loved each other with a fury. I do not deny that, but as the eldest, I remember many times when they also argued and fought each other with that same passion." He grinned. "Mama once used the coarsest sort of language with Papa. Words I had never heard before. They didn't realize I was in the room when they were arguing. I don't know what he had done, but she gave him a heated dressing-down—absolutely scalding, in fact."

Felicity folded her arms across her chest, hugging herself. "If you had never heard such words before, how did you know they were coarse?"

"Because Mama overheard me use those same words and washed my mouth out with soap from the laundress." He worked his mouth as if he could still taste it. "I never used those words again until university, and then my chums were quite impressed with my broadened vocabulary."

She hugged herself tighter. This conversation was not going as she had planned. "Your point, brother?"

"People who love each other do not always get on." He added milk to his tea and slowly stirred it. "Our married sisters would tell you the same, and you know it. How many times have they fussed and fought with the loves of their lives? Couples learn and grow as their relationship ages and becomes richer, like cheese or a fine wine."

"And how many times have *you* been in love, brother? How are you such an expert on marriage?"

"I do not claim to be an expert on anything other than my sisters, and I know what I have witnessed." He pulled three more letters out of the pouch. "These are for you. From Blessing, Fortuity, and Grace. I will bet you my favorite horse they are telling you the same thing I just said."

"I am not a fool, Chance. These letters have been opened."

He gave her the sheepish grin he always wore whenever caught doing something he shouldn't. "I failed to notice they were addressed to you and not me." His grin faded. "I didn't much like Wakefield until he saved your life." He patted the bulging leather mailbag again. "And any man who is thought well enough of to cause a merchant to forgive a sizeable debt deserves a second chance." He stared down at his tea and seemed almost sad. "We all deserve a second chance when we have chosen poorly with the very best of intentions."

Felicity studied her brother for a long moment, sensing this conversation wasn't entirely about her and Drake. "What have you done, Chance? When have you chosen poorly?"

He shook his head and started stirring his tea once more. "Many things were left unsaid between me and Papa." He shook his head faster. "Many things I should never have done. Things that made him ashamed of me."

Felicity reached across the table and took her brother's hand. "Papa loved you, Chance. You know that."

He twitched with a half-hearted shrug. "I know he loved me, but I never made him proud."

"You are doing so now." She squeezed his hand. "Even though you are impossible at times, I feel certain Papa and Mama both are pleased with you."

"I hope so," he said quietly, then leveled a hard gaze upon her. "Give Wakefield time to heal and explain himself fully, even though you think you know the entirety of his story. He deserves that much, Felli, before you fully condemn him. Both of you deserve that much, and then, if you still wish to end the engagement, do so."

"In other words, you refuse to let me go home?"

He nodded. "I refuse to let you hide until you have put your demons to rest."

"Fine." She would do as he asked. This time. She waved down the maid, motioning for her to come over. "Have you any eels? I need a bucketful."

"Felicity!" Chance pointed at her as if she were a naughty child. "Don't you dare."

She smiled, knowing all along she wouldn't take a bucket of eels upstairs to his bed. She hated the slimy things—but Chance didn't know that.

Chapter Seventeen

"WHERE IS SHE?" Drake asked the maid who had been helping Mrs. Bean take care of him for the past several days.

"Who, my lord?" The girl propped the window open wider, scooted a wooden rack over in front of it, then draped clean bandages across it to dry in the breezy sunshine.

"Lady Felicity." Drake tried not to snap at the servant, but the chit knew very well whom he meant. "The duke's sister. I have not seen her for days. Has she gone?" Gads alive, he hoped not. Not when he had finally decided to follow her around on his knees until she forgave him. They could not end this way. He needed to prove to her that he could do so much better.

When the maid didn't answer, he thumped the bed, flinching as the searing pain shot through his shoulder, reminding him he shouldn't do that. "You know bloody well who I mean. Where is she?"

"Mrs. Bean should be the one to tell you, my lord." The girl curtsied and hurried from the room.

"Damn and blast." Drake gritted his teeth and floundered to shove himself higher in the bed. He was sick of being flat on his back and weak as a kitten. He went still and held his breath as the door creaked open again, but it turned out to be the insufferable Mr. Warner.

"And how are we feeling today, my lord?" the surgeon asked

in a tone that clearly stated he couldn't possibly care less about Drake's well-being.

"I am shedding this bed." Breaking out in a cold sweat, Drake forced himself to an upright position, then swung his legs over the side.

"Take care now, my lord." Warner rushed forward and caught him just as he lost his balance and veered to one side. "Do you care so little for my handiwork? I removed your stitches only yesterday. If you fall, you will split the wound open wide all over again."

"Leave me, quack." Drake swallowed hard. Bile burned the back of his throat, churning his innards with a queasiness that would not bode well if it didn't settle soon. "I must rise. Strengthen myself. I have to return to Broadmere Hall."

"Why?" Warner didn't release him. Instead, the man had the gall to hold him there as he teetered unsteadily on the side of the bed. "If you wish to speak with His Grace, I can send a maid for him."

"Not that you have any right to ask, but I do not wish to speak with His Grace. I demand to see his sister, Lady Felicity."

"Demand?" Warner laughed. "I admire your spirit, my lord. A man in your condition issuing demands."

"Is she still here, damn you?"

"She is. In the kitchen, I believe. Showing our cook one of her recipes." Warner chuckled again. "Mrs. Warner cannot seem to get enough of her chocolate biscuits."

"I have not seen her in over two days." Drake didn't care that he sounded like a spoiled child. He wanted to see Felicity. "It is imperative that I see her."

Warner narrowed his eyes and grunted, an annoying habit Drake had noticed before. "You are weak, my lord, and cannot expect to roam the inn in search of her. If you would be so kind as to lie back down, I will speak with His Grace and inquire as to whether his sister might be fetched." After a curt shake of his head, he added, "I make no promises. One can predict nothing when it comes to women."

Not about to admit defeat so easily, Drake pointed at a small writing desk in the corner. "Help me sit upright long enough in this infernal bed to write to her. I beg you."

The surgeon scowled at him. "I do not recommend that just yet, my lord. You must be stronger first."

"I will never get any stronger if I do not push myself. Are you going to help me or not?"

Warner's usual scowl deepened. "Fine, my lord. Hold fast and let me know if you need the chamber pot."

Drake very nearly did cast up his accounts as the man helped him position himself back against the headboard with the support of multiple pillows. As the surgeon fetched quill, ink, and paper, he closed his eyes and sucked in deep breaths to regain control of the pain before his vision darkened any more with the threat of unconsciousness.

The cool rim of a cup was pressed against his mouth.

"Small sips, my lord," Mr. Warner ordered him, "and continue breathing deeply while I fetch the items you require."

"Thank you," Drake whispered. He would do this task. It could very well be his last chance to convince Felicity to bless him with her presence. Blinking away the sweat running into his eyes, he sipped the water as instructed and also noted the surgeon had placed a basin within reach.

"My wife insisted we put my old lap desk in this particular room." Mr. Warner set it across Drake's legs. "The woman amazes me at times."

"I appreciate her foresight." Drake concentrated on what he wished to write to the woman who held his fate in her hands. "This will not take long. I have repeated these words over and over in my mind several times."

This was his last chance. He dare not waste it.

THE YOUNG WOMAN cleared her throat with a loud *harrumph* and curtsied. "My lady?"

Kneading the dough as if it had wronged her, Felicity hadn't noticed the maid Chance had hired to help Mrs. Bean with Drake's care. On that, Felicity had remained steadfast. She had agreed to stay at the inn, but she would not be spending every waking moment at Drake's bedside. Her heart simply could not bear it.

Without taking her focus from the soon-to-be bread, she worked the dough harder. "Yes?"

"For you, my lady. From his lordship." The girl held out a folded bit of paper.

Felicity eyed it as if it were a viper. "From Lord Wakefield?"

The maid nodded. "He asked that I put it in your hands rather than leave it in your room."

"Did he now?" Felicity wiped her hands on her apron, then took it from the girl while trying to keep from shaking. "Thank you."

The maid curtsied again, then hurried away, leaving Felicity alone beside the kitchen worktable.

It took her a moment to realize she was the only one in the kitchen. "I sense a conspiracy," she told the bread dough as she unfolded the letter. "He must indeed be doing better." But it wasn't a letter. It was a poem from her eloquent, yet lying, earl.

*A **Gentleman's Plea** by One Most Contrite*

O fairest lady, whose tender glance once shed
A radiance brighter than heaven's own spread—
If, by my folly, chill silence and pride,
I dimmed the star that once in thy heart did bide,
Then here I kneel, with humble breath implore,
That your mercy lift me from death's dark shore.

No honor mine, who shattered thy trust;
My pride lies broken, naught but dust.

I let my tongue be bridled by fear,
When truth, not silence, thou didst deserve to hear.
Yet know, sweet love, my heart was ever true,
Thou art its liberty, its joy, its view.

Recall, my dearest, our walks 'neath lilac skies,
Thy laughter like larks when the dawn did rise.
Oh, let not shadows steal that tender bloom,
Restore me, I pray, from this self-fashioned doom.

Forgiveness! I beg thee but one word,
That hope may breathe again where despair has stirred.
Let mercy's grace thy wounded heart employ,
And I shall prove my love with steadfast joy.

For what is life, if not to love thee still?
And what am I, if not absolved by thy will?
Speak, beloved, and grant me but this grace—
To live redeemed within thy fond embrace.

"Bah! Most contrite, indeed." But his words touched her more than they should, making tears escape before she could stop them. *Do not be such a fool.* She squinted her eyes tightly shut and swiped the tears away. Whatever should she do? This poem captured her soul even more fiercely than his ode to her coddled eggs.

Fierce like a lioness. Not cowardly like a mouse. She clutched the poem to her heart, wanting to be courageous but not wanting to be a fool.

In their letters, her sisters had stressed that Drake's lies of omission were out of fear that he might lose her and not merely because of her dowry, which he had denounced, and remained firm on that count. The gossip about his proposing to other women had proven to be just that—gossip. He couldn't very well control what others said about him. And as each of her siblings had so boldly pointed out, if he had not dived in front of her, the bullet he had taken would have hit her.

She stared down at the poem, knowing she would cherish it forever. "Drat it all, I do love him. What the devil is wrong with me?"

Tapping the page with her thumb, she made up her mind. She rushed from the kitchen, calling out to the scullery maid peeping at her from the pantry. "Please finish the bread. I have a letter to write."

STILL SITTING UPRIGHT in bed with the lap desk beside him, Drake kept his focus locked on a crack in the wall across the room. Had Felicity read his plea, or had she tossed it into the nearest fire? "Let her read it," he whispered to any benevolent entities who might be passing through. "Let the words of my heart touch hers."

A tapping on the door interrupted him. It couldn't be Mrs. Bean or Edmund. Neither of them ever knocked. "Come in."

A different maid from the one who had carried off his original message entered. Gaze lowered, she paused just inside the door and curtsied. "A letter from Lady Felicity, my lord."

Both eager and yet dreading to read the missive's contents, Drake motioned the girl forward. "Thank you."

She hurried to place it in his hand, dropped a quick curtsy, then scurried back out again as if he were the devil incarnate.

After a hard swallow, he broke the seal and slowly unfolded it, fully expecting three simple words: *I reject you.* When the page revealed more than that, his heart pounded as he devoured every word.

The Lady's Reply *by One Not Easily Moved, Yet Not Unmoved*

Thou speakest now of love and rueful pain,

Of pride laid low and words thou wouldst reclaim.
Yet though thy voice with trembling sorrow pleads,
The hurt thou gave my heart yet softly bleeds.

For true love's hand should never wield a blade,
Nor turn from warmth till hearts grow half afraid.
Yet still—thine eyes hold embers, faint but bright,
A candle flickering through the tempest's night.

Thou called to mind the lilacs, and our spring,
The laughter that once made my spirit sing.
And lo—my heart, though bruised by folly's art,
Still leans toward thee, as flowers toward light do part.

I shall not yield with girlish sigh or feigned forget,
Nor let soft lashes hide my heart's regret.
But mark me well, if thou wouldst seek anew:
Love is not seized—it is earned, and true.

Rise, dear sir; thy penance but begins,
Not with fair vows, but deeds the day rescinds.
Let constancy guard thee, let honor guide thy tongue,
Perhaps then I shall see again the man I once loved.

Forgiveness awaits—not like a prize to win,
But as a hearth where warmth may grow again.
Tend it slow and steadfast, ever proving true,
And we may find the love we once knew.

Hands trembling, he reread the last stanza. "Forgiveness awaits," he repeated. Dare he hope and pray that this graceful response was the promise of another chance?

If he were strong enough, he would run to find her and drop to his knees. At best, all he could do was write her a response so heartfelt that it would surely bring her to his door.

Dragging the desk back onto his lap, he selected a fresh page from inside it, inked his quill, and stared at the paper for a long moment. Then the words came to him. Yes. Surely, this response would coax her to return to his bedside. He prayed it would, because nothing would strengthen him more than her presence at his side.

FELICITY SAT BESIDE the bay window in the inn's dining room, sipping her tea but not tasting a thing. For all she knew, she could be drinking water from a puddle on the lane. Her mind was a whirlwind, and her poor, battered heart was no better. How would Drake take her response? Would he understand the conditions she had woven through her poem? Would he realize how strongly she meant them? Yes, she loved him, but she needed to be able to trust him. Trust was just as important as love. At least, it was to her.

"I be going to check in on Lord Wakefield." Mrs. Bean toddled up to her, leaning heavily on her cane. "Be you coming, gal, or are you still making him stew in his iniquities?" With a weary grunt, the old woman lowered herself into a chair. "This town life be making me soft. I hope His Grace don't be finding me lacking by the time we get to your home."

"You could never be found lacking, Mrs. Bean." Felicity took another sip of her tea and noticed it had gone cold. "And I am uncertain whether I will visit Lord Wakefield today or not. It depends."

"On what?"

"How he responds to my letter."

Mrs. Bean eyed her with a confused scowl. "The man is abed in a room upstairs, and you wrote him a letter?"

"He started it." Realizing she sounded like a petulant child, Felicity cleared her throat and adjusted her tone. "He wrote me a poem, and I responded in like terms."

"A poem?" Mrs. Bean seemed most unimpressed before slowly shaking her head. "Appears to me that a man's actions say a great deal more than his words. He saved you, gal."

"I am aware of that, but his untruthfulness put me in that dangerous situation in the first place."

Mrs. Bean frowned, staring out the window while resetting her grip on the knobbed handle of her cane. "He told me about that." She barely nodded while thoughtfully pursing her lips. "Sounded genuinely sorry for all that happened and the *way* that it happened. I be thinking he meant well." She shifted her attention to Felicity. "He be a good man, gal. Just made some poor choices. Any of us might have done the same."

"Yes…well…" Felicity allowed herself a determined sigh. "He and I are attempting to sort ourselves through all that."

"Lady Felicity?"

Felicity turned to the maid, her heart leaping at the sight of the letter she held out. "Yes?"

"From Lord Wakefield." The girl handed it over, curtsied, then hurried away.

Mrs. Bean pushed herself up from her chair. "I leave you with your letter, gal. I hope you and his lordship can sort things out." She slowly toddled away, heading for the stairs just beyond the archway of the dining room.

Taking another sip of her tepid tea to wet her suddenly dry mouth, Felicity stared at the letter on the table in front of her. This letter, this reply, would decide her on what to do. She slid her finger underneath the wax seal and unfolded it.

His Vow Renewed *by One Reborn in Love's Light*

Thy words, though tempered and sweet, strike keen and clear,
A just command, which I hold most dear.
Thou asked not for vows in idle air,
But daily proof, in shadow and in fair.

So be it, my love; I cast aside the guise
Of silence easy and of comfort lies.
If time must weigh me, let the years proclaim
That I am worthy to speak thy cherished name.

At each new dawn, with reverence I shall rise,
And frame each word with care, not vain disguise.
No timid hush shall keep my truths apart;
I shall honor thee with deed as well as heart.

To tend love's hearth, as thou hast wisely shown,
I shall not bring flowers false, but bread well grown.
I will walk beside thee through sun and storm,
And guard thy soul, and keep thy spirit warm.

Not perfect—nay—but willing to amend,
Your faithful lover to the very end.
And shouldest thou, in thy time, call me to be thine,
No treasure on earth shall I more richly prize as mine.

"My faithful lover to the very end," she whispered. She traced the words with a trembling finger. He would guard her soul and keep her spirit warm. Walk beside her through sun and storm.

She hugged the note to her heart. This was as precious as a wedding vow. She fanned herself with the letter, determined not to weep in front of the inn's patrons. Ever so carefully, she refolded the precious words and, after a surreptitious glance around, tucked it inside her bodice next to her heart. It was time to go upstairs and speak with him face to face.

Her steps slowed as she climbed the stairs. How could his room possibly seem so far away? When he'd suffered with the fever, she had flown up and down this stairway, helping the maids fetch anything and everything that might help him heal.

He had very nearly died. She halted at that sobering thought. What if he had? She clutched a hand to her heart. Thank the

Almighty, he had been spared. Now, it was time to do something with this chance they had been given.

When she reached his door, she stared at it for a long while before summoning the courage to knock.

Mrs. Bean pulled it open barely a crack, rewarded her with a toothless smile, then swung it open wide. "Come in, Lady Felicity."

Lady Felicity? The term of address surprised her. Mrs. Bean had always called her *gal*, even after discovering her full identity. Felicity didn't mind. Mrs. Bean had become a good friend. "Thank you," she said as she stepped into the room, forcing herself to walk with a calm demeanor and not run to Drake's bedside. But when her eyes met his, a shuddering gasp escaped her.

He reached for her, his smile hesitant yet hopeful. "Felicity?"

"Your vow renewed," she said as she went to him and took his hand. "Did you mean it? Every word?"

"I would not have written it if I had not meant it." He pressed her hand to his mouth, closing his eyes as he treated her to a lingering kiss across the backs of her fingers. "I will prove I meant them. Each and every day for the rest of our lives."

"I be going to fetch more linens," Mrs. Bean announced in an overly loud voice. "A maid will be up soon with more water." She left the room, closing the door behind her with a soft thud.

"Thank you," Drake said in a hoarse whisper. "Thank you for the opportunity to make us right."

Easing her hand free of his, Felicity drew a chair closer to the side of the bed. While it was scandalous enough for her to be in here without a chaperone and her reputation already hung in tatters, she refused to sit beside him on the edge of the bed.

"Thank you," she said, "for saving my life."

"You are my heart."

Struggling to do more than sit there and lose herself in his hazel eyes, she forced her gaze away. But it didn't stray far. She boldly reached out and touched the perfectly sculpted line of his jaw. "You need a shave. That is more than a day's dusting of stubble." But she liked it on him. It lent him a wildness, a wildness that fit him well.

"Mrs. Bean promised to see to that this afternoon." He arched a brow. "There are not many whom I allow near my throat with a well-honed blade."

"You are highly thought of, my lord." She remembered what Chance had told her. "Once people realized you were not your uncle, they considered you a good man, like your father."

"His Grace told me about the merchants forgiving my debts." He slowly shook his head in disbelief. "They are too good to me. Especially after Uncle George took such unfair advantage of them."

"You paid them some of what was owed. They appreciated what you tried to do."

"If I am ever able, I will repay them in full. They are businessmen. Their profits feed their families." He held her hand tighter, lacing his fingers through hers. "Dare I hope this means we might progress with the reading of the banns?"

Struggling to overcome what felt like thousands of winged beasties fluttering in her middle, Felicity pulled in a deep breath, then slowly allowed it to ease back out. "Yes," she said, unable to speak above a whisper. "But I wish to marry in Binnocksbourne. Not here."

"I understand. It is enough to know we shall marry."

"Marry," she repeated, fighting the winged beasties with a hard swallow. "I usually plan the wedding breakfast for the bride, and now, I am finally able to organize my own." She held his hand between both of hers. "I fear coddled eggs and soldiers simply won't do, but I promise you something just as delicious."

"As long as I have you, I will have everything I need."

"I love you." The words sprang from her of their own volition.

Solemn as a slate gravestone, his eyes dark with emotion, he kissed her hand again. "I love you more and always will."

Chapter Eighteen

A PLEASANT BREEZE wafted through the open windows and doors of Binnocksbourne's only church, but beads of sweat still trickled down Drake's spine as he stood at the altar. Gads alive, was the place truly that stifling, or was he a coward at heart? Or could it be because he stood in front of Felicity's entire family? Her sisters, their husbands, and, surprisingly, their children, who appeared to range in age from less than a year old to the more mature Duke of Wolfebourne's siblings, who Felicity had said were nine years old each. Or was it ten? Among the children was an army of nannies, tending to their charges. And, of course, Broadmere, Felicity's brother, sat in the front row, stone-faced as always.

Drake resettled his footing and rolled his shoulders, trying to ease his tensed muscles, which stirred the ache in his healed wound that still twinged now and then. It didn't matter. All that mattered was that today, Felicity would become his wife. They had been through so very much and still found themselves here. He thanked the Almighty for making Felicity such a forgiving, understanding woman. For all the rest of his days, he would do his very best to give her the happiness she so richly deserved.

The vicar, Mr. Donaldson, joined him at the altar, and the man did not at all look pleased.

Unwilling to allow anyone or anything to spoil this day, Drake edged closer to the man and spoke in a hushed voice for the vicar's ears alone. "Is there an issue of which I am unaware, Mr. Donaldson?"

"This family's repeated insistence upon an *abbreviated* ceremony rather than the customary rites and words as are written in our *Book of Common Prayer* sorely grates upon my belief of that which is right and true."

A sense of relief eased Drake's nervousness. "Will we not still be legally wed even though we requested to speak the vows as our hearts wrote them?"

The vicar cleared his throat with an indignant *harrumph*. "That is not the point, my lord. Not the point at all."

Drake bit the inside of his bottom lip to keep from smiling and inciting Mr. Donaldson any further. "The Lord our God will surely forgive us for this slight change to the ceremony. It is most important to us, Mr. Donaldson, and we greatly appreciate your understanding."

That seemed to smooth the vicar's ruffled feathers somewhat. "It is indeed my hope that you and Lady Felicity are blessed with endless years of happiness, my lord." He gave Drake a long, pointed look. "The two of you have fought valiantly to reach this day."

"Indeed, we have, Mr. Donaldson."

The village musicians, a trio of men, one with a violin, one a flute, and one a cello, sent a bright, airy song through the tiny church, announcing to one and all that the bride had arrived and was coming down the aisle to join her groom.

A roaring in Drake's ears brought on by his pounding heart drowned out the sweet music. His Felicity, his precious, lovely bride, floated toward him like the angel he had always known her to be. Her wide blue eyes sparkled with love and happiness. The delicate headpiece of tiny white flowers and silky ribbons couldn't compare with the rich golden sheen of her curls. Her morning gown of white with the daintiest embroidered yellow flowers gracefully flowed around her. Those lips of hers, plump and red as sweet berries, made him wet his own and struggle to keep his thoughts as pure as this moment required. Gads alive, he loved this woman so very much.

When she reached him, he took her hand even though he knew it wasn't yet time. He couldn't help it.

Mr. Donaldson cleared his throat and fixed a pointed glare on their joined hands for a long moment, then gave up and rolled his eyes when they held fast to one another. With a resigned huff, he looked out upon the congregation and lifted the small, worn book in his hands. "Dearly beloved, we are gathered together here in the sight of God, and in the face of this congregation, to join together this man and this woman in holy matrimony; which is an honorable estate, instituted of God in the time of man's innocency, signifying unto us the mystical union that is betwixt Christ and his church; which holy estate Christ adorned and beautified with his presence, and the first miracle that he wrought, in Cana of Galilee; and is commended of Saint Paul to be honorable among all men: and therefore is not by any to be enterprised, nor taken in hand, unadvisedly, lightly, or wantonly, to satisfy men's carnal lusts and appetites, like brute beasts that have no understanding; but reverently, discreetly, advisedly, soberly, and in the fear of God; duly considering the causes for which matrimony was ordained."

He paused, pulled in a deep breath, and turned the page, making Drake wonder if the vicar had changed his mind and decided to plow forward with a full serving of the long ceremony contained in the *Book of Common Prayer*. But there was little he could do other than squeeze Felicity's hand.

The vicar continued, raising his voice, "First, matrimony was ordained for the procreation of children, to be brought up in the fear and nurture of the Lord, and to the praise of His holy name. Secondly, it was ordained for a remedy against sin, and to avoid fornication; that such persons as have not the gift of continency might marry, and keep themselves undefiled members of Christ's body. Thirdly, it was ordained for the mutual society, help, and comfort that the one ought to have of the other, both in prosperity and adversity. Into which holy estate these two persons present come now to be joined. Therefore, if any man can show just cause why they may not lawfully be joined together, let him now speak, or else hereafter forever hold his peace." Mr. Donaldson halted once more and looked out across the congregation, waiting for what seemed like forever. With a curt nod, he read on, "I require and charge you both, as ye will answer at the dreadful day of judgment when the secrets of all hearts shall be disclosed, that if either of you know any impediment, why ye may not be lawfully joined together in matrimony, ye do now confess it. For be ye well assured that so many as are coupled together otherwise than God's Word doth allow are not joined together by God; neither is their matrimony lawful."

Drake swallowed hard. The only reason he knew that they shouldn't be married was that he didn't deserve Felicity. Other than that, they should be good.

He stole a glance at her and was fortified by her reassuring smile. Was now the time they were supposed to speak their personal vows?

Apparently not, since the vicar cleared his throat again and turned another page. "Drake Bartholemew Pemberton, wilt thou have this woman to be thy wedded wife, to live together after God's ordinance in the holy estate of matrimony? Wilt thou love her, comfort her, honor, and keep her in sickness and in health; and, forsaking all other, keep thee only unto her, so long as ye both shall live?"

"I will," Drake said a little too loudly. The words rang through the small church.

Mr. Donaldson arched both eyebrows at him, then turned to Felicity. "Felicity Bethianna Jasmine Abarough, wilt thou have this man to be thy wedded husband, to live together after God's ordinance in the holy estate of matrimony? Wilt thou obey him, and serve him, love, honor, and keep him in sickness and in health; and, forsaking all other, keep thee only unto him, so long as ye both shall live?"

"I will," Felicity said, then squeezed Drake's hand.

The vicar snapped his book shut and once more scanned the congregation, which consisted wholly of Felicity's family and some of their servants. His narrow-eyed gaze seemed to settle on one sister in particular, but Drake couldn't tell which one. "Once again," Mr. Donaldson said, "an abbreviated and more personalized ceremony was requested." He blew out a heavy sigh. "And once again, my wife informed me I was not to refuse."

The quiet tittering of laughter swept through the pews.

The vicar nodded at Drake. "Now, my lord, and do not forget the ring at the end."

"I prefer to do the ring at the beginning, Mr. Donaldson." Drake smiled. "I am sure you understand."

"It appears I have little choice." Mr. Donaldson tucked his holy book in the crook of his arm and offered another curt nod for them to continue.

After Felicity handed her bridal bouquet of roses to Merry, she turned back to him with a shy smile.

Drake pulled the ring from his pocket, the precious gold ring his father had given to his mother on their wedding day, and one of the few things Drake had refused to sell. He placed it on Felicity's finger, smiling at the perfect fit. Their union was meant to be. His parents had blessed it.

Still holding to the ring, he said, "With this ring I thee wed, with my body I thee worship, and with all my worldly goods I thee endow. In the name of the Father, and the Son, and the Holy Ghost. Amen."

She caught her bottom lip between her teeth, her eyes shining with tears.

He kissed her hand, then brushed an escaped tear from her cheek, and brought it to his lips. "My dearest heart, before God and these witnesses, I bind myself to thee—not merely in duty, but in affection, admiration, and unwavering resolve. Thy happiness shall be my purpose, thy sorrows mine to share. I vow to honor thee, to guard thee, and to stand beside thee in every season and trial—until the stars dim and time forgets our names."

She touched his cheek and nodded. "My beloved, with full heart and steady hand, I give myself to thee—freely, wholly, and without reserve. Thy name shall be my comfort, thy arms my home. I shall walk beside thee through all of life's tempests and triumphs, ever seeking to bring thee peace and gladness. As long as breath is mine, my love shall be thine."

Mr. Donaldson cleared his throat yet again, but not with quite as much irritation as before. "Let us pray. Oh eternal God, Creator and Preserver of all mankind, Giver of all spiritual grace, the Author of everlasting life; send thy blessing upon these Thy servants, this man and this woman, whom we bless in Thy name; that, as Isaac and Rebecca lived faithfully together, so these persons may surely perform and keep the vow and covenant betwixt them made, whereof this ring given and received is a token and pledge, and may ever remain in perfect love and peace together, and live according to thy laws; through Jesus Christ our Lord. Amen."

He reached forward and joined Drake and Felicity's right hands together. "Those whom God hath joined together, let no man put asunder." Then he held a hand up and looked to the congregation. "Forasmuch as Drake Bartholemew Pemberton and Felicity Bethianna Jasmine Abarough have consented together in holy wedlock, and have witnessed the same before God and this company, and thereto have given and pledged their troth either to other, and have declared the same by giving and receiving of a ring, and by joining of hands, I pronounce that they be man and wife together, in the name of the Father, and of the Son, and the Holy Ghost. Amen."

He snapped his fingers at shuffling in the pews, then turned to Drake and Felicity as he continued, "God the Father, God the Son, God the Holy Ghost, bless, preserve, and keep you; the Lord mercifully with his favor look upon you; and so fill you with all spiritual benediction and grace, that ye may so live together in this life, that in the world to come ye may have life everlasting. Amen."

"Amen!" shouted one of the more exuberant children who had escaped the clutches of their nanny.

The church erupted with laughter and more shouts of "Amen!"

Drake took Felicity's hands in his and kissed them. "We are married, my angel."

"Married at last," she said. "Married at last."

The musicians struck up a lively tune, and the family swarmed them as they hurried down the aisle and swept outside to the cheering villagers who had gathered to wish them well.

Happier than he could ever remember being, Drake helped Felicity up into the ribbon- and flower-bedecked barouche that would take them to Broadmere Hall for the wedding breakfast that Felicity had planned but entrusted Cook and Mrs. Bean to prepare. As they rolled away from the church, Drake tossed handfuls of coins to the anxiously awaiting children. Felicity's brother had insisted upon providing bags of pennies, saying it was his right and place to do so. Drake had chosen not to argue, even though it had stung his pride until Felicity assured him it was the bride's family who usually treated the village children to the wedding scramble. Even though the tradition was more commonly known in Scotland, the young ones of Binnocksbourne caught on to it with great gusto.

"Have a seat now, my lord. Wouldn't want to tip you out on your wedding day." With a hearty wink, Drake's driver, John, tipped his hat, which had been decorated with ribbons and flowers that matched the ones festooning the carriage. "God bless you both, Lord and Lady Wakefield. I be wishing you endless years of happiness."

"Thank you, John." Drake settled into the seat beside his new wife, unable to imagine being any happier.

Felicity slid her hand into his, beaming at him with such love, he considered himself the most blessed man in all creation. "To endless years of joy."

He couldn't resist. He leaned forward and kissed her, breathing her in like a man starving for air.

Behind them, the villagers cheered even louder, sending them on their way with the very best possible start to their lives as husband and wife.

"YOU ARE SHAKING, my lady," Daisy said with a knowing smile. "Did your sisters frighten you with all they told you about your wedding night?" She unwound Felicity's hair and brushed it until it was a golden river of curls streaming down across Felicity's shoulders.

"I am not so sure *frightened* would be the apt word." Felicity pulled in a deep breath and rubbed her damp palms against the lace-trimmed chemise her sisters had presented for her to wear on her wedding night, along with their advice on what to expect. She almost wished they hadn't told her in such startling detail of all the reportedly wondrous feelings a husband and wife could share. "I am not frightened," she repeated, more to convince herself than to convince her maid. "I am simply nervous."

"All that matters is the love, my lady." Daisy set the hairbrush on the dressing table and stepped aside with a reassuring smile. "That's what my mum always said, and she would know. Her and my da never had much, but they always had love to spare."

"I know I love him," Felicity said, "and he loves me. I am sure of it."

"Good night, my lady." Daisy eased out of the room, closing the door behind her with a soft click.

Felicity remained sitting in front of the dressing table, eyeing herself in the mirror. Heart pounding, she wet her lips and tried to slow her breathing as she turned and looked at the door connecting her bedchamber with Drake's. This was home now, the home she and Drake would return to its former glorious state and fill with love and laughter.

She went to the door and took hold of the latch. How in heaven's name could she be so eager to run into the arms of the man she loved, and so reluctant at the same time? Were all brides this way, or was she simply mad? Well, if she was mad, then mad about Drake she would be.

After a deep breath, she squared her shoulders and squeezed the latch, only to find it locked. Locked?

"Drake?" She hesitantly rapped on the door.

"Come in, my angel."

"I cannot. The door is locked."

"Locked?" The soft thud of his footsteps grew louder, then the latch rattled. "Bloody hell." It rattled again, harder this time. "Damn and blast it all."

Felicity couldn't help but giggle. Their entire relationship had been fraught with mishaps. Why should their wedding night be any different?

The door shook with a hard bang as something quite solid hit it. "Damned English oak. You worthless piece of..."

Before Drake injured himself and swore any more profusely at the stubborn door, Felicity rushed out into the hall and hurried to his bedchamber door, which, thankfully, was not locked. "Drake?"

He had the iron rod from the hearth hooked through the latch of the connecting door and was about to pry the thing free of its frame. "Felicity." He dropped the rod and brushed his hands on the seat of his breeches, looking as sheepish as a schoolboy caught being naughty.

She bit her lip, trying not to laugh. "Did you hurt yourself when you hit the door? I assume you rammed it with your shoulder."

"I used my good shoulder." He ambled closer, making her catch her breath at the sight of him with his shirt open at the throat. "That door will be opened tomorrow," he said as he gently pulled her into his arms, "and it will never be locked again."

She hesitantly ran her hands up the ridges of his muscular chest, her breath hitching. "I know we are married, but this still feels quite scandalous." She brazenly pressed closer and offered up her mouth to him. "I do not mean to shock you, but I am most ready for more of your delectable kisses."

He grinned as he bent to brush teasing nibbles across her lips. "Delectable, you say?"

"Indeed, most delectable."

As he obliged and cupped her bottom with both hands, her senses reeled. She returned his kisses with a wildness that shocked her, but dear heavens, to be in his arms felt so indescribably right and made the room overly warm.

"Clothes," she whispered against his mouth.

He drew back and arched a brow. "Clothes?"

A furious blush had to be staining her cheeks, because they burned as hot as a stoked oven, but she pressed on, determined to be the passionate lioness rather than the skittish mouse. To force herself out of her temporary shyness, she cleared her throat. "We are wearing entirely too many clothes. Do you not agree?"

"I do indeed." He eased back a step while untucking his shirt, then stripped it off over his head.

She had seen his bare chest before while tending to him after the shooting, but this…this did not compare. The candlelight lent a golden glow to his skin that made her palms itch to touch him.

He unbuttoned his falls and let his breeches drop to the floor, revealing a masculinity the likes of which she had never seen in any painting or sculpture.

"Oh my." She pressed a hand to her throat, unsure exactly how they could possibly *fit* together.

He hurried back to her, pulling her into his arms and whispering, "It will be all right, my angel. We shall take our time and discover every joy we are meant to know." Ever so gently, he untied the neckline of her chemise and slid it off her shoulders, kissing a trail along her collarbone as he let it crumple lower. "My goddess," he murmured against her while teasing her to distraction with artful flicks of his tongue. "My angel."

Without warning, he swept her up into his arms and carried her to the bed, easing her down among the pillows. "I love you, my darling wife, forever and a day."

"I love you more." She reached for him, aching for more, longing to lose herself in his embrace. She buried her fingers in his thick hair as he kissed his way back down her throat and worshipped each of her breasts. "Oh, dear heavens." She wrapped her legs around him. The feel of him sliding against her inner thighs drove her mad.

Then he kissed and nibbled lower still while stroking his hands the length of her. Crouched between her legs, he paused long enough to blow a tickling breath of air across her most private curls while sliding his fingertips through the wetness in the place no man had ever touched before. Heaven help her. What kept a person from dying of such pleasure?

But then he slid a finger inside while closing his mouth around a part of her that felt ready to explode from such undeniable bliss. The more he touched her, the harder he sucked, the more the aching throbbed, making her heartbeat pound in her ears. A shriek burst free of her as the ecstasy spiraled out of control, reached its pinnacle, and shook through her in crashing waves of pleasure.

Drake kissed his way back up the length of her as the wondrous feeling ebbed but still vibrated through her, leaving in its wake a delicious sense of completeness. Well, almost complete. Even though he had sated her ache with expertise and delightful finesse, there was more she needed. She needed him to join with her, unite them, make them one rather than two.

"More," she whispered against his mouth while arching up to meet him. "Show me more. Make me yours."

He smiled down at her. "As I am yours, so are you mine." With a shift of his hips, he nudged against her, easing his way inside. As he tenderly kissed her, a groan rumbled free of him, and he pressed his forehead to hers. "Gads alive. You are so very tight."

"Is that bad?" she asked, a little more than breathless with each passing moment.

"No, my love." He pushed in deeper still, then paused again. "I simply do not wish to hurt you."

She smoothed her legs up and down his sides, unable to keep from wiggling beneath him. She needed more and needed it now. "My sisters said it's just a little sting and well worth it." Beyond the point of worrying about being brazen, she raked her fingers down his back and squeezed his buttocks. "More, my love. Take me fully. Please—I beg you."

With a quick thrust, he rocked into her, making her gasp at a sudden tearing sensation that was as bearable as her sisters had described. Immediately, he halted and stared down at her, his eyes filled with worry. "Are you all right, my love? Shall I stop and leave you be?"

"Do not dare leave me be, or I shall never forgive you."

"I could not bear to be unforgiven by you." He settled into a slow rhythm that promised the return of the earlier ecstasy.

A most unladylike moan escaped her, but she didn't care as she arched to meet him with every thrust. Yes, that wondrous bliss was well within reach, and this storm of passion promised to be even more satisfying than before. Much to her delight, the rhythm of the ancient dance moved faster, harder. Euphoria exploded, crashing through her like the waves of a stormy sea.

With a roaring bellow, Drake buried deep and held fast, shuddering with every muscle tensed. Then he collapsed on top of her, catching himself on his forearms to keep from crushing her. She pulled him down the rest of the way, reveling in the heat of his flesh sliding against hers. Now, she fully understood why mamas kept their daughters closely chaperoned and away from rogues and rakes.

He pressed a slow, tender kiss to her forehead. "Gads alive, woman. I love you more than you will ever know."

"Was I all right, then?" She knew it had been wonderful to

her, but would a man of experience find the same pleasure?

He rose and stared down at her, slowly shaking his head. "You were perfection itself, my love. Not merely *all right.*" He idly smoothed a stray curl out of her face, then traced his thumb across her cheek. "Never before have I experienced such a wondrous completeness, my love, all because of you."

She smoothed her hands up and down his sides, unable to get enough of touching him. "And to think, all this started with coddled eggs and soldiers."

He laughed and kissed her heartily enough to stir and reawaken that lovely ache at her core that he seemed to control. "To coddled eggs and soldiers, my love, the supper of lovers."

Epilogue

En route to Lady Joy's annual Yule celebration at Winterstone Estate
England's Lake District
December 1825

"WE MUST TURN around and return home. Immediately."
Drake held Felicity steady as she cast up her accounts
in the snow beside the carriage. "You are not well at all."

"The festive season will not be complete if we miss Joy's Yule
celebration." Felicity sagged against him, breathing as hard as if
she had run alongside the carriage rather than ridden inside it.
"Oh dear. Hold fast." She doubled over and retched again with
such force that Drake flinched.

"I forbid it," he said. "You are unwell and should be home in
bed, allowing Mrs. Pepperhill, Mrs. Bean, and me to care for you.
We are turning the carriage around."

"We are not!" Felicity burst into tears and vomited some
more.

Gads alive. Not more tears. She had been so weepy of late.
Drake felt the worst sort of lout for making his beloved angel so
unhappy. "Felicity, please. I am so concerned for you. Please do
not cry. It will only make you worse."

"I cannot help it!" She stamped her foot and glared at him.
"All of this is because I am with child." She poked him in the
chest. "But I didn't wish to tell you until Christmas Eve, and now,
you have ruined my surprise for you!"

He stared at her, uncertain he had heard her correctly.

"Well?" She covered her mouth with her handkerchief, her glare sharpening with a distinct glimmer of murder in her eyes. "Say something."

"Our child?"

"Yes. Our child."

"I am going to be a father?"

"If you live long enough," she muttered, then burst into tears again. "Oh, do forgive me for being such a sharp-tongued wretch. I cannot seem to control it."

He eased her into his arms, held her close, and tenderly shushed her. "You have every right to be a sharp-tongued wretch. Your husband is a bloody fool."

"So you *do* think I am a sharp-tongued wretch?" She keened with a louder, high-pitched cry, making the horses flatten their ears and prance in place.

"I think you are my beautiful angel," he hurried to tell her as he took her by the shoulders and forced her to look him in the eyes. "And I am awestruck and giddy beyond compare that you carry our child."

"Mrs. Pepperhill promised my temperament would improve." Felicity slowly shook her head. "But I hold little hope for your survival. Blessing was an absolute beast when she was expecting little Rorie. The devil himself couldn't get along with her."

Drake grinned. "All that matters is that you are not suffering from some deadly malady that is going to steal you away from me. I couldn't bear it, my love. You are my heart, and without you, I would have no reason to live." He wanted to roar to the world that this wonderful woman carried his child. His child. She was blessing him with a child. But he didn't wish to startle the horses any more than she already had. "We shall take the rest of the journey slowly and keep the carriage windows uncovered so you might breathe the fresh air. Will that help you make it to your sister's?"

She gave him a forlorn look and shrugged. "I do not know.

There is neither rhyme nor reason for when it chooses to hit me."

"What do you wish to do?" He hoped that was safe enough to ask. He also made a mental note to speak with Blessing's husband at his first opportunity for suggestions on surviving future fits of anger and tears brought on by this wondrous condition. Blessing's husband, Thorne, had successfully survived the fathering of two children. Drake considered the man an expert. He would also speak to Matthew, Wolfe, and Jansen for any advice they might have to offer, since they had fathered children with Broadmere sisters as well.

Felicity didn't answer, just stared downward, occasionally dabbing at the corners of her eyes with her handkerchief.

Ever so gently, he tipped her face up to his. "My love? What do you wish to do?"

She gave a heavy sigh. "Might we just walk for a little while?"

Rather than argue that it was cold and snowing, and the wind was picking up, Drake took her by the hand and wrapped his other arm around her, enfolding her in the depths of his cloak. "We shall walk alongside the carriage until you are ready to ride inside it."

"Are you sure?" The hopefulness in her eyes was his undoing.

"I am positive, my love." He kissed her forehead, then turned to John, where the man sat huddled deep in his coat. "We are going to walk for a little while, John. Be a good fellow and follow along."

John first puckered with a look of disbelief, then tipped an obedient nod. "As you wish, my lord."

"He thinks we are mad." Felicity blew out another heavy sigh that clouded in the frosty air.

"Perhaps we are, but what of it?" Drake pressed a kiss to her temple, unable to resist. "Everyone is a little mad about one thing or another, and I am so proud about the thought of becoming a father, I might just howl at the moon." Her color was improving, and her faint smile urged him on. "You have made me the happiest man in the world—yet again."

"Yet again?"

He nodded in time with their plodding steps, unable to feel his toes, but it didn't matter. All that mattered was Felicity and their child. "When you married me, and now that you carry our first child. I had no idea we would be blessed so soon."

She cut a sideways glance his way and snorted. "You turned me into a greedy wanton, my lord. What did you expect would happen?"

"We are newlyweds," he said, adopting a lofty tone. "It should be no other way." He leaned in and whispered against her ear, "And I can never get enough of you, my love, not ever."

Her cheeks reddened even more, and she shyly ducked her head. "Drake," she softly scolded him, but her voice had lost the sting from earlier. "Shh…John might hear."

Drake chuckled. "John and his wife raised five children. I feel sure he would understand." They continued in contented silence, the surrounding countryside hushed with its blanket of newly fallen snow and the delicate curtain of fluffy white flakes still falling. The holiday bells on the horses' tack softly jingled a merry tune as they followed along.

"It is so peaceful." Felicity lifted her face, smiling up into the gentle wintry storm. "I love this time of year." She snuggled closer, tightening her arm around him. "And I love you."

"I love you, my darling. More than you will ever know." He noticed the tip of her nose had gone quite red. "Are you warm enough?"

"I am lovely, other than my toes. I fear they have gone quite numb."

"Shall we walk a bit farther, or are you ready to attempt another jaunt in the carriage?"

"I feel I can ride now." She cast an uncertain look back at the conveyance. "At present, anyway. Hopefully, your son will allow it."

"And how do you know it is not my daughter causing you to

be ill?" He didn't care what they had as long as the babe and Felicity remained healthy and hale.

"It is a boy. I just know it."

Far be it from him to argue. "And when will our son be making his arrival?"

"Late spring, I believe. Mrs. Bean assured me her method of counting is ever accurate, and Mrs. Pepperhill seemed to agree." She wrinkled her nose. "They mentioned something to do with the phases of the moon and our tenant farmers' late lambing season."

Drake signaled for John to stop the carriage, escorted Felicity to its door, and helped her inside. Before joining her, he winked at the driver. "Fast as you can in this weather, John. My wife and our unborn child are getting cold."

John grinned and doffed his hat. "Congratulations to you and her ladyship, my lord, and ne'er you worry. I'll get you there posthaste."

Drake climbed into the carriage and tucked the heavy lap blankets around them, taking care to keep Felicity's feet well covered.

She snuggled into his embrace. "Just think, next Yule we shall have a child ready to meet all the cousins."

Remembering how loud the small church in Binnocksbourne had gotten with all the children, Drake smiled. "Another voice for the Broadmere sisters' choir."

"Merry is next, you know." Felicity yawned and shifted more comfortably against him.

"Next for what?"

"The next little Broadmere goose to take center stage in the Marriage Mart window, and then it will finally be Seri's turn to experience Chance's mad dash to get us all happily married." Her voice trailed off, and soft snoring followed.

A sense of completeness, of utter contentment, overtook Drake as he cradled her so her head wouldn't bob forward while she slept. He brushed a tender kiss to her forehead and whispered, "Thank you for loving me."

"Forever and a day," she sleepily muttered. "Will love you forever and a day."

THE END

About the Author

If you enjoyed FELICITY'S ELOQUENT EARL, please consider leaving a review on the site where you purchased your copy, or a reader site such as Goodreads, or BookBub.

If you'd like to receive my newsletter, here's the link to sign up:
maevegreyson.com/contact.html#newsletter

I love to hear from readers! Drop me a line at
maevegreyson@gmail.com

Or visit me on Facebook:
facebook.com/AuthorMaeveGreyson

Join my Facebook Group – Maeve's Corner:
facebook.com/groups/MaevesCorner

I'm also on Instagram:
maevegreyson

My website:
https://maevegreyson.com

Feel free to ask questions or leave some Reader Buzz on
bingebooks.com/author/maeve-greyson

Goodreads:
goodreads.com/maevegreyson

Follow me on these sites to get notifications about new releases, sales, and special deals:

Amazon:
amazon.com/Maeve-Greyson/e/B004PE9T9U

BookBub:
bookbub.com/authors/maeve-greyson

Many thanks and may your life always be filled with good books!
Maeve

www.ingramcontent.com/pod-product-compliance
Lightning Source LLC
Chambersburg PA
CBHW060354310726

48976CB00003B/813